Girl, Balancing

Helen Dunmore was an award-winning novelist, children's author and poet who will be remembered for the depth and breadth of her fiction. Rich and intricate, yet narrated with a deceptive simplicity that makes all of her work accessible and heartfelt, her writing stands out for the fluidity and lyricism of her prose, and her extraordinary ability to capture the presence of the past.

Her first novel, *Zennor in Darkness*, explores the events which led D.H.Lawrence to be expelled from Cornwall on suspicion of spying, and won the McKitterick Prize. Her third novel, *A Spell of Winter*, won the inaugural Orange Prize for Fiction, and she went on to become a *Sunday Times* bestseller with *The Siege*, which was described by Antony Beevor as a 'world-class novel'. Published in 2010, her eleventh novel, *The Betrayal*, was longlisted for the Man Booker Prize and shortlisted for the Orwell Prize and the Commonwealth Writers Prize, and *The Lie* in 2014 was shortlisted for the Walter Scott Prize for Historical Fiction and the 2015 RSL Ondaatje Prize.

Her final novel, *Birdcage Walk*, deals with legacy and recognition – what writers, especially women writers, can expect to leave behind them – and was described by the *Observer* as 'the finest novel Helen Dunmore has written'. In January 2018, she was posthumously awarded the Costa Prize for her volume of poetry, *Inside the Wave*.

Praise for *Girl, Balancing*

'This posthumous collection from the much-loved author ... is an act of tender commemoration ... there are new departures on the themes that preoccupied Dunmore: childhood, motherhood, war, friendship, forgotten lives. And where her subject is women under threat or siege, the writing takes off ... Compassion is one of her keynotes. She likes to give a voice to the voiceless.'

Blake Morrison, *Guardian*, Book of the Week

'Wisdom and wit shine out from Helen Dunmore's stories ... Great writers are always great readers, and Dunmore's literary meditations are illuminating. ... This book is the grace note to a lifetime of wonderful writing.'

The Times

'One of [fiction's] most eloquent voices. It was [Dunmore's] emotional concision that made her so exceptional, a quality on ample display in these posthumous short stories ... some absolute gems. Whether musing on a portrait of John Donne, describing two widows forming a friendship over the garden fence ... Dunmore always has something worth saying.'

Mail on Sunday

'With recurring themes of parenthood, secrets and painful reassessments of lives lived, Dunmore's skill as an observer and chronicler of human behaviour shines throughout this final collection of her fiction.'

Sunday Express

'This is the final collection of Dunmore's short stories in which she looks at love, friendship, betrayal and grief. Sharply observed, they're ideal holiday reading.'

Woman & Home

'It's notable just how many of these stories ... concern women achieving private moments of personal liberation ... In "Esther to Fanny," which feels like a metaphor for the way Dunmore's fiction operates, a woman in the present day finds such emotional parallels in a letter written by Fanny Burney detailing her excruciating mastectomy, she half-imagines herself to be the recipient. That's the impact of Dunmore's best work: we too imagine ourselves in the room with her characters, imagine they are talking, like friends, to us.'

Evening Standard

'Helen Dunmore has a particular flair for stories set in the past century, acutely conjuring up experiences that range from a Zeppelin raid to "a warm wriggle of olive oil" as a ticklish remedy for earache. At best, Dunmore's gift for period detail combines with the respect she has for her characters' inner lives to produce an effect that is oddly moving.'

Sunday Times

'This posthumous collection of stories by Helen Dunmore reminds us what a talent we have lost ... Many of the stories ... leave you with the hairs standing up on the back of your neck ... These stories are mostly tasters, amuses-gueules to tempt new readers, and remind old ones of the future works that have now, alas, been lost.'

Daily Telegraph

'Helen Dunmore's love of history glints and gleams in this elegant, posthumous collection. It is beautifully displayed in "Esther to Fanny", in which she celebrates the writer Fanny Burney ... in the glorious "Taken in Shadows", it's the poet John Donne who is subjected to a passionate and wryly speculative investigation. But it is the four Nina stories that shine, as a young girl learns the lessons of self-sufficiency and self-defence.'

Daily Mail

ALSO BY HELEN DUNMORE

Girl, Balancing

Helen Dunmore

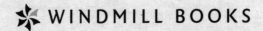
WINDMILL BOOKS

1 3 5 7 9 10 8 6 4 2

Windmill Books
20 Vauxhall Bridge Road
London SW1V 2SA

Windmill Books is part of the Penguin Random House group of
companies whose addresses can be found at
global.penguinrandomhouse.com

 Penguin
Random House
UK

First published by Hutchinson in 2018
First published in paperback by Windmill Books in 2019

www.penguin.co.uk

A CIP catalogue record for this book is available from the British Library.

ISBN 9781786090515

Typeset in 12.5/17 pt Sabon LT Std
by Integra Software Services Pvt Ltd, Pondicherry

Printed and bound in Great Britain by Clays Ltd, Elcograf S.p.A.

CONTENTS

FOREWORD

On the evening of 11th November 2016, when my mother was already very unwell, she asked me to sit with her to discuss the management of her literary estate after her death. Although she lived until June the next year, the unpredictable path of her illness meant we did not know how many more weeks or months she had left, and for her this was the time to get things in order.

We sat on her bed and I noted down what she told me: the processes she followed in doing her accounts, her instructions on what to do with the papers that were stashed away in many boxes in her office, passwords for her email, phone, Spotify account, Facebook, and that we might, perhaps, publish a collection of short stories after she died.

That next year, 2017, would see the publication of her final novel, *Birdcage Walk*, her poetry collection *Inside the Wave* and an illustrated children's book *The Little Sea Dragon's Wild Adventure*. Amongst the complex and

ix

interlinked feelings of impending loss, a less visceral yet still potent sense of waste was that the flow of Mum's writing was being cut off long before its time. Mum, though, was more philosophical about this. As always, ideas for the next novel were developing in her mind, but she felt satisfied with where she had got to with her work; there wasn't something particular that she wanted to achieve which she would not now be able to do.

'A collection of short stories at some point might be nice, though,' she said to me that evening.

It is almost twenty years since my mother published a full volume of short stories, but she did not stop writing them. She told me about a file on the floor by the narrow bookcase in her studio, a bird's nest over-looking Bristol on the eighth storey of a block of flats, and also gave me the passwords for her laptop and iPad. Some of the stories had been printed ad hoc in newspapers or magazines, or had been broadcast, and others had not been published at all. Those could be included, she said, but 'it depends how good they are'.

As I think is common for many people, the months after Mum's death were a frenetic period for me, prob-ably trying to counter or mask the loss of our mother with action. Yet I did not think about the short-story collection until visiting Keats House in London one weekend with my father, standing in Keats's bedroom there and suddenly remembering with vivid recall Mum's short story 'Writ in Water', about Keats's death in Rome. From that moment, putting together a collection of short stories 'at some point' became urgent, a project to focus on.

Not remembering at the time about the file by the narrow bookcase, I started a search of Mum's laptop, trawling through her many thousands of emails and document files. I was tentative at first, knowing that a person's privacy does not die with them, and that there would be many emails that Mum would not have wanted me to read. I glanced sideways at emails, skimming for signs that they might be relevant, before seeing that Mum's careful categorising of her emails made the task much easier. Those labelled 'personal' were out of bounds, those labelled 'work' I knew she would not mind me reading.

It was some time before I felt certain I had found everything. A number of the stories were already gathered into a collection that Mum had compiled in 2010, but not pursued any further. That was the year of the publication of her novel *The Betrayal*, of her illustrated children's book *The Ferry Birds*, and a year when she was working on the poems that would later be published in *The Malarkey*. The 2010 collection had sat there, waiting for its time, and clearly this was the starting point of what Mum had in mind when suggesting a collection. The decision on which stories would be included was made by my father, my sister and me, Mum's publisher and her agent, all of us satisfied the stories certainly met Mum's criterion of being good enough.

The prospect of editing this collection was daunting, although made much easier by the guidance of Mum's friend and publisher, Selina Walker, who published Mum's last three novels. Ordinarily the publisher makes suggestions to the author who then finalises the work. Here, I had to make judgements not about what I thought should or should not be edited, but about what Mum herself would have done. I felt neither qualified nor entitled to do anything to her work, yet once I had started my concerns dissipated. Probably this was because I have followed Mum's work so closely from the days as a child when she would read draft manuscripts of her children's books to me. Not that the stories required a great deal of work, almost none for some, and for others merely the lightest polish before publication.

There was also something special about reading work that I had not read before. Throughout my mother's writing life, I always anticipated the next work, which she would give to me as a finished manuscript or proof copy, or simply as an emailed poem or short story. When I read her final novel in manuscript, I thought as I finished the last page that I would never get to read new work from my mother again. Then, as I read these stories, here was that feeling; the pleasure of discovering something new. This is one of our reasons for publishing the collection, to share this work with Mum's readers, many of whom, too, must feel that their enjoyment of Mum's writing has been cut short.

My mother kept her own story to herself, feeling strongly that once she handed her work over to the public, it would take on myriad meanings that had nothing to do with the author. Yet it is inevitable that her writing holds something of her in it. The humour in this collection is very much of my mother. Always kind, she nonetheless had a keen eye for other people's less than benevolent behaviour, not least when they themselves were unable or unwilling to see it. In the sad, but comical story 'With Shackleton', the narrator's mother-in-law is skewered for her hurtful conduct towards her daughter-in-law. For my mother humour was one of the sides of a good life, especially in difficult times. This is shown beautifully in 'A Night Out', a story of two widows whose warmth towards one another and shared laughter give a shimmer of hope in amongst their grief.

The collection itself is Dunmore work through and through. Mum's writing has always been characterised by a preoccupying interest in the individuals who otherwise may not be noted by the hands that write our shared history. Many of her novels focus on the impact of historical events from the bottom up, but her interest in the individual was not limited to times of great upheaval. She recognised the work it can take simply to exist, for a person to make their way through their own life and the interactions that come together to shape a human experience.

Each of the stories focuses sharply on the individual, perhaps most movingly in the Nina Stories, in which a young woman has to take responsibility for her own protection, her knowledge of how to stretch her small budget to feed herself almost as vital as her instinct for danger. She is a girl, just about balancing. Or in 'Esther to Fanny', in which Fanny Burney's astonishing bravery in undergoing violent nineteenth-century surgery for breast cancer extends her life for twenty-nine more years. The story is Fanny's, not that of the pioneering surgeons.

Most important, though, is the writing. The poetry of my mother's observations is as present here as in any of her work, the sometimes ethereal quality of a world seen through a lens that catches minutely the harsh realities of our existence, but also the endless beauty of the world and the people in it. In the wonderfully titled 'Portrait of Auntie Binbag, with Ribbons', you sense the hidden riches of life, which perhaps is how you might describe my mother's philosophy. As she wrote in one of her final poems, 'The Shaft':

> Who would have thought that pain
> And weakness had such gifts
> Hidden in their rough hearts?

If you stop to look, as my mother always did with intense curiosity, you will see beauty. We are glad to be able to share these stories and we hope that Mum's readers, whom she valued greatly, will take as much pleasure from them as we have.

Patrick Charnley, 2018

Girl, Balancing

THE NINA STORIES

CRADLING

❦

Nina didn't know that she had earache. She'd woken up in the bottom of her bed, trapped in folds of blanket, on fire. They heard her crying and came in smelling of the time that happened after she went to bed. Their mouths breathed out smoke and cider when they said she must hush now because her sister was still asleep.

Nina batted her hands at her hair because the pain was somewhere inside her head. They pushed back the hair that was stuck to her face with crying, and knew straight away what was wrong.

'It's those blessed ears again.'

Her mother was already in the kitchen, lighting the gas, fetching out the little bottle of olive oil she'd bought from the chemist last time Nina's ear hurt. There was a special spoon with a groove where the oil could drip out. Nina kept her eyes shut and listened. Her father carried her into the sitting room and sat back in his

5

armchair, pulling her against him. She cried on but not panicky now, just letting him know how hard it was hurting her.

'It's the same ear,' said her father. She heard his voice through his chest, not through the air. 'The right one.'

She could sense her mother above her, with the spoon, hovering.

'I'll do it,' said her father.

She felt him free his hands, but she stayed as still against him as if he were still holding her. He was testing a drop of the oil on his hand to see how hot it was. She'd seen him do it before.

'Keep still, Nina.'

The back of the spoon was hot as it went into the cup of her ear. She moaned although it didn't hurt. In a moment a warm wriggle of oil went deep inside her. It nearly touched the back of her throat even though it was going into her ear. Her father was holding her arms to his body, not hard but firm enough that she knew she didn't have to battle. She could let it happen without fear. The warm oil spread inside her. The bolt of pain weakened a little.

'I've put a cloth in the oven,' said her mother.

Her father held Nina, rocking her so that the oil would find its way deep into her bad ear. She heard the thick, warm sound of his heart inside his body. She curled herself right up so that she was as close to him as possible, like a snail inside its shell. She heard the little pock sound of someone lighting a cigarette. Her mother lit cigarettes for her father when they were in the car, and then passed them to him. She was doing it now, in the house.

Her father smoked steadily, blowing the smoke away from Nina, over her head. The wireless was on in the corner, playing band music. Once she had seen her mother and father practising the cha-cha with the rug rolled back.

She heard her mother dig the shovel into the coal-bucket. She would be getting the right mix of large pieces and small. Coal rattled as it fell back into the bucket, and then there was the sound of it going on to the fire and the smell of coal-dust. Before they went to bed her father would put the slack on the fire and beneath its crust the fire would sleep all night, ready to wake in the morning. The stove in the kitchen had to be fed too or there'd be no hot water. Sometimes Nina heard the noise of riddling and stoking through the floor when she was in her dreams.

'Hell's bells, I've forgotten that cloth,' said her mother.

She had to wave it about in the air to cool it. There was a singed smell, but not as bad as burning. Nina had one eye open now, her right eye. The other stayed shut, pressed into her father's pullover. Her mother did a little dance with the cloth to cool it faster. There was a glass with cider in it on the table and her mother picked it up and drank some. Nina thought: This is what they do at night when we're not here. They make a big fire and then they dance.

'Keep still, Nina,' said her mother. Nina closed her eyes meekly and the warm cloth came all over the side of her face. Ease spread through her.

'That's better,' said her father, as if he knew.

'It's such a nuisance, this ear,' said her mother.

Nina was never ill. She had slept through the night almost from the day she was born. She ate everything. She was a Trojan. But the coils of her ears were too narrow, that was what the doctor said. Sometimes, without knowing it, Nina heard almost nothing at all. She sat behind the bathroom door, looking at her pop-up book, while they shouted for her. In a minute or a minute more, the people in the pop-up book would come alive.

'It's hardly surprising this child can hear nothing. Her ears are completely blocked.' The doctor had pumped warm water into Nina's ear until it felt as if he was holding her down to drown her. Clots of wax had poured out in a swill of clouded water. Since then Nina had had ear infections, one after the other.

Her father began to sing a little song:

> 'Chin Chan Chinaman
> Bought a penny doll,
> Washed it, dressed it,
> Called it Pretty Poll,
> Sent for the doctor,
> The doctor wouldn't come,
> Because he had a pimple
> On his thumb thumb thumb.'

A giggle stole into Nina's throat. She knew that the last word didn't have to be *thumb*. It could be *bum*.

'She's feeling better,' said her mother.

But her father stayed where he was. He wasn't rocking her any more, although the noise of his heart made it feel as if he was. It was slow and steady, much slower than her own. That was because he was twenty-eight. Next birthday he would be twenty-nine, and after that, thirty. She had counted all the way up from nought for him, but he hadn't been pleased.

'Bloody hell. You might as well put me in my coffin straight away.'

When Nina's sister was born, her father had had to telephone one of his own sisters, because her mother had never looked after a baby in her life. He said, 'You'll have to come, Sheila, because Cathy has no idea which end of a baby is which.' Her father knew which end was which, because there'd been eleven babies younger than him, but he had to go to work.

'Are you going to put her back?' asked her mother. Nothing moved except for a stir of flame in the fire.

'In a minute,' said her father. 'When the cloth's gone cold.'

THE TOWEL

༄

That first night, Nina dried herself on a piece of striped Madras cotton. She'd packed it because she had the idea of spreading it across the armchair. But although the armchair was dark with use it looked worse with the fabric lying limply across it.

The bathroom was down a half-flight of stairs. There was a notice on the door. 'Upon vacating the bathroom, please leave the door ajar.' When Nina went downstairs, the bathroom door was firmly shut. She went back to her room, and waited behind the door for sounds. She would give it twenty minutes. That was a fair time for someone to have a bath, even if they were old and had to haul themselves in and out, groaning and sloshing water over the enamel lip.

Mrs Bersted had shown Nina how to use the geyser, but only once. Nina was not quick with things like that. The pilot was always alight, she remembered that, and there was a whump as the flame shot up and filled the geyser window.

She knew, even from upstairs with her own door shut, that the bathroom door hadn't opened. She would go down again with her sponge bag and the Madras fabric. The turn of the stairs was dark and a heavy smell of food hung in it. There was a smell of Jeyes Fluid too. She went right up to the bathroom door, put her ear against it, and listened. Nothing. Perhaps someone had drowned in the bath. She tapped once, very lightly, on the oily dark green paint. Nothing. It ought to be like a public toilet, with a slot where you pushed in the penny. You'd know where you were then.

Far below in the house, a door opened. Nina took fright. If someone came up and saw her standing here—

She rapped smartly on the door, and when no one answered she turned the handle and pushed it open. The bathroom was quite empty. She put her stuff on the chair, and quickly bolted the door.

The bath was bone-clean.

'Turn the knob of the geyser until the flame ignites, then adjust until desired water temperature is achieved,' said the notice on the wall which Nina had failed to notice earlier, in her panic of attention to what Mrs Bersted was saying.

She took off her clothes and folded them carefully on the chair, as if someone were watching her. Her legs looked very white and naked. Gingerly, she took hold of the knob, and turned it as she thought Mrs Bersted had done in her demonstration. Nothing happened. She turned the knob a little farther. There was a sudden, frightening hiss of gas, but no flame. Only the puny pilot light, crouched down in the heart of the enamel geyser. She fumbled in her rush to twist the knob back. There was sweat prickling in her armpits and her lips moved as if she was explaining herself to someone.

She would have a cold bath. That would be much better than trying the geyser again. Nina ran a few inches of water and swished it about to make it warmer before she climbed in. She could not sit down; it was much too cold. She knelt, shivering, sweeping a little water over her skin with her flannel. The soap slipped out of her hands. She wanted to mew like a cat from the cold but there might be someone else on the landing now, waiting silently. She stood up and rubbed the Madras cotton over herself. It seemed not to dry her but to spread the moisture more evenly over her body. Her nipples stood out, hard and dark. The bath mat was slimy under her feet but she had her flip-flops under the chair and soon she was wriggling the rubber thong back between her toes.

The bath emptied itself with a noise like an old person clearing catarrh in the morning. Nina swilled the tub with cold water, and then she noticed a tin of Ajax and a bath-scourer on the windowsill, beneath another notice, which read: 'Please leave this bathroom in the state you would wish to find it.' She shook the tin cautiously over the enamel. Nothing came out, so she shook again, harder. The cardboard lid flew off and a cascade of dirty white powder dropped on to the bottom of the bath. A hot wave went over her skin. She began to shovel the powder back into the tin, using her hand and the lid. It gritted her finger-ends but she captured most of it, forced the lid down again and replaced the tin on the shelf so that it faced the same way as before. The bottom of the bath was covered with dull grey streaks. She let loose another flood of cold water and was still scouring at the enamel when there was a bang on the door.

'Anyone in there?' called a man's voice.

'Just a minute,' she called, scuffling into her pants and bra. Her jeans were splashed all over with water and some of the white powder had fallen on her T-shirt. She looked around quickly. The bathroom had lost its pure dry cleanliness and she didn't know how to put it back. The doorknob rattled. Nina pulled back the bolt and opened the door, keeping her eyes down on her heap of wet Madras cotton and sopping flannel.

'You've forgotten your sponge bag,' said the man as he barged into the bathroom. He held it out to her backwards, as if it were something contaminating. 'Thank you,' she said, not looking up at him. She smelled his sweat. He's just come in from work, she thought. He had his right to the bathroom, ahead of any schoolgirl, and he knew it. She backed away into the stairwell, clutching her possessions, and waited until the bathroom door slammed before she went upstairs. She didn't want him to know where her room was.

But he would know anyway. The boarding house wasn't that big. She was right at the top. Opposite, there was a blank door.

'Oh no, that room's not let,' Mrs Bersted had told her with a grim smile. 'It's not fit for habitation.'

Nina spread the Madras cotton out over the back of the wooden chair she was to sit on when she ate. There was a table-flap which came down from the wall with a sudden bang; but she had mastered it. She had spent 14/6 on food: tonight she would have baked beans, with some cheese grated on top. There was a food safe outside the window for 'perishable items'. You had to pull the sash right up, then open the little wire cage door and slip in your bottle of milk or a piece of cheese. Nina's room faced north, so things would keep nice and fresh.

Nina had two saucepans: her mother's old milk pan, and a new, thin, shiny aluminium pan for everything else. She stabbed the tin opener into the baked-beans tin, twisted it and, after a false start, she found the steady jagging rhythm that would take her all the way around the tin and open it.

She ate carefully, sopping her bread in the sauce. The Baby Belling didn't have a grill, but there were two rings on top, and a small oven. Next time she would slice the bread and put it into the oven, which would be just as good as toast. She had bought three tins of beans, one of which had pork sausages hidden in it, two of tomatoes, several packets of dried soup and a Vesta chow mein. She had even remembered about washing-up liquid, and had already tried out the Ascot water heater with success. It occurred to her that if she could never get the geyser to work, she might carry pans of Ascot-heated water downstairs to take the chill off her baths. At least that way she would be able to wash her hair.

The street lights were coming on outside. They were a rough, angry orange. She closed her eyes. When she opened them, the street and its lights would have disappeared. She would hear an owl.

'Now, are you sure you're going to be all right, Nina?' her mother had asked. She was already picking up her things, and the empty suitcases which she was taking back with her. Nina could not remember packing. There were gaps like that all over her memory at the moment. But she had thought ahead: in a side pocket of her case there were four packets of her father's cigarettes. She had slid them out and into a drawer while her mother was talking to Mrs Bersted. Four moist, yielding packets which would release the sweet breath of tobacco as soon as Nina stripped off the cellophane.

'Now, are you sure you're going to be all right?'

They looked at each other. Her mother's eyes were evasive, pleading. The family was leaving again, only this time Nina wasn't going with them. She was too old to be crammed into the back of a car with the little ones and driven a hundred miles to the next home. She had found a bedsit and would get a part-time job.

There was nothing to say. Nina turned and smoothed out fresh sheets of newspaper to reline the drawers before she put her clothes away. One day people would take out those sheets and read the paper and marvel at how long ago it all was.

Her mother's hands were moving quickly into her purse. Nina watched through her hair as her mother took out four pound notes, put one back and placed three on the bed, for Nina to find when she was gone.

Nina chased the last baked bean on to her knife, ate it and pushed the plate away. She would have a cigarette now. She fetched the heavy Senior Service ashtray, her cigarettes and matches. The cellophane was off, and then the guardian strip of silver paper. Nina breathed in. She took out a cigarette, feeling the others loosen in the packet, and struck her match.

The first drag, that moment of calm, of absolute release. From the time she was fourteen it had never failed her. Nina drew in the smoke. But there was something wrong this time: the smoke tasted sour, the peace spilled away, her lips twisted as if she'd put something vile into her mouth instead of the virgin cigarette. She got up with the cigarette in her hand and went to the window. All she needed was some fresh air. But she still couldn't smoke, and after a while she returned to the table.

Nina stubbed out the half-smoked cigarette. For a long time she remained quite still, watching the yellow nicotine mark in the middle of the filter as if she expected something to happen. It was quite dark outside now, and the draught was cold. In a minute she would close the window and draw the curtains. She had plenty of shillings for the gas fire: six at least. It was just that she didn't feel like putting it on yet.

She had to buy a towel. That was the real problem. She hadn't thought ahead. But she had money: the three pounds. If she had a towel she could wrap herself up in it.

Her gaze crept back to the window. How orange those lights were. She could feel it beginning in her shoulders. Alone now, the dark of fear was rising. She closed her eyes and listened for the owl. It was a crisp cold night and she was running down the lane, her satchel banging, late home from school. Soon she would come to the turn, out of the trees. A long race downhill, along the wall, and then she would see the house. Lights would be on in the kitchen. She would pull open the back door and shout, 'I'm home!'

She would go out, now, this minute. There was a late market on a Wednesday night, not the proper market but a few stalls huddling over by a wall. They were kept by big, hard women who were always calling and laughing to each other even while they were selling something to you.

Nina thought of them and the darkness inside her began to retreat. She had her money. She would buy a towel.

THE WHITE HORSE

∾

Tony was standing outside Yates's Wine Lodge, his hands deep in his pockets. The fog was thick now. His head was wreathed in it.

'Have you seen the others?' he asked as Nina came up. She wasn't sure what others he meant. With Tony, she rarely asked questions, in case they were stupid ones which would make him whistle through his teeth and then say, 'Little Nina,' in a way which even someone who wanted to couldn't possibly think was affectionate.

'They're probably inside already,' he went on, moving towards the entrance.

Inside, the man with the violin was playing. He wore a shabby loose-sleeved coat which he never took off. His face was morose, but when his bow whipped and skidded, the music which came off it was bright. You would imagine a quite different player if you closed your eyes.

'He's getting past it,' said Tony.

'What?' Nina was too much astonished, and so the question jumped out of her mouth. It was Tony who'd told her that the violin man had played with Toots Thielemans once. Yates's would be nothing without him.

'Little Nina,' said Tony. His eyes were scanning the upper floor. 'There's Chris.'

There were five or six of them at the table, but to Nina it was dozens. Maggie moved up and made room for her, and a packet of cigarettes was thrust towards her. She took one and sat back, hidden in smoke. Bodies pressed in on either side.

'Did you move in all right?' asked Maggie.

'Yes.'

'Good.'

Maggie was twenty-five. She was in love with Tony, or at least Nina thought so.

'You want to get your own stuff up on the walls,' said Maggie. 'That'll make it feel better.'

'Posters, you mean?'

'Yes, posters.' Nina heard a tang of impatience in Maggie's voice.

'I know a guy who works in advertising,' said Chris, leaning forward out of the noise. 'He could get you a poster, Nina.'

'You don't know anyone who works in advertising,' said Maggie, half closing her eyes.

'He pastes the adverts on to billboards,' said Chris.

'They'd be a bit large for Nina's room.'

'They come in sections. He's pasting up whisky ads at the minute.'

'Whisky ads,' repeated Nina.

'White Horse,' said Chris.

'Oh!' She thought of a white horse, as big as the side of a building, galloping across Mrs Bersted's wall. Or even a section of a horse. Its head, perhaps, or a pair of flashing hooves.

'I'll ask him for you,' Chris promised. 'What've you done with Mal?'

Nina said nothing. She hadn't heard from Mal for a week.

'He's gone to Leicester to score some dope,' said Tony.

'I shouldn't have thought there was any necessity for that,' said Maggie. 'All he has to do is walk around the corner.'

'Afghan gold,' said Chris, and tapped the side of his nose. 'Are you not drinking, Nina?'

'She's waiting for someone to buy her a drink,' said Tony.

'I'm not!' said Nina eagerly. 'I've got money, I'll buy you a drink.'

'We don't want her going up to the bar,' said Maggie quietly.

Nina took one of the pound notes out of her bag and pushed it across to Tony.

'What do you want, then?' he asked her.

She couldn't think of a drink in the world that she wanted to put into her mouth. She stared at the walls for inspiration. There was a metal plaque with 'Stone's Ginger Wine' embossed on it in curling letters.

'I'll have a glass of ginger wine.'

'Don't waste your money, it's not even alcoholic,' advised Chris.

Tony shrugged. 'It's her money,' he said.

'You have a drink too, Tony,' said Nina hastily, 'and Maggie and Chris – and everybody.' She had forgotten the others' names.

Tony took the order for the table, and went to the bar.

'You don't want to go buying drinks for everyone,' said Maggie. 'It's not as if you're earning.'

'It's all right,' said Nina, but already her mind was making quick, panicky scampers. If each of them had a pint of beer, that would be ten shillings, and then her own drink too. She didn't know how much ginger wine cost. Maggie would only have a lemonade or something like that. Perhaps it would be all right. She could get by for a week on a pound, as long as she ate as much as possible at school dinners. She would have two bottles of milk at break.

Maybe Mal would ask her to Sunday dinner at his place. She'd been there once before. His mum served up the roast and then they all took their plates through to the lounge so they could watch a film while they ate. Mal's mum put her feet up on a leather pouffe which was seamed with deep cracks. Sometimes she made a comment about the film, and Mal's thin dark face eased into a smile. Nina kept very quiet, on the sofa next to Mal.

'Here's your ginger wine,' said Tony, and put down the glass in front of her on the table. It was full up and had an oily wobbling surface. 'First time I've ever asked for that.'

He had carried four pints to the table first, balancing them carefully, frowning when Maggie moved to help him. Then there was a small glass of tonic water for Maggie, who never drank alcohol.

Nina waited for Tony to reach into his pocket for the change, but nothing happened. She stared down at the surface of her drink. Her ears hummed. With a flourish, Tony produced a bag of crisps and dropped it in front of Nina.

'Little Nina,' he said.

Maggie eyed him, but said nothing. Tony smiled, as if he was waiting for something. Nina sipped from the top of her drink.

After a minute Tony said, 'It's Peter Stuyvesant you smoke, isn't it, Nina?'

'Number Six.' She was not going to explain that she only smoked Peter Stuyvesant when she had taken them from her father.

'Pity,' said Tony. Like a conjuror, he produced four packets of Peter Stuyvesant and held them in front of Nina. She made no move. 'Don't you want your change?'

Nina's lips hurt. Probably it was the ginger wine. She swallowed down the taste. 'Thank you, Tony,' she said. Maggie shot Tony a dark look.

It was two days later that she met Chris in the Black Olive. He was carrying four long rolls of heavy paper. 'Here's your white horse. No, don't unroll it now.'

Nina was sitting alone. She knew Chris wouldn't stay. He hated cafés like this, full of students. She stroked the smooth back of the paper. It was time for her to go. Last time she'd sat for more than two hours over a cup of coffee, doing her art homework in the warm, before the owner came over and asked if she was going to pay him rent for the table, seeing as she wasn't buying anything. There were some friends of Mal's over in the corner, but they didn't speak to her and she didn't speak to them.

Nina looked up. Through the window she saw a girl coming down the narrow passage to the entrance of the café. Her head was bent over something she was holding. Nina saw a smudge of white through the fuggy glass. The girl's face was small, narrow and very calm. It was a girl called Sarah, who'd had to leave in Upper Sixth because she was pregnant. She was two years ahead of Nina. She came in through the door and looked around the café. From the corner table a man raised his hand and beckoned.

Nina hadn't expected the unwieldy rollicking of the posters as she unrolled them on the floor. If she could get all four of them laid out flat together, like a jigsaw, she could see how big the whole picture was and work out how to fit it on her walls. But as fast as she weighed down a corner with a book or a bag of sugar, another corner broke free and began to roll up. The room filled with a sickly smell of printers' ink and new paper. The posters would never fit on her walls, even if she could get them to stay there. She decided to concentrate on the rectangle which showed the horse's head with its mane flying free, and blue sky behind it. The wallpaper was old and pitted, and had come away from the skirting board. She would stick up the fresh new poster with Sellotape.

She crisscrossed it at the poster's corners, and ran strips along the edge. She had to bend down to fix the bottom and when she straightened up her head filled with blackness. She stood quite still, waiting for her vision to clear. When it did, there was the white horse, nostrils wide, glaring at her. Its head seemed angry at the separation from its body.

But it was better than before. Now she would boil her egg. The reason she felt dizzy was that she was hungry.

The eggs looked smaller than Nina thought eggs ought to look. 'Pullet's eggs', her father would have called them. They were dead white, and cool from being outside. She cradled one in each palm, then lowered them carefully into the roiling water. A plume of white ran out, coagulated and began to whirl as she quickly turned down the ring to two. She buttered three slices of bread and cut them into fingers. It was three minutes for a just-set egg, she knew that, but these were so small that perhaps she should allow less time. Her alarm clock had no second hand, so she counted aloud, 'one and two and three and …', and then she lifted the eggs, one by one. The best thing to do would be crack them open and mash the soft-boiled egg.

She took her plate over to the table counter and began to eat ravenously, cramming the food into her mouth. Egg dripped off her fingers and she wiped up the drops and licked them. She finished both eggs and took another piece of bread out of the packet to wipe the plate. Suddenly her stomach clenched. Sweat started out on her forehead and she sat very still, clutching the sides of her chair.

There was a sound. A corner of the poster detached itself and began to roll up, slowly but with an authority which could not be interrupted. The poster moved across the wall like a wave, cleansing it. The horse's head had almost disappeared. There was a final small sound and then the last bit of blue sky vanished as the poster fell right off the wall and disappeared behind Nina's bed.

She had left the saucepan of boiling water on the ring. The Sellotape had steamed off. There was a fine film of moisture all over the surface of the wallpaper.

Nina went to the window and opened it as wide as it would go. The iron smell of the eggs left her. Outside, the fog that had hung over the city for days had all blown away, and there was a cold, wild look to the sky.

GIRL, BALANCING

❧

The wardrobe was sticky black, as if someone had tried to polish it with cough mixture. Nina looked inside and racks of old-lady clothes bulged into the room. She shoved them back, forced the door shut and locked it with the rusty little key.

She had picked the wrong room. The house was tall and narrow and there were six bedrooms. It belonged to her friend Edith's great-aunt, and Edith had been coming here for holidays all her life. Now the great-aunt was dead, and the house would soon be stripped and sold, but Edith could have it for Christmas week. It was better than having it lying empty, for squatters and thieves.

Nina went to the window and looked out over the surging sea and the broad empty promenade. A gull flew and then sank down almost to the water. The wind was cutting the tops off the waves. It came straight from Siberia, Edith had told her that. The house creaked coldly and the windows rattled.

She would choose another room. Nina scooped her stuff off the bed, crammed it back into her bag, and went up to the attics. The stairs were bare wood and her feet clopped on them. At the top there were three doors, all closed. She tried the knobs, one by one. Locked. Locked. But whatever happened she wasn't going back into that room which smelled as if someone was still dying in there. And then, like a sudden warm miracle, the china knob of the third room door turned. She paused. Far below in the bowels of the house she could hear Edith singing and banging pots. The sound gave her courage and she pushed open the door.

It was the smallest, whitest room. It looked as if someone had scrubbed it bare from ceiling to skirting boards. It was like being on a ship, Nina thought. Up here the house was left behind and you were halfway out to sea. She went to the round window. The glass bulged and distorted the line of the horizon and the iron railings of the promenade. From here she could see the humps of boats hauled on to the shingle bank.

There was no bed. She would drag a mattress upstairs, and she had her sleeping bag. Edith had said to bring it. Nina began to spread out her stuff in neat piles at the side of the room. Her clothes, her hat with her money tucked inside it, her roller skates. She had plenty of money. She was working at the Gaumont cinema and, with all the Christmas shows, there had been plenty of extra shifts. She could more than pay her way. They would have to buy bags of coal, and wood. There would be the gas for cooking, and the food.

She heard Edith's footsteps coming all the way up the house.

'I'm here!' Nina called down. 'I'm in the attic.'

There was a pause, and then Edith clumped upwards again. She stood at the door, her cheeks flaring scarlet. 'I've got the stove lit,' she announced.

Nina stared at her in admiration.

'There was coke in the cellar, but there's no coal. You brought your skates, then.'

'Yes.' Nina lifted her roller skates. They were old and the red leather was rubbed, but her feet hadn't grown since she was twelve and they still fitted.

'We'll go skating before it gets dark,' said Edith, and her eyes flashed boldly. 'There's a shop on the corner that sells bags of coal. We can carry a big one between us.'

They lugged the coal home, grunting and heaving under its weight. The shop man watched them ironically, without offering to help. He seemed to know Edith, but she was cold with him. As they left, Nina smiled back over her shoulder, abjectly.

'You want to watch yourself with him,' said Edith before they were out of the man's hearing.

'Why?'

But Edith just glanced, sniffed and said nothing.

Nina had the gift for lighting fires. All her life she'd known how to coax flame and make it roar. In her bedsit she was thwarted, because there was only the gas fire with its mean blue jets. But here, there were fireplaces in every room. Even in her attic there was a small black iron grate. Edith was going to make soup, she said, and Nina could light the fires.

Nina found a pile of old newspapers, and began to make coils. First you rolled up a sheet of newspaper, then you coiled it round and twisted the ends until it was as firm as a bird's nest. She began in the front room, which was the sitting room. The fireplace was big, cold and lined with beige tiles. There were no tongs or shovel; Edith said people had taken most of her aunt's stuff. Nina laid a pyramid of paper coils, balanced kindling from the shop into a pyre, and placed small lumps of coal delicately all over it. She sat back on her heels, laid several larger lumps of coal ready, and reached for the matches.

She held the match to the edge of a coil at the back of the fireplace. Through the kindling she saw the flame grow from blue to yellow and then stretch up to lick the wood. She dropped the match, lit another and held it to the deepest coil at the right back of the fireplace. Another touch, and another. The flame puckered and crackled on the wood. It was lit. It was going. She leaned forward, feeling its heat, urging it on. The wood settled; the coal slipped. She laid more coal jewels, dropping them on to the cruxes of the kindling. The damper was right out and the chimney was drawing. More coal, bigger pieces. There was heat in it now as well as flame.

Nina went from hearth to hearth, starting fires in the back room, in Edith's bedroom and in her own. She would get all the fires roaring and then she would bank them down with slack so that they would stay alive while she and Edith were out. She went out to the coal bunker. It was empty of coal, as Edith had said, but there was an old shovel left in there and an iron bucket. Nina scraped for slack on the floor of the bunker and thought of the sound the coalman made when he delivered his sacks, walking to the bunker bent double, then heaving the sack off his shoulder, opening it and letting down the coal with a rattle and then a rush. You could tell how full the bunker was from the sound. Back and again the coalman trod the path until he had delivered all the sacks. And then you were safe for the winter.

They sat over the fire, still in their coats, and ate the soup Edith had made. It was thick with onions, fried until they were brown and meltingly sweet. The smell of coal-smoke and onions was slowly hiding the old, dead smell of the house. Behind it all Nina thought she could still taste the faint tang of the sea.

Nina wouldn't be allowed to make such soup in her bedsit, even if she knew how. Boiled eggs, toast and baked beans passed muster, but anything fried or foreign was out. Nina had learned that after her attempt at curry brought Mrs Bersted prowling upstairs, sniffing at the doors until she found Nina's.

'I'll get bones from the butcher tomorrow,' said Edith. 'He'll be all right, as long as he thinks we're getting our Christmas meat from him.'

'Aren't we?' asked Nina.

Edith shifted and looked at the fire instead of at Nina. 'It's not really worthwhile getting a bird for one person,' she said.

'We could make sandwiches from the leftovers.'

'I'll be sick of the sight of a bird by then, after the turkey at my sister's. One year it was so big she had to break its back to get it in the oven.'

'That's only one meal, though. You'll be hungry again.'

Edith looked deeper into the flames. 'She wants me to stay over,' she said. 'She doesn't want to drive me back on Christmas Day. And then they always go for this long walk on Boxing Day, so it would mess that up if she had to drive all the way over here first.'

'With the baby?'

'Oh, they wrap the baby up and he goes in one of those carrier things, on Simon's back.'

'So you're staying over on Boxing Day too?'

'I'll be back really early the day after, Nina. You know what it's like. Simon's not much of a one for people. He's a musician, you know.'

Yes, Nina knew. She looked down, flushing at her own stupidity. When Edith had said, 'I'll be going to my sister's for Christmas dinner,' she had thought:

Christmas dinner, that's only three or four hours. Edith will be here in the morning, and she'll be back in the evening. It will still be a proper Christmas.

'You'll be all right, won't you?'

'I'll be fine,' said Nina. 'I'll get some sausages.'

She was glad no one else had heard Edith's words, or her own thoughts. If Tony was here he'd smile in that way of his, a bit mocking, and say, 'Little Nina.' If Mal was here he would stretch and yawn like a cat, and walk away because he didn't want to think about Nina, not when she was like this. 'You want to keep your feelings inside you, where they belong,' he'd said to her once. Remembering it, she flushed more deeply.

The good thing about Christmas, thought Nina, is that it comes when the days are very short. Once it was dark again she could curl up by the fire. In the old days, she thought, people probably never left their beds all December. They wrapped themselves in their wolfskins and dreamed all winter long. They let their flame burn low, saving themselves for summer. By four it would be thickening into dark, and she could say to herself, 'Christmas Day is over now.'

Edith had left at nine. Her sister didn't come to the house, because you couldn't bring the car on to the front. Edith was meeting her outside the corner shop.

Nina cooked the sausages early. It was either a late breakfast or an early lunch. She cut up an apple and grilled slices alongside the sausages. She and Edith had bought a big net bag full of tangerines. Nina thought of squeezing tangerine juice over the sausages, for a change of taste, but decided against it. Instead, she went into the small, grim garden behind the house and picked a few grey heads of lavender to put them in a jar. She looked up and down the row of houses. There were some lights on in the back windows, but not many. A string of coloured fairy lights flashed, four houses along. The garden could be beautiful, Nina thought, if it had the right plants in it. The shape of it was good, and even though you couldn't see the sea from here, you could smell it and hear the gulls.

The day was still and cold. She would go out later. It was all right to go for a long walk on Christmas Day; it was what people did. She would build up the sitting-room fire and then she would go out and walk for miles and miles.

No. She would skate. Edith said that the promenade went on for miles, until it faded into the road that went over the marshes. And the country was perfectly flat. You could see for miles, Edith said, over the salt marshes and down the coast. In the old days, when it froze hard, people used to skate along the drainage ditches.

Nina had never skated on ice, but on roller skates she was a demon. She'd practised all her childhood, backwards, forwards, turning, jumping, doing arabesques on one leg. She raced, she skated long distances over the clickety pavements, she practised figures on the smoothest and oiliest piece of tarmac she could find.

Her skates wore out and she begged another pair for her next birthday. They were metal skates with hard rubber wheels, a laced toe-piece and an ankle strap. You could adjust the length by unscrewing and screwing a metal nut.

Edith was no good on her skates. They'd tried on that first day. She wobbled; she messed about like an adult playing a child's game. Nina tried skating with her but it was unbearable. She longed to strike off alone, free, but out of politeness she held back and took off her skates at the first opportunity, saying it was too cold to stay out any longer.

Now, Nina washed up the sausages, banked the fires and put on her coat, her scarf and a striped woollen hat Edith had knitted for her. She picked up her skates, and locked the house.

There was no one on the promenade. The sea lay flat, as if a huge hand had stroked it in the night. The horizon was wintry, bare of ships. Nina's heart lifted. Leaving her skates by the railings, she ran down the steps to the beach, across the shifting, crunching pebbles, to the edge of the water. There it lay, barely breathing. She knelt on the shingle and reached out her hands. The cold water sucked her fingers, then slunk back on itself. She licked the salt taste, dipped her hands again, licked more salt and then slowly she rose from her knees and turned to go back up the beach.

There was a figure leaning against the railings, watching her. A stab of recognition pierced her. It was him. Surely it was Mal. Scarcely daring to believe, she peered through the thick, cold air. His hair had fallen forward, hiding his face. Yes, it was Mal's hair, the two dark wings of it, almost meeting.

She scrambled up the beach, hot, hasty, breathing hard.

'Little Nina,' he said.

'Don't call me that. I don't like it.'

He raised his eyebrows, smiling with a crooked corner of his mouth. 'Nina, then,' he said. 'After all I suppose you are seventeen.'

She came up the steps, watching his face all the while. 'How did you know where I was?'

'I've been here before.'

'With Edith?' she asked quickly, and then wished she hadn't.

He nodded, indifferently.

'But I thought you were spending Christmas with your mother,' she said in a rush.

'I was, but I changed my mind.'

There was something in his face which made her say, 'You haven't eaten.'

'I borrowed Tony's van,' he answered.

'I've got some sausages.'

He shrugged; then, as he moved his feet, something clinked. His feet had knocked her skates, on the edge of the promenade where she'd left them.

'Some kid's left her roller skates behind,' he observed, looking down.

She nearly disowned them, but his look made her sure he already knew. 'They're mine,' she said, 'I'm skating to the marshes.'

'Can I come too?'

'You haven't got any skates.' And then she thought of Edith's. Edith's feet were big, size eight. Mal's were small, considering his height. 'I suppose you could borrow Edith's,' she said.

They went up to the house. It seemed very dark and quiet inside, with the fires sleeping in their grates. Nina's heart was beating with excitement now. They would skate side by side. He would match his strokes to hers. Mal would be a good skater, she was sure of it. She found Edith's skates and with the key she adjusted the metal base to its maximum length. She could have done it in complete darkness, she was so used to it.

There were a few more people about when they set off. Thick, bundled figures in groups, staying together as if they had brought their indoor closeness with them. But she was with Mal. When Edith asked what she had been doing, she would say, 'Mal came over. We went skating.'

Mal was no good at skating. Not as hopeless as Edith, but bad enough. It astounded Nina to find herself doing something better than Mal. There was no chance of their skating arm in arm: he needed both arms to flail and balance himself.

She skated much more slowly than usual, but tried to look as if she was putting in an effort. Mal was doing better now.

'I used to skate when I was a kid,' he puffed, coming up to her, and she nodded. Really she had no patience for people who said they used to do things when it was obvious they had only ever done them once or twice, but she let it go for Mal.

They skated on, until they had passed all the people. The houses thinned away. There was a bus shelter, and then a bunker from the war. Only the tarmac continued doggedly as if whoever planned the town had intended to pave the coast for miles. It was rough and potholed in places now, but you could still skate. The air stung her cheeks. It felt as if it carried grains of ice. Mal had no hat. Perhaps they shouldn't skate so far, she thought, but she could not stop herself. It was like when she was a child and would skate on long after it was dark, by the light of the street lamps. Even when her mother called for her she would shout that she was coming, but she never would. They had to come out and fetch her. At the thought she skated faster, unconsciously, speeding on until she became aware that Mal had fallen behind. She spun into a turn, and waited.

'Do you want to go back?' she asked.

'Do you?' He was panting a little. It was more effort for him than for her.

'Not if you don't.'

'We'll go on then.'

Marram grass grew on their left. The town had faded now; its lights were all behind them. One or two solitary lights showed across the marsh, from distant farms. On their right the sea dragged at the pebbles. The light was already weakening. The path was narrow now, but still tarmacked. It might go on forever, Nina thought, or at least to the next town. She could hear the grass hissing.

The sky seemed to be coming down all around them. They were specks in it, barely moving. Suddenly she swooped back into herself, her blood tingling, every inch of her alive. The path was widening ahead of them. The tarmac was becoming a pool. It was the end.

She stopped first, and waited for him. He skated up and put his hands on her shoulders. She turned her toes in to keep balance; very probably he didn't know how to lock his skates.

'Where's this place then?' he asked.

'I don't know.'

'It could be anywhere. Anything might happen here, Nina.'

His lips curved but she wasn't sure he was smiling. The sea was behind him, flat and grey, moving to its own tide pattern, she knew that, but seeming to be still. Mal's face twitched.

'I hate Christmas,' he said.

'Do you?'

'It doesn't mean anything.'

'Won't your mum mind? I mean, you coming here.'

'She doesn't know. Anyway she'll be pissed by now.'

'Oh.'

'Yeah. What is it, three o'clock? She'll be drunk as a monkey.'

His hands were tight and heavy on her shoulders. She was always wishing Mal would touch her but now she wanted him to take his hands away. As if he'd heard her thoughts, he lifted his right hand and put it on her neck. Gently, he stroked her. Nina's whole body went stiff.

'Don't do that,' she said, her lips barely moving.

'What?'

'I don't like people touching my neck.'

His hand went still. He frowned and then suddenly his thumb went deeper, pushing into the base of her throat. She gagged, and tears sprang to her eyes.

'Don't you trust me?' he asked, speaking as softly as she had done. Speechlessly, she shook her head. Seconds pounded in her head.

'You don't think I'm going to hurt you, do you?'

This time she barely moved. Something deep in her body fired into life. She kept her eyes on his face but she seemed to know, like an animal, everything that was around her. The empty sea. The marshes and the grass making its whisper. The bare path with no one on it. Edith doesn't know he's here. His mum doesn't know he's here. *Mal's got a temper*. They all said that. She had seen it, but only in distant flashes, never close to herself. You must do something now, her body said. If he goes any further he won't be able to come back. His eyes did not look quite as if they saw her clearly. He was tired and he'd had no food. Perhaps he was on something. You never knew, with Mal.

'You don't think I'm going to hurt you, do you?'

She mustn't answer that. She must take him far away from that question. She half lowered her eyes. The pressure on her neck was steady but not as hard now. She must lift him away from this dark place.

'Do you want to see me do something?' she asked him. She saw a spark of reaction. It wasn't what he'd expected.

'What?' he said.

'Something on my skates. This place is perfect for it.'

'Like a trick?'

'No. Just something I learned when I was little.'

She felt him take a deep breath, almost a gulp. The twitch came again, clinching his eye and then releasing it. The hold on her throat was easing, easing. She smiled, putting all her innocence into it.

'All right,' he said, and he let go of her. She stood quite still for a moment, in case the idea of her escaping should enter his mind, and then, very slowly, she skated backwards a little way.

'You'll need to give me room,' she said, preparing herself, and, like a member of an audience told to take a different seat, he skated to the edge of the tarmac.

She needed to build up speed first. Round and round she went on the circle of tarmac, until Mal's face blurred. But she was still not fast enough. She was low down, racing. Suddenly it came, the moment, and she balanced herself, jumped, came down on her left skate, lifted her right and made a perfect line of arms, body, leg, skate. It lasted only a few seconds and she was out of tarmac, turning, gaining speed again. She couldn't help herself: she laughed aloud, all of her blazing and triumphant, before she swerved on to the path and, picking up speed, began to race for the town.

She could out-skate him easily, but it wasn't until she reached the lights of the town and the promenade with its lingering crowds of Christmas walkers that she slackened speed. Dusk was coming down. She looked back through the graininess of it and far behind she saw the speck that was Mal, labouring along the path. She slowed further. An old couple went by, leaning over a little girl on a bike with stabilisers. The grandma looked up at Nina as she skated by and gave her a creaking smile. There were people all around her, tired of their houses and eager for the cold air. They were offering smiles now, and Christmas greetings, as if they were all survivors of a wreck and had been hauled up on to the same raft.

She would go into the house, lock the door and break up the crust of the fire in the sitting room until the flames leaped. She would stoke the stove and cook herself a meal. Mal had meant nothing; she was sure of it. He had only wanted to frighten her. He would bang on the door and she would keep it shut against him until he went away in Tony's van, back to the city. He was finished for her; he had given her that. She would carry a shovelful of burning coals up to her room and light a fire in the iron grate, and while she fell asleep she would see flames reflected on the white walls.

Tomorrow she would oil the skates, so that they'd go even faster.

THE PRESENT

TAKEN IN SHADOWS

❧

Beautiful John Donne. Who wouldn't want you? You lean slightly forward, arms folded over your body as if to protect it from all the women who might otherwise tear off your clothes.

And yet, now that I look closely – and I do look very, very closely, John – there's a teasing touch of something I can only call … *readiness* … in the way you're sitting for your portrait.

Take your eyes. They are clear hazel, brooding on something that is beyond me and a little to my right. What has caught your gaze? How many generations of women – and men too, I'm sure, men too – must have longed to make you turn to them. But your gaze has never shifted. Not once, in over four centuries.

Your mouth is red. The shadow of your moustache – so dandyish, so eloquently shaved into points! – serves to emphasise the perfect cut of your upper lip. Your lower lip is full, sensuous. Red lips, hazel eyes, arched dark eyebrows. Your jaw is a line of perfection. The shadow of your broad-brimmed hat can't hide the modelling of your temples. Your long fingers rest on your sleeve's rich satin. You gleam in light from a source which is forever invisible, outside the frame. And then there's the fall of your collar, the exquisiteness of lace thrown over darkness.

You're in your glory. From where you sit inside your portrait, it's the present day. The present moment, even, and you're caught in it. Your right ankle itches, but you suppress the urge to scratch. Your heart throbs with its own quick life. Soon the sitting will be over, but you don't mind the time you spend here. The artist is anonymous to me, but not to you. You know him well. This portrait is important to you and you'll keep it with you all your life.

The moment I look away, you smile, stand up and stretch like a cat. The artist, of course, has taken careful note of your pose before it dissolves.

'Until next time,' he says, wiping a brush.

'Until next time,' you agree.

You've given me the slip again, John. You're back in your own world. It's 1595, a date which I know well. I've studied your period, and I dress you in my rags of knowledge. I can analyse your social status in the light of your lace collar. You are history, John. You wouldn't like that, I know. The fact that I can speak and you cannot would seem quite wrong to you, given the relative values of what we have to say.

You know 1595 from the inside, by the touch of satin, the warmth of a spring day, the gamey smell of your own body, the bite of a flea at the nape of your neck. For you, the door is about to open into a stream of May sunshine that will make you blink. For me, it has closed forever.

The Elizabethan age has eight more years to run. The old Queen has kept the show on the road so much longer and more brilliantly than anyone had a right to expect. She has united the country. Those who are not united are dead, imprisoned, exiled, silenced or lying very low indeed.

You're in your glory, but also in those shadows that wrap themselves around you like a cloak. Your mother has gone into exile, and your brother died in Newgate two years ago, because he harboured a priest. Your fellow Catholics are food for the scaffold. That is what hanging, drawing and quartering is all about. It does so much more than kill: it turns a protesting soul into blood-slimed joints of meat, laid on the block for the public appetite.

You don't yet know for sure that England will not return to the faith, not soon, not ever, but I should say that you've already made an educated guess. You have, as we know, a great deal of imagination. You will do nothing which will allow your body to be seized, racked, beaten, imprisoned, to die in its own shit and blood and vomit on the clammy ground. You will not be carted to Tyburn to be pelted with the crowd's insults, spittle and rotten fruit before you are lynched. Nor are you willing to endure the long, dismal martyrdom of being jobless, without influence, friends or position, bled dry by penal taxes. You are already preparing to leave the home of your soul, and find another if you can.

I look at your long, slender fingers. Perhaps you played upon the lute as well as upon the emotions of a hundred women. Beautiful, beautiful John Donne. How were you to know that there'd be generations snuffling greedily over your portrait? How could you estimate the wolfish hunger of a public not yet born? You couldn't guess, any more than Sylvia Plath guessed what would happen to her image after the lens clicked, her radiant smile faded and she got up from where she'd been sitting on a bank of daffodils with her infant son in her arms.

You and Sylvia are the kind we really love. You make us feel that we can climb right inside your lives. The only frustrating thing is that you keep looking at things we cannot see. You will never meet our eyes.

Listen, John, I can tell you what's going to happen to you after you take off that lace collar. You're going to screw up on a royal scale. You'll fall in love with the wrong girl, miscalculate about her father coming round to your secret marriage (he won't, not for years). You'll find yourself in a cottage full of children, most of whom have coughs or colds or sweating sickness or some other early-seventeenth-century malady for much of the time. Life will become an everlasting winter, smelling of herbs, baby shit, sour milk and dirty clothes.

> John Donne
> Anne Donne
> Undone

I wonder what your wife thought when she read that little epigram? Some of your children will die, or be born dead. With any luck, you won't feel it as we do these days. Poor little rabbits, you'll be sorry enough for them while they're alive, screaming their heads off, wanting all the things that nobody's able to give them, such as antibiotics, central heating and a trip to Legoland.

I expect your wife will have to sell that lace collar to pay for one of her confinements. You'll lose your job. Everyone who owes you a grudge will take the chance to kick you now that you're down. You'll be out of favour for years. For all the effort you've put into avoiding martyrdom, you'll achieve your own not very glorious exile in a borrowed cottage in Mitcham.

But none of this has happened yet.

'Come and look,' says the artist, and you saunter round to his side of the easel. Next week he will begin to paint your hands. It has already been decided that you will wear no rings. You don't need to trumpet your status or your prospects, and besides, the artist prefers not to mar the effect of your long, elegant fingers.

You stare thoughtfully at your unfinished portrait. You do not know that it will wreak havoc for generations, that painted face, that cohorts of fifteen-year-old girls will fall for you and feel for you, as you struggle in the swamp of domesticity. *His wife had a baby a year, isn't that gross? She must of been pregnant, like, all the time.*

But your true lovers are more sensitive. We know the inside story. You were undone indeed, you and Anne. A piece of her soul went awry when she married you, and a piece of your soul left your body to meet it. You were never intact again. You tried to write with the noise of your little ones ringing in your ears. You went upstairs, you went downstairs, you went up to town and down to the country, you went to my lady's chamber but there they still were, babbling, squabbling, screaming and squawking, catching quinsies and spotted fevers and scarlet fevers and marsh fevers.

You had no money and each child cost so much. Months of sickness and weariness for Anne, heavy clambering of the stairs, dull aches that heralded the rack of labour. The children's voices floated, skirling. George fought with John, Constance bossed little Mary.

Mary died. Baby Nicholas died. The stillborn unnamed baby died. They floated off, little vagrant souls who had found flesh, but not for quite long enough. They were turned out of their bodies like tenants who hadn't paid the rent. They left fragments of themselves: their blind, eager sucking, the drum of their feet inside the womb. Mary's first words drifted around your house like feathers.

I was one of those fifteen-year-old girls, of course, and head over heels in love with you. You were so unhappy. With what brave grace you wrote of your 'hospital at Mitcham' where the children grew and the poems shrank. You were kept busy writing begging letters. You had to have patrons, even though so many had turned their backs. No one wants to be contaminated by social failure. You'd stepped out so boldly and now you had to fight for a foothold somewhere, anywhere.

I would have done anything for you, when I was fifteen. I even made friends with your wife. Yes, in that hasty, obsequious way of a very determined girl when she pits herself against a grown woman and a mother. I could babysit for Anne perhaps. Surely she would like to have a nice sit down? I shepherd little Constance and John and George and Mary into the other room, sing sweetly to them, give them their dinner and wash their bare, rosy feet. A curl of green snot crawls in and out of Mary's nostril as she breathes. I find a rag and wipe it away tenderly.

There is silence from the bedroom. Anne must be sleeping, I think, and no wonder. Her pregnancy looks like a growth on her skinny body. Her skin is blue-white. She wears a married woman's cap and the hair that escapes from it is thin and lustreless.

I wonder, by my troth, what thou and I
Did till we loved?

Let Anne sleep for a while, poor thing. I don't want the children to wake her, so I hoist Mary on to my knee and begin to tell a story. She twists round in my lap and presses my lips together with her fingers. The others pinch and poke and whinge. I can't even come up with a nursery rhyme. It is time to wake Anne up again.

I tiptoe to the door of her bedroom. Your bedroom too, but I prefer not to think about that. I hear something I didn't expect: laughter. A slash of dread goes through me. You've got in there somehow. You are laughing with her, privately. But no. I peep through the gap in the door and there she is, quite alone, sitting up in bed and reading. She laughs again, and looks up with vague shining eyes as if she is expecting someone. She doesn't see me, of course.

I put a stop to all that sort of thing. I'm not fifteen any more. The past is the past and it's better, much better for everyone, if it doesn't come alive. I don't want to see your beautiful face grow old. I don't want to see your wife's plain, worn features light up when she thinks I might be you, ready to share her laughter. I went too far that time, but I've pulled myself back and I'm in command again. You are history, John. You've written all your poems. Your tongue is still. I refuse to be coerced into seeing things your way.

You're back inside the portrait frame, beautiful and contained. Your red lips. Your high cheekbones and the pure almond cut of your eyelids. It's no surprise that you liked this portrait so much. What a blend of sexual magnetism and intellectual glamour. But I've just noticed something else that I've never seen before. There's a glint of humour in your eyes, as if you're wondering how many more centuries of devastation you'll be capable of before your painted magic fades.

There are just the two of us, John. Why won't you look at me? Why won't you tell me what you see?

ESTHER TO FANNY

❦

I am an orphan. I say these words aloud to myself and hear them move around the room and then disappear into the carpet. They sound like a lie, even though they are true. An orphan is small, scared and hopeful, battling bravely in an institution or bowling along a country road in a dog cart towards a new home where she won't be wanted at first. Orphans have red hair, wide vocabularies and a carpet bag containing their earthly possessions. An orphan is a child with a destiny.

I know the literature. 'Orphans of the Storm: the journey to self-actualisation in literature for children'. We don't yet teach a module with that title, but we may well do so one day. It has exactly the right ring to it. Our students like modules which demand opinions rather than extensive reading. My studies in English Literature have brought me here, to this room where words sink into the cord carpet, to this university staff flat in a concrete block full of students.

They are arriving now. Parents are unloading cars, lugging TVs up echoey staircases, checking the wiring on the communal microwave, opening and then quickly closing the bathroom doors. Soon they'll be gone and the kids will be on their own. Big, bonny temporary orphans with credit cards.

My mother died during the summer. I practise the words and they too disappear. When last term ended I was a woman with a mother whom I visited each weekend. Some colleagues knew why, others didn't. I had learned a new vocabulary. I would say, 'Macmillan nurse,' and on one or two faces there would shine complete understanding. On others, not a flicker.

Esther to Fanny, this is Esther to Fanny, come in.

I listen. I'm not daft enough to think there's going to be any answer. My name is Esther. My mother's name was not Fanny.

Last term I read out to my students a letter from a woman with breast cancer. This letter was addressed to a woman called Esther. The writer's name was Fanny, Fanny Burney, and in her letter she described a mastectomy performed on her without anaesthetic, in 1811.

I came across Fanny Burney's letter by chance, while I was searching yet another website for information about mastectomy. And there was Fanny Burney's portrait. Her face was composed but she looked as if something had amused her very much a few minutes earlier. I began to read her letter to Esther.

The eighteenth century is not my period, but it has always appealed to me. There is something about those small, fierce, brave people who dressed elaborately, smelled awful, gushed about feeling and worshipped Reason. Fanny Burney, for all she lived forty years into the nineteenth century, is one of them to the bone. I am glad it's not my period. I wouldn't want to add to it, deconstruct it, contextualise it, demystify it, or explain it in any way.

I didn't ask my students to analyse Fanny's letter. It didn't fit into the module at all, but I thought it was worth reading to them, all the same.

I read it out to them, that's all. They are too big and bouncing, healthy and beautiful. They frowned and shifted in their seats and flinched and probably felt glad that things like that only happen to really old people. Fanny Burney was fifty-nine! No wonder she got ill, what else could she expect? Besides, at fifty-nine, should you really care so much about your life any more? It is the deaths of children and young people that rate as tragedies, just as it is children who make real orphans. Fanny Burney's mastectomy, performed without anaesthesia, gave her another twenty-nine years of life. I watched my students doing the calculation, and reckoning that it was hardly worth it. Who wants to suffer in order to be old for even more years?

No, I am not doing them justice. They flinched, as I did. Unconsciously, some of the girls brought up their hands to cover their breasts, as I'd done. Fanny got through to them.

'I don't see why she agreed to have the operation. I mean, I'd rather die than go through that!' one girl said after I had finished reading. 'I mean, she wasn't young, was she?' she added, glancing at me.

Esther to Fanny. No, you weren't young. My mother wasn't young, either. She was even older than you. She was seventy-three. If she didn't receive the very best of modern medical treatment, she certainly had the nearly best. She had a mastectomy, radiotherapy, chemotherapy. Two years later she developed a secondary in her left lung. She had more radiotherapy, oxygen, a nebuliser, massage, physiotherapy to keep her lungs as clear as possible. They gave her baths in a Jacuzzi at the hospice. She liked the Jacuzzi, or at least I think she liked it. She was so polite that it was hard to tell.

My mother had everything. GP appointments, clinic appointments, a second opinion, referral for rehab, referral to pain clinic, a place in a trial, a re-referral, another X-ray, a series of blood tests, a change of consultant, a lavender massage, a Macmillan nurse, a commode, a bell by her bed and a tube up her nose, a bed in the hospice. She was so lucky to get it, that bed in the hospice.

Esther to Fanny. You had none of that. Each doctor in your story had a name. They trembled, or grew pale, or stood aside hanging their head at the thought of the pain they were about to give you. They colluded with you in sending your husband out for the day. They knew, as you did, that he would not be able to endure witnessing your operation. They told you the truth: 'Je ne veux pas vous tromper. Vous souffrirez, vous souf-frirez *beaucoup*!'

Yes, they were clear about it. They were men of the eighteenth century, even though the century had turned. They told you that you would suffer a great deal. They told you that you must cry out and scream. They stam-mered, and could not go on, because their sensibility was as powerful as their sense of reason. When the moment came for the operation to begin, you wanted to run out of the room. But Reason took command in your fierce, bright eighteenth-century mind, and you climbed on to the bedstead where your breast was to be amputated. There were seven men around your bed. I wonder how they smelled, and how often they washed? They were the greatest doctors of their age, but probably they didn't even wash their hands before they cut off your breast. They put a cambric handkerchief over your face, and through it you saw the glint of polished steel.

But they also cured you. They cut off your living breast and scraped you down to the bone to search out the last cancerous atoms. You screamed all the time, except when you fainted. You recovered, even though everyone concerned in your operation was left pale as ashes, in their black clothes. You saw the blood on them as you were carried back to your bed. You were about to live for another twenty-nine years.

It's a strange story to our ears, Fanny. How exquisitely you act out the hard logic of the eighteenth century, and keep your eyes open under the cambric handkerchief. It is only semi-transparent anyway, so you see most of what goes on as the men prepare to operate upon you. They could have found a thick black piece of cloth and tied it around your eyes as a blindfold, but they didn't. I have the feeling that they respected you too much.

And the emotion around that bed! Imagine if one of the doctors treating my mother had turned ashen, and wept. If he had told her the truth. 'Vous souffrirez, vous souffrirez *beaucoup*!'

Nobody said it. But you suffered, Mum. You suffered a great deal. There was a smell in the hospice which we never mentioned, although I know you smelled it as well as I did. It was the smell of death, literally: it was the smell of the cancer in the old man who shared your two-bed room. He was curtained, out of sight, but we could smell him. I had never known that such a thing could be. Sometimes I would gag, and turn it into a cough.

'It's not very nice, is it?' you whispered once, sadly, pitifully. But in a very soft whisper, so no one else would hear.

Esther to Fanny. I am glad that you screamed throughout the twenty minutes of your operation, except when you fainted. To restrain yourself might have seriously bad consequences, your doctors told you beforehand. What miracles of sense and feeling those men must have been! Knowing that you would scream, you must scream, and anticipating it by actually charging you to scream and informing you that to do otherwise might be dangerous for your health. Knowing that you would have enough to contend with, under that semi-transparent cambric handkerchief, without any false shame.

My mother hated to make a fuss. She was very grateful to all the doctors and nurses. If they didn't do their jobs well, she had an answer for it. They were understaffed, run off their feet. 'That nurse over there, Esther, she's got an eight-month-old baby, she's been up half the night with him cutting his molars. I don't know how she does it.'

I wanted to shake that nurse until her teeth rattled. She was late with the drugs round. My mother was waiting, waiting. There was sweat on her yellow face but she wouldn't let me ring the bell.

'For God's sake, Mum, it's what they're here for. They're supposed to be taking care of you. That means bringing your tablets when you need them.'

But my mother turned her head aside wearily. 'It doesn't do to get across them. You don't know, Esther.'

Esther to Fanny. You were utterly in those doctors' power, just as Mum was. You saw the flash of steel through your cambric handkerchief. You felt and heard that blade scraping your breastbone. You were a heroine and the doctors treated you as one.

We have moved on. We have chemo and radio and prostheses, and scans to show the travels of those 'peccant attoms' of cancer which your doctors feared so much that they scraped you down to the bone. What can I say? I can't reread your account without flinching. You couldn't reread it at all.

Mum is dead and I'm an orphan. Two things that don't sound as if they can possibly be true. Mum didn't want to cause any trouble, and she didn't cause any trouble. The doctors barely noticed her really.

My students are pounding up and down the stairs with their posters, IKEA lamps, armfuls of CDs and clothes. They are flushed, healthy, on the whole averse to study but only too pleased to be back at uni with all their friends. Some of them will choose my module on Elizabeth Bishop. These days it is perfectly possible to get to the end of a degree in English Literature without venturing into the eighteenth century at all.

Esther to Fanny. At the end of your long letter you apologised to your sister. 'God bless my dearest Esther – I fear this is all written – confusedly, but I cannot read it – & I can write it no more …'

I put my hand out to touch that semi-transparent cambric handkerchief which time has laid across you. Your letter cuts like polished steel, although I am not, dear Fanny, your Esther at all.

WHERE I KEEP MY FAITH

❦

When we were children and our badness jumped out of our hidden hearts and showed itself in bold words, Grandpa would raise himself from his chair. His shadow would fill the doorway as he went into the yard to cut a switch. When he had found the right one he would call us outside. Five strokes on our calves, no more. Each one was a sharp, hot, single pain. I would stare down to see if my badness was flickering away across the dust like a snake. Maybe if I looked hard enough I would see the moment when the shadow of it left my body and slipped to the earth.

My grandpa never hurt us hard. My mind was always quick and alive, not swallowed up in pain the way I know that a mind can be beaten until darkness overcomes it. But Grandpa made me think about badness: where it came from and how it could be seen in a person's eyes or in his voice or in his smile. It might be

64

hidden but it would never be hidden enough, not from my grandpa or from the eye of God.

One night Grandma showed me something that looked like a star. She got me to fix my eyes on it and then she told me that it wasn't a star, but a satellite made of metal and plastic.

'Who put it there?'

'The Americans put it there.'

'Why?'

My grandma shrugged. 'Who knows?' she said.

I wondered if one day a satellite might take out God's eye. If so, He would be able to see nothing. I thought about God seeing nothing and waiting blindly to be told what had happened in the world. The angels would be His messengers, and perhaps some days they would be tired or bored and they would fail to tell Him of every little piece of badness wriggling across the dust of the earth.

I was grown up before I knew that it was the other way around. Something had taken out the eye that would show us God, and only faith would help us in our blindness. The word of God was so clear that it dazzled me.

I was grown up some more when all this changed again. Blindness and hiddenness were in me and all around me. The words I had stood up for in church were far away. The sound of my voice praising the Lord was silent.

Where is a person's faith? Where does she keep it? I have been thinking about this question for so long.

However much it wearies me, it will not go away. The more I think, the less I can answer. Even the word itself begins to have a strange sound in my mind. *Faith*. You might tell me that it is obviously kept in the soul, and then we can talk about what the soul is made of, and whether we can see it, and where it goes after death. Or perhaps it is in the heart. The heart is closer and more familiar. We are used to it knocking against the ribs when we are afraid, or melting tenderly at the curve of a baby's head. Perhaps faith is in there too, sometimes knocking and sometimes melting.

But I don't think so. I've had a long time to consider it, and many alternatives have presented themselves to me.

Firstly, the hair. Unlike the heart and perhaps unlike the soul, hair continues to grow long after we are dead. It is not a pleasant thing to imagine hairs pushing through the skin, wriggling out into the white shroud. Even if a woman has always coloured her hair, she won't be able to fool anyone after her death: the hair that grows will be grey. Grey and tired-looking and without lustre. Sometimes I imagine all the hair that is growing all over the planet, from the recent dead.

Hair is not a safe place to keep your faith. It can be cut off against your will. It can be torn from your scalp. But on the other hand, hair can be plaited so tightly that the pattern endures for weeks. Perhaps faith would be happy there, planted deep in a maze.

It is a long, long time since anyone plaited my hair, although I can remember sitting between my grandma's knees while she combed and separated and twisted. She had strong fingers but she never hurt me.

'What's the hurry? We have all the time in the world,' she used to say.

My grandma liked to stroke the curve of my cheek with her finger. She told me that I was like her garden after rain had fallen on it, because I was young. 'Look at my face. This is how a garden becomes when rain refuses to fall.' She laughed and all the gullies in her face crinkled, exactly like the channels that ran down to the dry river.

You might think it would be possible to keep faith in my grandma's lines. Surely it would be safe there. An old woman's lines will only grow deeper and provide a safer shelter. But even apart from the fact that my grandma is dead, I don't think it would be possible. We shed our skin every seven years. The faith would flake away invisibly into what we call dust.

I am supposed to sign a letter, renouncing my faith. I have spent a long time thinking about what this means. If you renounce something, then it goes away from you and you no longer possess it. But where does it go? The letter has been written on a computer. If I renounce my faith, will it go into the fibres of the paper, or will it hop back to where the letter was conceived and lodge itself in the computer's memory? Where exactly will it go?

What is supposed to happen is this. They bring me out of my cell into a room where I have been brought many times before. It is a small, dirty room with a desk and a chair with a man sitting in it. He is dressed in his army uniform. The uniform is clean and stiff. It looks as if its pleats and folds would have the strength to cut. His boots are also clean. His boots and his face glisten like land where rain has fallen. My feet are bare. The skin is grey and the veins are knotted. I have no mirror but I know that my hair does not shine. I have an infection in one eye which refuses to clear. I am not clean and so my body smells. I see his nose wrinkle. I am forcing him to do things he doesn't want to have to do. All that is necessary is for me to sign his piece of paper and then sensible things can begin to happen.

Each time it happens I look down at my feet. On my right foot, the big toenail has gone. Obviously I did not keep my faith in that toenail. I almost smile, but without changing the expression on my face.

It is stupid, all of this. It is so stupid. They make that clear to us. There are four of us keeping our faith not in our souls or our hearts or our hair or our toenails or our grandmothers' wrinkles. Sometimes we are kept separate and told that all the others have signed the piece of paper and gone away. They have been given food and a shower and shoes and clean underwear and even a small roll of notes so they can buy a bus ticket home.

When the men say this, we just wait. We don't look believing and we don't look disbelieving. Even though I know it isn't true, my stomach hurts because of the thought that it might be only me left. I fear that the others have been killed. I see them so rarely and we never have time for more than a few words. It's better if we aren't together, in case we give something to one another. Our badness maybe, or else our faith, which we ought to give to the white sheet of paper.

I think of a thousand falling at my side, and ten thousand at my right hand.

I am not the material of which martyrs are made. I have always known this. The others say that they are the same. It's just that we took a step, and then another step, and these steps brought us here. But in fact it's not possible to count the steps. And you can't take them back again, because in order to do that you would have to unmake everything. I would have to become a woman with ten toenails and ripe, moist skin and hair the colour of earth after heavy rain has fallen on it.

Sometimes I imagine myself lying on the ground, clinging to the big shiny boot of the man who brings in the piece of paper. Rubbing my cheek against the leather. Saying that I will do anything he wants.

But what would be the good of that? I would have to get rid of my faith first, and I am unable to do that until I find out exactly where it is.

In my skull perhaps. I have a bony cave of secrets under my scalp, just like everyone. They could dig their way into it, but that would be the end of me. No chance of a pen in my hand then. No words on paper. *I give up. I renounce. I have no faith any more.*

I understand completely that it would be gratifying to kill me. I am an annoyance, as well as a source of undesirable odours. I get in the way of what ought to happen next. Sometimes I find myself completely in sympathy with their point of view.

Perhaps my faith is in my elbow. Elbows are awkward things, jabbing out into the world, making space for themselves. They are also far from beautiful. The only elbow it's possible to love is the elbow of a baby, so soft and dimpled that it fits into your mouth like a plum.

My elbows are dry. When I hold my arm out straight in front of me, wrinkled skin hangs. Sometimes it seems very funny to me that once I had those plum elbows too. At other times I feel as if time has stopped moving in a straight line and is zigzagging back and forth like a snake on the floor. I feel my grandma's hands in my hair. I hear her voice vibrate against the back of my head. I watch my grandfather throw his switch on to the earth and walk back inside.

Without question I am lucky that I have no children. My little son with the plum elbows was never born. But sometimes I forget it. I feel the tingle of milk beginning in my breasts. I feel my belly lift and tighten as if someone is about to be born. After a while I come back to myself and I am glad that I am alone, that my grandparents are dead and that everyone in my family has signed the piece of paper. Or have they? Perhaps they never needed to, because they were clean of faith.

I remember everything about when I was taken away. There were six of us in a room, and the Lord was with us. Wherever two or three are gathered together in my name.

This is why they keep us alone most of the time, so that two or three cannot gather together. But being alone does other things as well. It makes time whip backwards and forwards like a snake about to strike. It makes a baby come to me.

Of course I pray. I say words, as if my faith were in my mouth. The others tell me: 'I will pray for you,' and I say: 'I will pray for you.' It makes our prayers sound like wheels, rolling across the world and touching on one another.

But my faith is not in my mouth. I pray less than I ever did.

My voice was beautiful. I was a praise-singer. I used to rise up, and then raise them up. The sound would grow from deep inside me and swell richly until my forehead was slick with the dew of praise. I sang for hours and never tired. My voice was a gift and I gave it back to the Lord seventy times seven.

Yes, I thought a lot of myself, the way a woman does when her skin is ripe and soft and her voice sways a roomful of hearts.

Now I look back at that singer with her blaze of a smile at the end of a song, and I'm watching a child dance in imitation of a grown woman. My voice has dried up. All last winter I had a cough from lying on the ground. I don't worry about it too much. My voice will come back, or else it won't. I used to think that my faith was in my voice. It made people turn to me like flowers. They called my voice a gift from God.

I won't sign the piece of paper. This is not something I've decided. It has come to be true for many reasons which are all one reason. My missing toenail, my knotty hair, the veins on my feet, my disinclination for prayer. The sound of the switch and the slam of my head against the wall. The grey hairs that'll still be growing after I die. My elbow joint, working away like a knuckle under the flesh. My brain which says that the men are right, and what I am doing is not sensible.

The Lord refusing to be with me, then suddenly giving me a child.

The smell of myself.

The fact that I can't, anywhere, find where I keep my faith.

A THOUSAND ROSES

∽

I'm driving in the dark. There's not another car in sight. I haven't seen one for miles. Only my own headlights, brushing the loneliness. You wouldn't believe how this road chokes in summer. Miles and miles of glittering cars, stuck together in a glue of heat and exhaust. The mist is coming down. Dad listened to the forecast earlier. *Mist and fog patches over high ground and in coastal areas. Driving conditions may become hazardous.*

'Surely you can wait until the morning?'

'No,' I said, turning away so he wouldn't see my face. 'I've got to get back.'

'You know best, I suppose,' he said, not looking at me either. I'd been very careful, but he'd picked up something. Like a smell or a slick of sweat on a palm.

'It'll only be a few days, Dad. You sure you'll be all right with Johnny?'

'I'm his grandad, aren't I?'

Dad knows that flesh and blood make everything all right. Whether you approve or disapprove, whether you like or dislike, you love. Love isn't an idea to Dad; it's as strong as stone.

Dad goes to bed at ten and rises at five, summer and winter. He kneels down slowly, his joints cracking, and sets a match to the fire he's built the night before. When the flame spurts, Dad warms his fingers. He'll be asleep by now, on his back with his mouth open. Johnny will be sleeping too. Safe, both of them, now that my car's not parked outside the cottage, and I'm not there.

'Jacinta, are you there? I need to speak to you.'

Khalid's voice, on the answerphone. Dad raised his eyebrows, because I didn't cross the room to pick up.

'Are you there, Jacinta? Are you in your father's house?'

Khalid waited for a long moment; then there was a click.

I asked Dad to call him back. 'Say you don't know where I am.'

'You're asking me to tell a lie, Jacinta.'

'Dad, please. Just say it. Say we're not here. Say you thought I'd gone to Wales.'

Dad shook his head. 'Why can't you speak to him yourself?'

'You don't understand, Dad. There are things you don't know.'

'Then tell me.'

Inspiration flashed through me. 'It's to do with Johnny.'

'Oh.' Dad's face sagged. He would do as I asked now.

I should have been in Wales. Carola and I had booked a two-day canoeing course on the River Wye, our first ever weekend away from the children. Carola's mother was going to look after them. We'd got the hotel and railway tickets on a cheap deal.

Dad sighed heavily. 'I suppose you know what you're doing, Jacinta.' Dad had met Khalid, and decided he was all right. 'He's training to be an engineer,' he said to me. 'He's already got a degree in mathematics from his own country.'

'Just phone him back, Dad. Please. Now.'

'You know best,' he said at last, coldly. He would stretch his conscience for my sake, and Khalid would believe him, because Dad was a man of his word.

A few minutes later he came out to the garden where I was pushing Johnny on the swing.

'Your answerphone was on.'

'Did you leave a message?'

'Yes.'

I put Johnny to bed early, and Dad came out to the car with me. Already, night had fallen.

'Get Shep and Jasper in now, Dad,' I said. 'You ought to put your bolt across, these dark nights.'

'We're safe enough here. The dogs come in at ten and not before.'

'You will lock up properly?'

'You don't need to worry about Johnny. He'll be all right with me,' said Dad. He was still angry that I'd made him lie. He'd understand later. I put my hands on his shoulders and felt his bone and smelled his oldness. We said goodbye.

My car is a small box, trapped in the huge box of night. Suddenly the mist is everywhere. I turn on my fog lamps.

I try to breathe deeply, steadily. I make my fingers relax on the steering wheel.

Johnny. Think of Johnny.

There's always mist up over Bodmin. Once I pass Colliford Lake and the road drops, it will clear.

The needle of the speedometer is falling. I can't see the side of the road now. The slower I go, the worse the engine sounds. My tyres rasp on the safety strip and I haul us back on to the tarmac. I must keep to the crown of the road. I shouldn't be driving in this.

Crawling now. Twenty miles an hour, eighteen, sixteen.

Soon you'll be going downhill and the mist will clear.

I know the road too well. The bare browns of the moor, the little lake, the sweep of bog and grazing. Small clusters of trees, wire fences, thorn bushes around lonely farms. Wind always blowing, even when the mist is heaviest, and a lick of wetness in the air that tastes of salt. Always the noise of the wind.

If I stop the car, and roll it into the verge, the mist will hide me. No one will guess where I've gone.

Johnny. Think of Johnny, fast asleep in my old bed. He's safe. Khalid won't come looking for me there. He'll believe my father.

Lights. Lights behind me. Too late to turn my headlights off, too late to roll into the side of the road and hide. Panic jolts thoughts out of me in sparks, like live wires brushing.

Lights, full glare. Too close. Right up behind me. Khalid. He's not in London at all, that's why Dad got the answerphone. He's here. His lights fill my car. He'll see me.

So close, too close, it's dangerous.

Oh God, he's going to go into me, push me off the road. That's why he's up so close. He's trying to push me off the road and then he'll get me out of the car. He's flashing his lights. He wants me to stop. I will not stop.

He's falling back now. I clutch the wheel and won't look. They say don't look back, don't catch their eye. It makes them more angry.

And then he does it. His lights are there again, blinding, and he pulls out with a surge of speed and he's alongside me, very close, sounding his horn to make me move over. And I look, I do look though I know I mustn't, and I see the men crammed into the car, two in the front, two in the back.

Their car passes me and accelerates away. For a few seconds its rear fog lamps are bright, and then it fades in the murk.

I'm shaking too much to keep driving. I pull over and switch off the engine, and then the lights. I open the window wide and the cold air pours in.

I hated hide and seek when I was a child. I would walk out of my hiding place and face the seeker, rather than wait to be caught.

Coming, ready or not …

I'm ready. Come and get me. I can't take any more. It's less than a day since it began, but I can't take any more.

Three months ago it was high summer. Johnny was in the paddling pool from the moment he came home. Yes, that's how it was all summer. The splash of water, the smell of plants drinking, Johnny laughing, the rush of the hose. Our garden is tiny, but in the evening light it looked green and gold, like paradise. Our new lodger stayed in his room, working. He was a mature student of engineering, quiet, considerate, polite. The perfect lodger, I thought, after the first week.

I'd put Johnny to bed one evening and I was watering the garden when I heard the front door open. It was Khalid, on his way up to the small room that had been collecting heat all day.

I brushed my palm over the lavender bush, and went into the house.

'Khalid!' I called softly. Upstairs, his door opened.

'Yes?'

'It's so hot, I wondered if you would like to sit in the garden.'

A pause. Maybe all he wanted was to rest, alone.

'Thank you. I am taking a shower now, and then I will come down.'

I stood in the hall, looking up the narrow stairs. I could hear every sound he made. The house was so small, so cheaply built. Every sound that Johnny made was familiar, grooved into me so that any break in the pattern sent me running. But the footfalls of a grown man were as strange as the smell of another adult in the house.

I could hear everything. Khalid's shower, the flush of his toilet, the clink of the mug where he kept his tooth-brush. I hadn't guessed that taking a lodger would make me think so much about the work of caring for a body. The time it takes, flossing and brushing, pumicing dead skin and putting plasters on corns, each of us intent in our separate rooms. Hairs caught in the plughole, soap scum and toothpaste scum, nail clippings, soggy towels drying on the heated rail I forgot to provide until he asked. Khalid was to give me his bedding to wash once a week.

'You're welcome to use the washing machine any time,' I'd told him. 'I'll peg out your washing if you're not at home, or put it in the dryer.' But he was too private for that.

'I will use the launderette.'

He came out into the garden, damp from his shower, in a fresh pale blue shirt and chinos. He was not much taller than me – five eight or five nine, maybe – but he was strong, stocky even. He carried a newspaper. Maybe I had created awkwardness for him with my invitation. He might have preferred to stay in his room. He'd thought, I'll bring a newspaper, and then I won't have to talk.

Khalid stood at the open French windows, looking around the garden, letting his eyes rest on one thing and then another. He stepped forward, on to the flags, and pointed at the apple trees.

'What is that shape in English? The way it's cut to fit the wall?'

'Espalier. The branches grow along those wires – see?'

'Yes. So, you have an orchard,' he says, smiling faintly.

'I've always wanted one,' I say. 'Full of fruit and flowers.'

'My friend had an orchard,' says Khalid abruptly. 'It belonged to his family for many generations. His mother was the last person to grow fruit there, after his father's death. But they lost the land.'

'What fruit did they grow there?'

'Pomegranates. My friend told me a poem his grandfather had written, about this pomegranate orchard.'

'Do you remember it?'

'I remember only some of it. My friend was young when the grandfather died. You know that pomegranate flowers come at the end of the little branches? Sometimes they are single, and sometimes they bunch together. They are very bright, the colour of fire. The poem was about this pomegranate fire.'

'What happened to the orchard?'

'It's finished. All the trees pulled up and burned.'

'Was that in your country?'

'No.'

Pomegranates. On that warm summer night the word seemed to open like a flower. Khalid's face lightened, and he smiled at me.

'Have you mint in your garden?'

'Yes, it's there, in a pot behind the lavender.'

'If I pick some, I can make *shay na'na*. Moroccan tea. I have green tea in my room. Wait one moment.'

We sat drinking tea. Khalid smoked.

'It's good,' I said. 'The tea, it's very good. It's so refreshing.'

He smiled again. 'It's whatever you want. Sometimes refreshing, sometimes relaxing. It changes to what you need.'

And there you were, Khalid. You changed to what I needed. Suddenly, in that moment, the change happened, and it couldn't be put back. But I don't know if I changed for you. Did I, Khalid? Or was your rage still burning in you when you looked at me, like the fire of pomegranate flowers on the end of a branch?

The mist is so heavy that I can't see what's ahead of me and I can't see what's behind me. There's nothing but mist and silence, now that I've switched off the engine. I'm cold, but I don't close the window. I'm listening for the sound of a car, coming closer, closer.

It was yesterday evening. I was packing for Wales. Stuff all over the bed, Johnny in the bath, the phone ringing, spaghetti sauce burning ...

'It's OK,' said Khalid. 'Leave it to me. I'll pack your case so everything comes out perfect.'

'It's all such a mess. I hate packing.'

'Where I come from, we are always packing our suitcases. Always preparing to go away. Packing and unpacking and getting ready ... Because there is nothing for us at home.' He smiled. His eyes were soft and warm. 'I'll finish everything for you, and strap the case.'

He was right; his packing was perfect. When I unstrapped the case and opened it, everything was immaculately folded and fitted together like an expensive jigsaw. It was a shame to touch it, but Khalid would never know. I'd forgotten to put in my new electric styling tongs. After a day on the river, my hair would need work. I'd wedge the box right down at the bottom. I could lift Khalid's layers without disturbing his packing—

My fingers met something hard that they didn't recognise. Gently, I shifted a rolled-up shirt. In the heart of my packing, there was a strange shape. I parted the clothes.

It was gift-wrapped in shiny red paper. A present. A present from Khalid, for me to discover in Wales. I smiled, already imagining how Carola would watch as I opened it. 'He's fantastic, imagine him thinking of this, he's so different from any man I've known before,' I'd say.

Very carefully, I slipped my hands under the package and felt its weight. It was dense. Heavy. Too heavy, when for once I could travel light, without all the stuff you need when you have a child. Khalid was so lovely, so generous ...

I listened. I could hear him downstairs, talking to Johnny. He was so good with Johnny. You'd think they'd known each other for years, not three months. Quietly, I opened the bottom drawer of my chest, slipped the package into the back and covered it with clothes.

I went downstairs. Khalid was carefully spooning the non-burnt layer of spaghetti sauce into another pan, but he turned to smile at me. 'All you need to do is eat,' he said. 'Your packing is done. I have strapped up your case.'

'Maybe I'd better just check in case there's anything I've forgotten,' I said, to tease him.

'No!' His spoon stopped scraping. 'It is all done, Jacinta. Everything that you need. Don't you trust me?'

'Khalid, what a question. Of course I trust you.'

'Don't you think I will look after you?'

'Of course, of course I do—'

His emotion surprised me.

'We have to trust each other,' he said, stepping forward, cupping my face with his free hand. 'Don't you see that? Without trust, there is nothing.'

'Khalid, what's the matter? It was beautiful, the way you packed—'

His hand, his eyes were frozen. 'You opened the case?'

'Well, yes—'

'You looked? You took things out?'

'No. It was only that I'd forgotten my styling tongs.'

His hand dropped to my shoulder, digging, squeezing. He said nothing. His eyes scoured my face. He said nothing, but I stepped back.

'Khalid, I'm sorry, I just put the tongs on top, I didn't mess anything up.'

He thought I'd found his surprise. He was wounded, angry. He was … what was he? I had to make him believe I hadn't found it.

'You did a great job,' I said, keeping my eyes on his, showing him through my eyes how much I loved him. Slowly, slowly, the hand gripping my shoulder relaxed.

At eight, Khalid went to his study group. He never missed it. 'They are my brothers, Jacinta. We study together, we help one another.' He'd creep in later, because I needed an early night. I only had to check Johnny, and put out my clothes for the morning.

The phone rang. Carola.

'For God's sake don't forget your waterproofs, Jass. I nearly left my cagoule on the peg behind the door.'

'It's all in. Khalid packed my case so beautifully. It looks like one of those magazine features.'

'Lucky we're not flying.'

'What?'

'You know, all that stuff. "Did you pack your bag yourself? Are you carrying anything for another person?"'

I pause.

'Yes,' I say.

'You OK, Jass? Don't worry, Johnny'll be fine with Mum.'

Her voice boomed in my head as I split into two people. One was on the phone to Carola; the other was silent, hearing echoes that spread like rings from a plunging stone.

Did you pack your bag yourself?

Almost midnight. Khalid wasn't back. I went to my drawer and lifted the clothes that hid the parcel. I could scratch off a corner of the paper. I could look inside.

No. I have to trust him. I have to believe.

Just a corner.

Did you pack your bag yourself? Could anyone have interfered with your bags? But they don't ask questions like that on trains, and they don't look inside your bag.

People don't do things like that. Not us, we live together. He loves me, we trust each other—

They are my brothers. We help one another.

Johnny cried out, and I went to him. His forehead was moist, but he wasn't really awake. I said to him what I always say: 'It's all right, Mummy's here.'

He settled into sleep again. *Mummy's here. Mummy's here. Did you pack your bag yourself? It's all right, Mummy's here.*

My mind changed by itself. I didn't have to change it. I lifted Khalid's package from my drawer. My fingers opened the straps of the suitcase, lifted the layers of clothes, and repositioned the weight of Khalid's surprise back into its place in my case. My fingers were as light and terrified as my breath. I packed another bag, with Johnny's things and some of my own. I woke Johnny and wrapped him in his duvet and carried him down to the car.

I left the suitcase on the bed. I didn't leave you a note, Khalid. Maybe your present was a thousand roses, packed so tight that the parcel weighed like lead.

HAMID IN THE PLAYHOUSE

❧

'Is it going to snow, Nan?'

'It looks like it. I'll have to get that sledge down from the loft.'

His small hand squeezes mine. He won't keep his gloves on, even when it's as cold as this.

'Are we just around the corner now, Nan?'

'Yes, just around the corner, Lewis.' I've said that to him since before he can remember, I suppose, on our way home from the shops.

There's a big silver van slewed across the street. Dreadful parking. Some builder who can't find a space and thinks it's all right to block everyone else. I'm still thinking that when I see the black figures swarming out of the back of the van. I pull Lewis against me.

'Nan, who are those men?'

Before he's finished saying it, I've understood. Black meshy suits like bikers, big helmets, visors down over their faces. Shouldering out of the van, moving fast.

87

Some at the door of the flats, some by the van. More and more of them pouring out. Two heading for the back, but the wall is too high. They don't know that they have to go down the alley, off the main road. They run back to the van, and come out with a ladder. How many seconds does that take? Two, four, six, eight. More men. Eight men at least now, moving so fast I can't count them properly. No markings on the van. Ladder against the wall. The first man goes up it, too fast, gets his weight wrong, the ladder tips, the other man catches it. They shout all the time. Now he's up. Razor-wire on the top, surely he must have seen that before he started climbing.

They've got guns.

'Nan, I want to go to your house.'

'In a minute, Lewis.'

'Are they baddies?'

He pushes in close to me, face in my coat. The men swarm. Another two charge forward with something I don't recognise until they run it into the front door of the flats. A battering-ram. A window on the top floor flies open and a woman leans out.

'What the fuck?' she shouts. She isn't dressed; you can see that. A young girl, not a woman, clutching a towel round her.

'Police! Get away from that window!'

'Are those men police?' asks Lewis.

'I think so.' My heart is thundering. Fear. Anger. Disbelief, as the door cracks and comes off its hinges.

Surely to God they could have rung the bell and that girl would have put on her dressing gown and come down to open it.

'Come on, Lewis, we're going back to the shops. You can have a hot chocolate.'

Lewis crouches down, grizzling. He doesn't want to walk any more. He wants to go home. 'Nan, why can't we go to your house?'

For heaven's sake, I think, lifting him into my arms, he's only three. The shops are half a mile away and he's already tired. We can squeeze past the van on this side. He wants the warm, and his toys, and his tea. 'You be a nice quiet boy for Nan. We'll be home in a minute.'

They're inside the flats now. Two are left by the van, looking up and down the street. I wrap Lewis in my arms. No, it wouldn't be safe to try and slip past the van. They're so keyed up, any movement and they might let fly. Instead, I keep my distance and call politely, 'Excuse me?'

They whip round. I can't see them taking me in, because of the visors, but I know what they see. A nan. Sixtyish, overweight in spite of religious attendance at Zumba in the church hall, wearing glasses, clutching grandchild. Worried, conciliatory expression.

'Excuse me, officer,' I go on, 'I live down the end of the street. My grandson's not very well and I need to get him into the warm. Would you be kind enough to help me through?'

It works. I'm not a threat, and I don't want to get involved. Through the broken door, I can hear the girl shouting – screaming, really – but I carry on regardless. 'Just that house down there, the end terrace.' I point. They look at each other. For a few seconds, the carapace cracks. There's no one else around. No audience, no one to play up to, or down to.

'All right, love. Quick as you can, and stay indoors once you're there.'

I keep Lewis in the back, away from the windows, until Rachel comes to pick him up at six o'clock. She's all nerves, grabbing hold of Lewis and squeezing him hard.

'There's police all over the end of the street. Yellow tape everywhere. They wouldn't let me bring the car through. I thought there'd been an accident. Are you OK, Mum?'

'Everything's fine.'

'Someone said it's the anti-terrorist squad.'

'It's the "late for tea and turn on the blues-and-twos" squad as far as I'm concerned. Frightening people like that.'

When they've gone, I can't settle. I go upstairs, and without turning on my bedroom light, I pull up the sash and peer out. The van is still there. I go downstairs, and decide to light a fire. I don't have one very often, but it makes the place cosy. I keep bags of smokeless fuel outside the back door.

It's very cold, and just starting to snow. Lewis will love that. A white world, when he wakes up. We can make a snowman tomorrow – I've got that old red and black scarf somewhere—

I stand quite still. My hair hackles. I can't have mistaken it. A cough, quickly smothered. It came from Lewis's playhouse, at the end of the garden.

I'm standing on the tongue of light from the doorway. If I scream they'll hear me from the end of the street. Someone's in the playhouse. Pretend not to have heard. Go back into the house, lock the door. Call the police. Say: *I'm probably being stupid, but I thought I heard something ...*

It's so cold. Too cold for anyone to sleep out. Why would a burglar go and shut himself up in a child's playhouse? I go back inside and fetch the brass candlestick from the hall table. Ugly old thing. Heavy as lead. I get the torch, switch it on, and then, without giving myself time to think, I go straight out of the back door, across the lawn, and I pull back the door of the playhouse.

'Oh my life,' I say, for there he is in the torch beam. Hamid from the flats, jammed into the playhouse like something out of *Alice in Wonderland*. He's wrapped himself in the old dhurrie from the floor. He rears up, squinting against the light.

'What are you doing here, Hamid?'

For a moment, all I can think of is that he must have had a row with his girlfriend, and she's locked him out.

'Please!' he says in a desperate whisper. 'They will hear you.'

I know Hamid. He's been in the flats more than two years. He's a postgraduate student at the university. Social sciences, I think. He plays football with Lewis sometimes, on the bit of tarmac they've got at the side of the flats, for parking.

'Get up off the floor, you'll freeze to death down there.'

'I cannot. Please, turn off the light. They will see.'

I get him into the house. He is so stiff with cold that I have to give him my shoulder to lean on. I run upstairs, fetch my duvet and prise the edges of the dhurrie out of his hands. It falls to the floor. He is wearing a bright red dressing gown with the words 'Santa's Sweetheart' blazoned across it.

'It is my girlfriend's,' he says apologetically as I wrap the duvet around him.

I make him a cup of tea and put three spoonfuls of sugar into it, and then I remember the snow. Our feet will have left a trail. I run to the back door, but the snow is coming down heavily, wiping away our footprints.

That dhurrie needs to go under the stairs. And Hamid ...

'Why were they looking for you?' I ask as I fill my hot-water bottle for him.

'They have also been to the university. They say I am in contact with proscribed groups, but it is for my research project.'

I am not naïve. I know that terrorists may also be young men who play football with the children of their neighbours, and pass the time of day pleasantly.

'Hamid, you're shaking. Are you still cold?'

'I am claustrophobic.'

I bought the playhouse in a kit, for Lewis. The instruction sheet was all diagrams, and I couldn't make it out. Hamid was cleaning his motorbike, so I showed him the sheet. He said it would be no problem to put the playhouse together. He could do it in half an hour.

'I expect they only want to question you,' I say, and think of the battering-ram.

'They can keep me for many days. Fourteen days.'

Lewis will be here in the morning, I think, at quarter to eight.

'You can stay tonight,' I say, 'but you'll have to be gone before Rachel brings Lewis in the morning.'

Hamid's asleep now, in the back bedroom. He wouldn't give me his girlfriend's mobile number. He said it wasn't safe. He threw away his own mobile when he climbed out of the back of the flats, he said. They can track you, even if it's switched off. He seems to know a lot. Too much? I feel dizzy, as if I haven't eaten all day.

The van is still there, but they've pulled it over to the side of the road. Through the window I see lights on in the flats. It's still snowing. I suppose in the morning he could go into the cupboard under the stairs, like

Harry Potter. Lewis wouldn't think of looking in there. But Hamid's claustrophobic, he said.

The way they came swarming out of that van. They all had guns. You wouldn't want to get in their way. When I was a child, the Prime Minister could walk in the park with a single policeman.

All right, love. Quick as you can, and stay indoors once you're there.

Up the road I went with Lewis, while they watched me. I know what they saw. A little boy and his nan, grateful and bit cowed. I don't think they'll come here looking for terrorists.

Hamid's fast asleep in that ridiculous dressing gown. I wish he had something else to wear for tomorrow. It'll show up so bright against the snow.

Once, long ago, before I was a nan, I saw a newspaper photograph of a huddle of men advancing out of an alley, waving a white handkerchief dipped in blood. I was a student then, like Hamid. Everything was in black and white in those days, even Bloody Sunday. The day after, we held a protest march, flanked by police who didn't think much of us. It was a snowy day then too, and they were ordinary police, in their helmets. Riot gear and kettling hadn't been invented yet, not on the mainland. A speech crackled through a megaphone, but I could barely make out the words. One sentence, however, has always stuck in my mind:

'Everything that's happening over there, will happen here.'

Police in full riot gear, bursting into a suburban street. Guns, roadblocks and helicopters overhead. Machine guns at airports. If they've made a mistake, there will be an apology. People who have nothing to hide have nothing to fear.

I'm a dot in a line of marchers, protesting, black against the rawness of snow.

I'm a nan, drinking tea in my own kitchen, with a young man in a Santa's Sweetheart dressing gown asleep in my spare room. At least, I hope he's still asleep. It gives me time to think what to do.

WHALES AND SEALS

❧

Shannon cuts the boat's engine, and here we are, drifting on the Pacific Ocean. Without the noise of the engine it's clear how fragile we are, just a speck of metal and flesh in a wilderness of water. But the thought doesn't trouble me.

'We're in US territorial waters now,' says Shannon. She's a tawny-skinned New Zealander with a beautiful smile and a passion for marine biology. The amount she's told us already would fill a guidebook, and I haven't listened to all of it. But I've kept a listening look on my face, because I like Shannon. She's working her way around the world, and then she'll do her PhD on Baltic herring.

'Baltic herring, Shannon?'

'Yeah, crazy, isn't it? Maybe it's because my father's Estonian.' Shannon gets up from her seat and beams at the rest of her passengers. 'We're in US waters now, guys! Got your passports handy?'

The man in front of me lifts his camcorder and begins to film the flat silvery US ocean.

'You can go out on deck if you like,' says Shannon.

The deck is tiny. If we're polite and not pushy there's room for the ten of us, and because of the big silence lapping round us it doesn't feel crowded. Everyone's mind is away out there on the ocean. We've seen sea lions, and cormorants, and a school of Dall's porpoises that rushed the boat. I was afraid of the boat injuring them, but Shannon said it wouldn't happen.

'They like to ride the bow wave,' she said. 'They like the feeling of it. Sometimes they'll get on to the bow wave of one of those big freighters and ride it for hours. Maybe it conserves energy. Maybe they're just playing.'

We haven't seen whales yet. I look across the water at the Olympic mountain range. The mountains are snow-covered, and a breath of chill comes off the Pacific water. The water is cold and rich, packed with chains of life that man hasn't broken. Not here, not yet. Shannon tells us that an orca can eat four hundred pounds of salmon in a day. The only way I can imagine that quantity of salmon is to build a tower of supermarket steaks in my mind. Three hundred, maybe? I used to buy four salmon steaks and they would weigh maybe a pound and a half. One for Luke, one for Jasmine, one for Don, one for me. I would ask the assistant to make sure the steaks were the same size. If one steak was bigger than the others I would cover it with sauce to hide the fact.

Maybe we aren't going to see any whales, not today. The man with the camcorder is asking Shannon if she thinks they'll come.

'Yes,' says Shannon. 'They're around. They were here this morning. This time of the day, they're feeding. I'll have a listen.'

She goes to the back of the boat and fiddles with the underwater acoustic device which she's already explained to us.

'Listen,' she says. All of us fall silent and listen obediently to noises which sound like music you'd turn off on Radio 3.

'They're hunting salmon. Hear that clicking? There's one quite close. Fifty metres off, maybe.'

We're all staring out at the bald silver sea, willing it to yield up a whale. I hold my breath. The boat twirls slowly on a current I can't see. Land is far off. Please, I say inside myself. *Please.* Our boat bobs like a little ark of prayer. All of us holding our breath; all of us wanting and waiting. Do the whales come at all? Is this whole trip a gigantic pretend, like putting your baby tooth in a glass of water by your bed so the tooth fairy can replace it with a coin, or staying awake on Christmas Eve to catch a glimpse of Father Christmas? I've been the fairy myself too many times. I've filled those stockings. Why am I holding my breath like a child?

Shannon scours the waters with her binoculars. I turn away. I'm not going to look any more. I'm not going to let those whales know that I'm desperate.

Suddenly, casually, on the other side of the boat, the whale is there. A black curve breaks the water. Much too big for a porpoise. Sleek and streaming and then it's gone. I pull at Shannon's arm.

'There. There. Over there. It's a whale. I saw a whale.'

'Hey, you did?' She acts thrilled and surprised, and I know she's never had any doubts. Of course the whales would come.

'Hey, guys, over here,' says Shannon, lifting her voice, and everyone stares at the water where the whale was. And then the water is alive with whales. A back shows above the water again, a fin rises, a tail lifts in the perfect forked whale shape we all know from a thousand pictures.

'Over there. Look. It's another. It dived, just there.'

No one calls out or rushes to the side. Calm spreads over the boat and the water as the whales show themselves more and more. They are playing, I'm sure of it, not hunting. They are playing with us. I stare, trying to print it on my mind forever. Whales in the grey, shining Pacific which turns dark in the distance. Their clicking sounds bubble through the acoustic device.

'There's Shaker,' says Shannon.

'Shaker?'

'Yeah, it's him. His mum'll be around here too.'

'Do you give them all names?'

I'm not sure I like the idea of naming whales.

'Yeah, pretty much. Shaker's really playful.'

'Is he a baby whale?' I ask foolishly.

'Nah, he's twenty-five, twenty-six. But these whales stay with their mothers all their lives. He's got a sister in this pod too. If his mum dies he'll stay with her.'

'All their lives – really?'

'If you think of it, it makes sense,' says Shannon. 'Their home is the pod. They won't leave unless there's something seriously wrong.'

'Like what?'

'There was a big story last year about a whale that got separated from the pod. Boats were tracking it; people were wanting to reunite it. But it wasn't lost. It had something wrong, some genetic issue, and the pod rejected it. That can happen.'

'Oh.'

'That's tough,' says a young woman in a red jacket.

'No sentiment in the animal kingdom,' says the man with the camcorder.

'I don't know,' says Shannon surprisingly. 'Whales have deep feelings; I do know that.'

She lifts her binoculars again, and is silent. She's a sensitive girl. She wants this to be our experience, not hers.

The whale she called Shaker has disappeared. There are two more whales moving through the water in the distance, west to east, sometimes showing, sometimes not. They travel purposefully. Even though I can see them clearly, it doesn't make them any less mysterious.

Everyone in the boat is filming or taking photos. I take some photos myself and think of showing them to

Luke. But they won't come out the way it was. My photos rarely do. I'm always having to explain what's in them.

See that shape there, Luke? No, not there, there. That's part of a whale. Which part? Um, well, maybe it's the back. Or it could be the tail …

The young woman in the red jacket taps my arm. 'You want me to take a photo of you with a whale in the background?'

Close up, I see how bright and eager she is. It would be churlish to turn her down.

She takes a long time, trying to get the best shot, waiting for a whale to rise behind me. At last it's done.

'He was distant, but it should come out OK.'

'Thanks a lot. Do you want me to take one of you?'

She hands me her camera. 'It'll be something to show my kids. They're back at the hotel. They're so jealous of me for taking this trip, but three and five, they're pretty young for it. And it's expensive …'

'You have every right to take a trip on your own,' I say firmly. 'That's what I'm doing, too.'

'You got kids?'

'Two.'

'I'm Julie. I'm from Moose Jaw. Yeah, I know. It's a real place; that's what it's called. I was born there. You're British, right?'

By the time we've all finished taking photos, a wind off the mountains is chopping up the water. The whales have hidden themselves. It's time to go back inside.

We settle ourselves in the cramped cabin. Shannon starts the engine and our boat bucks and slaps across the water. The engine noise makes me sleepy, but Shannon is telling us something above the racket.

'We'll be going by a seal colony on the way back. I'll cut the engine and take you as close as I can, but we don't want to scare them off the rocks.'

She tells us about seals, how the seal pups are independent at six weeks, and how the transient killer whales work together to hunt them. One group of whales scares the seals off the rocks, and another group waits for them to slide into the water on the other side.

'Six weeks!' says Julie. 'Seal mums sure get a better deal than whale mums. Didn't you say that Shaker was still hanging out with his mother at twenty-five?'

'He'll still be hanging out with her at forty, if she's alive,' says Shannon.

'Oh my Lord. Forty years. Can you picture that?'

My answering smile is as quick as I can make it.

When Luke is forty I shall be sixty-six, and still able to take care of him, unless something happens. Luke will be forty and probably his hair will be grey. My child's hair will be grey.

'How old are your kids?' asks Julie.

'Jasmine is nineteen, Luke is twenty-three.'

'They've flown the nest, then.' Like most parents of small children, she still sees their upbringing as a finite task. They will get to the sunlit uplands of adulthood at eighteen and that will be it. Job done.

'Jasmine's at uni. Luke is at home with us.'

And as her expression changes slightly I decide to tell her.

'He was in an accident last year. A car accident. He wasn't driving. He had head injuries.'

'I'm so sorry,' says Julie. 'How is he doing?'

'Better than we thought. Much better than we thought. But he won't be able to manage on his own. Not for a while.'

Luke's face rises in my mind. He is wearing the strange, lost look that comes over him sometimes. I am afraid that this look comes when he remembers that it wasn't always like this. Most of the time the facts of his former life are like a story to him. He went to university, he shared a flat, he studied sports science and psychology and played in the university hockey team. One day last month I found him standing by the washing machine with his cereal bowl and coffee mug.

'Mum,' he asked me. 'Do I know how to operate this article?'

I cannot get his frowning, pained look out of my head.

'It's great that you took this trip,' says Julie. For a moment her warm hand covers mine. 'You'll be able to tell Luke about the whales.'

'Yes.'

I will tell him about the cold, dark Pacific water, the American mountains, and the silence when our engine stopped. How fragile our boat was on the water.

ALL THOSE PERSONAL
SURVIVAL MEDALS

❧

'So what's the memory that really makes you flinch?' asked Liz. Melanie and Ros looked at her.

'Flinch?' said Ros.

'You know, like this.' Liz shrank and shrivelled, hands over her face, body twisting away. 'I don't mean serious stuff, I mean those stupid things that last a lifetime. Mine – I'm not saying what it is, but if I ever stop dead and start moaning "Oh no, oh no!" for no apparent reason, that'll be it.'

'How long ago was it?'

'Nineteen ninety-one.'

'So you were still a student.'

'Yes. Twenty-one. Peak time for collecting those "Oh no!" moments, wouldn't you say?'

'Definitely.' Ros, sitting across the table from Melanie, began to spoon organic plum purée into the mouth of her baby, Lucas. Her late baby, as everyone still thought of him. Ros had pulled a fast one on the others, settling all those arguments about whether or not they should slip in one more baby before the guillotine of the menopause crashed down. Perhaps Lucas had been an accident; Ros wouldn't say. All the other children were between eight and twelve, long-legged, independent and way down the beach in their wetsuits, body-boarding. The lifeguards weren't there at Easter, so the two fathers, Liam and Carl, kept watch at the water's edge. Lucas, six months old, lolled in his mother's lap.

'If they hadn't changed the rules about pensions, you'd have been able to collect child benefit at the same time as the old-age pension,' said Melanie suddenly, as if out of long thought.

'Only for a year,' Ros said, so quickly that it was clear the same idea had struck her, too, and been worked out as Ros worked everything out.

'Better than nothing,' said Liz, rather bitterly. Everybody seemed to do better out of the system than she and Carl. Melanie no doubt had all those child tax credits now that people talked about: Melanie worked four days a week as a legal secretary. Gary, although the owner of a successful sports shop, had appeared to have very little income when it came to working out child support.

Everybody had liked Gary, and the divorce was so recent that its shadow hung over them all. The fact that he had fallen in love with the dental nurse during a complex, costly implant procedure added a touch of the ridiculous which made things even worse for Melanie. How the hell, they asked themselves, could anyone fall in love when he had a suction tube in his mouth? As for the girl, she must have been very determined, that was all Ros and Liz could say. They would have to meet her some time, of course; Gary and Carl played squash, Liam and Gary went to football together, and all that wasn't about to come to an end just because Gary had been playing away. But for the time being they all wanted to show Melanie that they were with her, on her side 100 per cent in the miserable battle over the children, the house and Gary's final-salary pension scheme.

Melanie stared out to sea, shading her eyes against the harsh April light.

She's looking older, thought Ros, and then quickly, loyally: But of course we all are. The fortieth birthdays were over, and the rash of celebrations. Ros felt easier in the foothills of the forties than when she'd clung to the precipice of thirty-nine.

'I feel so old,' said Melanie. The light had made teary streaks on her face.

'You're not old, what rubbish,' said Liz stoutly, but Ros wiped her baby's mouth and said:

'It's the spring. People think they're glad about spring, but really they want to stay wrapped up in winter.'

'We do, because we're old. Getting old,' Melanie corrected herself. 'I hate having to take clothes off these days. Bare legs ... my God!'

'That's where wetsuits are so good,' said Ros, putting the baby up on her shoulder. 'I used to dread, positively dread, walking down to the water in a swimsuit.'

Liz suppressed the thought that Melanie was going to have to take her clothes off at some point, if she were ever to replace Gary. But that was different. It could be done in the dark; or, at the very least, in careful lighting.

'What you need to do,' instructed Liz, 'is pretend in your mind that you're ten years older than you really are.'

'What – fifty-two? How's that going to help?'

'Well, then you think: I'm fifty-two, just imagine how great it would be if I could wake up and find I was forty-two.'

There was thoughtful silence.

'I wonder if it would still work when you were, say, ninety-two?'

'I expect it would,' said Ros with automatic, encouraging cheerfulness. She stood up carefully. Lucas was dropping off. She rocked back and forth, shielding his head from the wind with her body. She was glad she'd brought his blue hat. Her mind emptied, drowsed. There were her children, somewhere in that cold, surging sea. Specks of life that she'd made. But so strong and solid now, busy with the sea as they were busy with everything. They would come rushing to her later with some plan: a ring of stones with a fire inside to cook sausages, or a deep-dug rock-pool hospital for injured crabs. Their long hair would be tangled, slapping against their neoprene shoulders. Yes, Lucas was asleep. She wondered what Liz's memory was, the one that made her flinch.

It was easy enough to remember her own.

She was back in the classroom. It was just gone half past three, and they had put their chairs up on their tables. Mrs Curtis was talking to two boys who'd been messing about with water – or worse – in the cloak-rooms, so she didn't notice Kimberley Hilton come prancing back from the cloakroom with a sheaf of party invitations in her hand. They were coloured envelopes, with stickers on them.

Kimberley went from table to table. As far as Ros could see, everybody was getting an invitation. Kimberley was the queen of the class. The Queen Bee, Ros's mother called her. She was smiling, sparkling, in her little black furry coat – no one else had a coat like Kimberley's – with her very pale hair pulled tight back into a ponytail and her sharp eyes going big as she gave out each envelope and then small again as she considered the next face in front of her. They were going swimming at the Oasis, with burgers and chips afterwards, then a few of Kimberley's special friends were going back for a sleepover. Ros knew there was no chance of her being asked to the sleepover. But she'd invited Kimberley to her party, and let Kimberley open the presents.

She was getting close. She was in front of Ros. She had an envelope in her hand. She was smiling and sparkling and her eyes were big. She wagged the envelope, stretching out her hand. Ros reached out too. 'Thank you, Kimberley,' she said, her voice too loud, clumsy with relief. The envelope quivered. Kimberley's eyes widened farther in a pantomime of surprise. 'Oh, sorry, Ros, I didn't mean you! It's a swimming party, and you can't swim, can you? This is Clare's. I was just going to give it to her.'

Everyone had seen. Ros heard giggling. 'Ros Howden can't even swim and she thought she was coming to Kimberley's party!' She stood there, red and ugly, as Kimberley danced on.

It was over. Kimberley was forty-two, for God's sake. Probably divorced. Ros held Lucas to her. She had the children. She had Liam. There were Liz and Melanie, close enough friends to come away together for an Easter break, all eight kids crammed into two narrow loft bedrooms, knowing that it didn't matter if quarrels broke out, because Liz or Melanie would settle them in the same way as Ros would.

Why the hell did it matter? It didn't, not by any possible scale of things that mattered.

'Ros,' said Melanie, shading her eyes again, her voice tight. 'Isn't that Amy on that dinghy?'

'What dinghy?'

'There.' She pointed; Ros followed. A small yellow dinghy was bobbing just beyond the surf, with two little black figures in it.

'But we haven't got a dinghy,' said Ros stupidly.

One of the little figures in the dinghy stood up, wobbled, sat down again. It was Amy.

'Where are Carl and Liam?' asked Liz. But the men were looking the other way, at the bodysurfers. Ros barely thought. She pushed Lucas into Melanie's arms and ran down the beach. Her breath was hot; her feet flew. She was so close now that the dinghy was hidden by the surf. If the wind veered – if an offshore gust sent the dinghy scudding out across the bay – if Amy panicked – why hadn't Liam been watching her—

Faces gaped as Ros plunged, fully dressed, into the Easter-cold water. She waded out, the sea dragging at her. She was too slow. She duck-dived under the surf, pushed herself down through the boil of the water, kicked out.

She rose, threw her hair back, trod water, pushing herself up to see beyond the next wave that was swelling towards her. She wasn't far enough out. She dived again, swimming hard and strong underwater as the wave passed overhead. She was beyond the breaking waves. There was the dinghy, bouncing on the swell. There was a man with it, holding its rope, swimming. She saw the white, scared face of a strange child in the dinghy.

'Amy!' she screamed and the man looked her way but he couldn't do anything, he was pulling the rope, hauling his own child to safety. 'Amy!' The man was pointing. Ros looked to her left and a dark head popped above the surface and went down.

*

Amy hadn't been drowning. She made that clear to Ros afterwards.

'I'm a good swimmer, Mum.'

She'd jumped out of the dinghy, because it was going the wrong way and she and the other girl – Talitha, she was called – couldn't make it turn back. But Talitha didn't jump even though Amy knew they could easily swim back to shore from there.

But she said all that afterwards, when they were on the way home. After Ros had towed her back to shore, after the doctor who happened to be on the beach had checked Amy over, after they'd all stopped shaking with cold and shock, after Amy had at last stopped crying and holding on to Ros's waist as if she would never let go. Ros kept running the same loop over and over. Amy going down. The surface of the sea with no Amy. The grapple for her underwater, nothing there but the sea. And then, as Ros dived for the third time, Amy rose.

'He was very apologetic, that other father,' said Melanie as she ladled sugar into hot coffee from the beach shack for Ros. 'Trouble was, he's here on his own with three of them to keep an eye on. He's divorced.'

'I don't blame him,' said Ros, although she did.

'They live in Bristol too.'

Melanie's eyes were bright. And yet she's a good friend, one of my closest friends, Ros thought. Aren't people extraordinary? Thank God I did all those personal survival medals. And the lifesaving course.

Kimberley Hilton flashed into her mind, still smiling and sparkling, with that neat little blonde head, and big eyes. Still waving that envelope after all these years. 'If it hadn't been for me, Ros Howden, you'd never have learned to swim properly,' she said, and then she laughed, and danced away.

A NIGHT OUT

The green beast squatted in the sun, grinning at her. Ruth climbed back on the seat with the instruction booklet, and went through it all again. Brake engaged, blades disengaged. Choke halfway out. For the fourth time, she turned the ignition key. For the fourth time the engine caught, vibrated and died.

Ruth's heart pounded. She got off the mower, drew back her foot and kicked the green flank as hard as she could. Pulses of pain shot up her leg, but the mower wasn't even marked. Hot, choking fury filled her throat. Now she was pummelling the metal with her fists, yelling words that the beast would never have heard from Donald in a million years of mowing.

Her hands hurt. She wasn't shouting any more. She was crying, leaning against the beast, crying in huge, painful jags that had never come in all the six months since the funeral.

'Mrs Carver? Ruth!'

A face was peeping over the high fence. How had she got up there?

'If you want, I can help with your lawn tractor,' said Aruna Patel, as if she hadn't noticed tears, thuds or swearing.

'It's a ride-on mower,' said Ruth mechanically.

'I am very familiar with them. Wait one moment.'

The face disappeared. The Patels had been living next door for two years: a professional couple, always extremely busy, leaving for work at 7 a.m. in expensive cars, and the young man's widowed mother, Aruna. Ruth and Donald had tried to be friendly, of course.

She was at the gate.

'It's very kind of you, Aruna.'

'Not at all.' Aruna was as businesslike as her son today.

Ruth stood aside. 'I know there's enough petrol in it,' she said, trying to sound competent.

'But not enough oil. There is a safety cut-out to protect against damage, if the oil level is low. See, the warning light is on.'

So it was. 'You seem to know a lot about these things. My husband – Donald – would never let me near it. He was like a child.'

'My son is the same. Exactly the same. However, he is out all day and I like to know how things work.' She laughed, and Ruth found that she was smiling too. 'We have oil in the garage. I will get some for you.'

'Don't bother now. The grass can stay long for one more day.'

'But you have such a beautiful lawn. I have often admired it.'

'It would make a great campsite,' said Ruth, surveying it. She had often thought that, but there was no chance that Donald would ever let tents be pitched on his precious lawn. When they had grandchildren, she'd thought, he would change his mind. But Donald would never see his grandchildren.

'He was only fifty-eight,' she said, very quietly, as she had said it so often to herself.

'My husband also,' said Aruna. 'Heart attack. He was fifty-six.'

The two women were silent. The glossy green of the mower blurred as Ruth said, 'There were so many things we were going to do. I took early retirement ...'

'We had the business. We could never go away together.'

It took them the rest of the day to mow the lawn. Aruna waved away Ruth's protests, and once the oil was topped up the mower ran like a dream.

'Now your campsite is ready,' said Aruna.

The expanse of grass suddenly looked enormous to Ruth. Ridiculous, for one woman. Why was she doing all this? Keeping on with everything. Everybody said you had to keep going. What for? But then the sweet smell of cut grass caught her so strongly that she felt dizzy. It reminded her of Guide camp. Blaise Fields had just been mowed when they pitched their tents. Ruth had woken at dawn, crawled over the others without waking anybody, and put her head out of the tent. Everything was grey, and wet with dew. It smelled wonderful.

Aruna was staring at the golden tops of the trees, her eyes half-closed. 'When I was a little girl,' she said, 'we had a most beautiful garden.'

'Did you grow up here, or in India?'

'Oh no, we were in Uganda. Our house was a bungalow, with a big verandah running all around. On hot nights the servants would push my bed out. I would wake up in the night and see the stars. I always preferred to be outside. Running and climbing and getting in the way of the garden boys.'

'I was a tomboy too. My own daughter was just the opposite. Everything had to be Barbie pink.'

'I know! It is like a disease. Mine was the same. But now she is living in Tasmania, so she has to be practical.'

'Lucy's in New York.'

The two women were silent, thinking of faraway, beloved daughters, and the endless Skyping and emails that never quite filled the gaps.

'I must be going home,' said Aruna briskly.

'I've still got the tent,' said Ruth, as if to herself.

Aruna's expression sharpened. 'Have you? How big is it?'

'It's a two-man tent. Donald and I – but that was years ago. I expect it's fallen to pieces.'

'You could look, perhaps?'

Next morning, Ruth looked. Dear, careful Donald had rolled it away immaculately, as if it was never to be used again. It was a very low-tech tent. Ruth remembered how she used to wrestle with its poles and guy-ropes.

I'll put it up, just to see how it looks, she decided.

The sun was hot on Ruth's back as she hammered in the last tent-peg. The cream canvas was spotted with age and damp, but the fabric remained strong. She crawled inside. It was very warm. A blackbird ran across the angle of her vision, a few feet away. She'd forgotten how close birds came, when you were camping. She would make a cup of tea, bring it out, and watch.

As Ruth emerged from the tent, she heard the clip of secateurs. Instantly, she knew that Aruna was in her garden, too. Aruna would have heard the hammering. But she would not come, unless Ruth asked.

I could sit in the sun with my tea, Ruth thought. She was getting used to being on her own. Make the tea, perhaps a couple of biscuits, wash it up, think about cooking, decide a boiled egg will do, email Lucy, save it as a draft because emailing every day is too needy, think about joining a book group, decide to leave it until the autumn, see what's on TV …

'Aruna?' called Ruth. 'Aruna, are you there?'

Seconds later, Aruna's head popped over the fence.

'How do you get up so high?' asked Ruth.

'I have steps for trimming the hedges.' Aruna's eyes brightened and widened. 'My goodness. I see that you know what you are doing when it comes to tents.'

'It's old-fashioned, but quite roomy inside. Come and have a look.'

Aruna's sari did not seem to get in her way as she crawled into the tent and then twisted herself into a sitting position. Her gold bangles chinked as she waved her hand admiringly. 'There is so much space! You would not believe it from the outside.'

'I'm going to sleep out in it,' said Ruth suddenly.

'Alone?'

'I'll be perfectly all right in my own garden,' said Ruth.

'Of course,' said Aruna, looking away, her voice suddenly distant, and Ruth realised once again that Aruna would never – not without being asked …

'Although I would feel much more secure if I camped with someone else.'

'That is very natural,' said Aruna.

'And I wondered if perhaps … You did say you liked sleeping out?'

'You mean that I should camp here?' asked Aruna, and her voice sounded so surprised that Ruth wondered if, in some way she didn't understand, she had offended her neighbour.

'Well – yes. But it was only an idea. Probably not a very good one—'

'And see the stars …' said Aruna dreamily.

'Well, maybe not through the canvas. It's quite thick.'

'I will peep out of the tent-flaps in the dead of night.'

'I'll buy those blow-up camping mattresses. Alex says they're wonderful.'

'No, please! Allow me!'

They wrangled gently over mattresses, camping stove and sleeping bags. They made lists and discussed timings. Aruna learned the route to Ruth's downstairs cloak-room. It became clear that Aruna's son and daughter-in-law were to know nothing.

'I will simply slip back into the house when morning comes.'

And here they were, side by side in sleeping bags, with the tent-flaps open to the warm night. Aruna wrote her diary in the fading light – 'Just two sentences. I began it years ago to practise my English.' How strongly the garden smelled of earth and falling dew, of cut grass, flowers and the distant compost heap. Ruth lay on her back and watched an ant on its slow journey across the pale curve of the tent. The light was nearly gone …

She woke, because Aruna fell on top of her. 'I am so sorry! So sorry! I lost my way to your cloakroom and there was a fox or some night animal running across the grass so I hurried into the tent rather quickly—'

Ruth could not help it: the vision of Aruna scrambling into the tent pursued by a night animal was too much for her. She laughed until she had to roll on her side to ease the pain in her stomach. Thank heavens, Aruna was laughing too.

They didn't go back to sleep. 'It's a beautiful night, full of stars,' said Aruna, and turned her sleeping bag round so she could lie on her back and watch them through the tent-flaps. They talked as the grey of dawn took away the starlight, and while the sun rose, creating unfamiliar shadows across the lawn. They talked about Donald and Manu, about Lucy and Jyoti, about time zones and funerals, about daughters-in-law and tree-climbing. Their voices rose and fell as the birds woke and took over the garden with their song.

It was Ruth who heard the click of the gate. She sat up, skin prickling. Much too early for the postman or deliveries—

It was the young man from next door, walking across the grass. He saw Ruth peering out of her tent and asked politely, 'Excuse me, have you seen my mother?'

'It is my Devan,' said Aruna, and she wriggled out of her sleeping bag and stood to face her son.

'Mother!'

'What is it?'

'I woke up and your bed was empty. I thought something had happened to you, and then I heard all this talking and laughing.'

'So you came to investigate,' said Ruth.

'But, Mother …' The young man's arm swept out to indicate the tent, the garden, the sleeping bag and his mother with her long plait over her shoulder. 'What are you doing here? Why are you not at home in your bed?'

He looks so bewildered, thought Ruth. Like a little boy. Aruna must have seen it too, for she said soothingly, 'I will come home, Devan. I will come now. The night is over.'

Hastily Aruna gathered her things, nodding at Ruth as if to reassure her, too. 'I will come later and help you to take down the tent,' she promised.

'I might keep it up,' said Ruth.

She watched them walk away, mother and son. It had only been one night, after all. He had nothing to worry about.

It was when Ruth was shaking the sleeping bags that Aruna's diary fell out and lay open on the grass. You must never read people's private diaries, but as Ruth bent over to pick it up she could not help seeing the two lines:

'I am camping in a tent with my friend Ruth. We are hoping to see the stars.'

PORTRAIT OF AUNTIE BINBAG,
WITH RIBBONS

❦

Mags, Kaff, Didi, Stu and Binnie. My mother, her two sisters and her two brothers. My mother was Mags. She's Margaret now. She stopped answering to Mags when she went to college to study book-keeping. Margaret, Catherine, David, Stuart. And Binnie. My Auntie Binnie, the eldest of the five. She didn't look the eldest, with her large, soft face and her round-toed babyish shoes. She didn't look any age at all. Mum and my aunts and uncles talked about her as if she was still a child.

'Binnie's so stubborn. She gets an idea in her head, and there's no doing anything with her.'

'She lives in a dream half the time.'

You could talk about Auntie Binnie in a way you wouldn't dare talk about any other grown-up. She was just Auntie Binnie. Or Auntie Binbag, sometimes, on account of her clothes.

'She gets dressed with her eyes tight shut.'

'She feels around in the wardrobe until she finds something.'

We mimicked Auntie Binbag, our arms thrust out stiffly and our eyes screwed shut. We understood that it was all right to do this in front of Mum, even though Auntie Binnie was Mum's sister. Mum would say, 'Stop it, Sarah, Jessie. That's enough,' but not in a way that meant anything.

What made us cruel was that we loved Auntie Binnie as much as we were embarrassed by her. When we were little we sat on her knee and patted her large, gentle face. We admired the scarves that trailed from her, and the ornaments she bought us from charity shops. Auntie Binnie didn't bother about presents being for birthdays or Christmas. In fact she was likely to forget your birthday altogether. Once she gave me a glittering china fairy with pointy toes, sitting on a bunch of china flowers. I had never seen anything so beautiful.

Auntie Binnie didn't have a proper job, or a husband, or children. My mother had all three, which was why she never had the time to go looking for treasures such as my fairy with her golden hair and bright cherry lips. It was also why Mum was more important than Auntie Binnie. When Auntie Binnie gave me the fairy, Mum explained that Auntie Binnie didn't have much money, and that was why we had to say an extra special thank you when she gave us a present, even if we didn't like it.

But I loved my fairy. I threw myself at Auntie Binnie and thanked her a million zillion times. It was my most beautiful possession in the whole world. It was only months later that I began to see a certain foolishness in the fairy's bright face. It must have been about the same time that I stopped begging Auntie Binnie to leave me her scarf collection when she died. Mum never wore scarves, or things that trailed. Everything about Mum had a clean, clear edge to it.

Auntie Binnie lived with an old lady called Mrs Bathgate. She was Mrs Bathgate's companion. She did the shopping and fetched the prescriptions and answered the phone and did the housework. If Mrs Bathgate rang her bell in the night, Auntie Binnie got up and went to her, and made hot drinks and moved pillows about. If it was a very bad night, Auntie Binnie would have forty winks on the sofa the next afternoon, while Mrs Bathgate was reading aloud. Even though Auntie Binnie was the companion, it was always Mrs Bathgate who did the reading aloud, and Auntie Binnie who did the listening.

Mum said it was quite ridiculous in this day and age, like something out of a novel by Charlotte Brontë. Mrs Bathgate was a mean old devil and knew when she was on to a good thing. What did she pay Binnie? Peanuts. But Binnie was so obstinate that she wouldn't even tell Mum how much she got paid.

Auntie Binnie would trail off in one of her dangly dresses to collect yet another prescription for Mrs

Bathgate. And then people would say to Mum, 'Oh, I saw your sister Binnie today, in Boots.'

They would sound as if they pitied Auntie Binnie for fetching Mrs Bathgate's prescriptions, and maybe as if they pitied Mum, too, for having a sister like Binnie, who didn't know that you don't wear a magenta satin skirt with the hem hanging down in the middle of winter.

Magenta was one of Auntie Binnie's favourite colours. Her bedroom, at the top of the house where Mrs Bathgate lived, was very small and crammed with bright cushions and ornaments and scarves. Crimson was another of Auntie Binnie's colours. Scarlet, petunia, lilac, mauve, flame. When I learned at school that the phoenix's nest was made of flames, I thought of Auntie Binnie's bedroom.

Next to the little bedroom there was another room which Auntie Binnie used for her painting. Mrs Bathgate didn't know about the painting, because she couldn't climb stairs and her stairlift only went up to the first floor. The stairlift whizzed Mrs Bathgate up or down the stairs, whenever she wanted. Auntie Binnie longed to try it out herself, she told Mum, but she'd never dared. Mrs Bathgate had a terrible tongue.

'Why do you let that woman bully you?' shouted Mum.

In her painting room Auntie Binnie painted one picture after another, whenever she had an hour free from Mrs Bathgate. There were no fairies in her paintings, no people, flowers or landscape. Just crowds of different colours, sometimes fighting one another, sometimes agreeing. Auntie Binnie spent hours and hours painting. She didn't bother to keep her paintings when they were finished, and no one ever asked if they could have one. I didn't like them much, but I admired the way she kept right on filling up the paper with colour until there wasn't any white left.

When each painting was done, she put it behind her wardrobe for a while, and when enough were stacked there she carried them downstairs and put them beside the wheelie bin. The binmen always took them. Auntie Binnie did all this with a gentle smile on her face, as if she enjoyed the act of putting her paintings out with the rubbish.

I was eleven when Mrs Bathgate died.

'Of course she won't have left Binnie a halfpenny,' said Mum.

Auntie Binnie went to the funeral in magenta and apricot, and Mum accompanied her, dressed in black. It was a beautiful sunny day.

'Do you know,' said Mum, 'Binnie was smiling all through the service. She was sat in a shaft of light coming through the chapel window and she smiled as if she was on the beach. "Isn't it a lovely day?" she said to Mrs Bathgate's son-in-law. He didn't know what to say. Not that they were a close family. I can count on the fingers of one hand the times they came to see Mrs Bathgate, in all those years.'

Mum took off her high black shoes and rubbed her feet. 'I don't know what we're going to do about Binnie,' she added with a sigh, as if I was a grown-up too. 'Twelve years she's been with Mrs Bathgate.'

The way Mum spoke, it sounded as if Mrs Bathgate had been looking after Auntie Binnie, not the other way round. But Mum was wrong about the money. Mrs Bathgate left Auntie Binnie a thousand pounds, and wrote in her will that Auntie Binnie could stay in her house until it was sold.

'Mean old devil. Mean as mustard, the lot of those Bathgates, always have been and always will be,' said Mum. 'A thousand pounds!'

It sounded a lot of money to me. I wondered what Auntie Binnie would buy with it. Dozens and dozens of scarves and ornaments. Maybe even some new clothes instead of old ones that smelled of other people. Or things for her painting. Auntie Binnie had confided in me once that she would love to paint on canvas, if only she had the money.

'I suppose she'll have to come here,' said Mum. 'We can put you girls in together, and Binnie can have Sarah's room—'

'*Mu-um!*'

'Or maybe you'd rather share with Binnie.'

But Auntie Binnie didn't come and live with us. The Bathgate house was on the market, and Auntie Binnie showed everyone round personally and told them everything about it. She even demonstrated the stairlift, but still nobody bought the Bathgate house. A month went by, two months.

'Would you believe what Binnie's done now!' Mum exploded. She couldn't explode too loudly, though, because she had the car keys between her teeth. 'Just let me get these bags down—'

Mum dumped the shopping, dropped into a chair and stared at us dramatically. 'She's only spent that thousand pounds already.'

'What on?'

'Would you believe it – art classes.'

'But Auntie Binnie can paint already.'

'Can she,' said Mum grimly. 'Well, she's enrolled as a full-time student at the Folk Centre, whether or not.'

'An art student? Is Auntie Binnie going to be an art student?'

'Apparently,' said Mum. 'And don't eat those biscuits out of the packet, please.'

Auntie Binnie hadn't spent all the thousand pounds, however. She gave Sarah and me a twenty-pound note each, and bought Mum a huge camellia in a pot. It was called Himalayan Fire.

'Oh Binnie, you shouldn't go spending your money on us,' said Mum.

'It flowers in January, after everything else,' Binnie said. 'The man told me.'

'It must have cost a fortune,' said Mum later. 'I hope he didn't diddle Binnie.'

Auntie Binnie was at the Folk Centre every single day. When she wasn't having classes she was working in the studios. You could work in the studios all evening and at weekends if you wanted, and Auntie Binnie did want. We hardly ever saw her. I had to wait nearly three weeks before I could ask her what being an art student was like.

'It's a traditional skill-based course in one way,' Binnie said, in the voice she used when she was repeating what the lady in Boots had told her about Mrs Bathgate's prescriptions. 'Although each of us is on her own journey.'

'But what do you do?'

'Lots of things,' said Auntie Binnie. 'We're having an exhibition at the end of term.'

'Can I come?'

But Auntie Binnie looked doubtful. Didn't she want us there? Her own family?

'You can if you want, Jessie,' she said at last. 'But don't …'

'Don't what?'

'It's not the sort of thing your mum's going to like.'

Naked ladies! I thought gleefully. Auntie Binnie's been drawing naked ladies. Or even bare men.

'I won't tell Mum,' I promised.

It was a couple of days later that Mum said, 'Jessie, did Auntie Binnie ask you about the photographs?'

'No. What?'

'She came round when Sarah was in and asked if she could go through all the old albums. She's took away lots of old photos of herself when she was little, Sarah said.'

'She didn't ask me. I wasn't even here,' I said, automatically defending myself.

'But Binnie's *never* been interested in photos. She didn't even want a copy of that studio portrait we had done of you and Sarah. She's got no sense of family like that.'

'You could ask her what she wanted them for,' I suggested.

'Don't be silly, Jessie.'

The day for the bare men and naked ladies was drawing near. Auntie Binnie didn't say anything more to me about the exhibition, but I saw a poster outside the Folk Centre. Saturday, 7th December. The exhibition would be open all day, and tickets cost two pounds.

I'd never been inside the Folk Centre. None of us had. I paid my two pounds to a lady with funny hair and then I went inside. I was early and there weren't many people there. The big echoey rooms were full of paintings and drawings and things made out of clay and wood and newspaper and metal. I looked at all the name labels but none of them was by Auntie Binnie. There were lots of drawings of a bare man who looked as if he didn't know he hadn't got any clothes on. Some of the drawings made his legs look strange, but some of them were good. None of them was by Auntie Binnie.

A lady was kneeling down on the floor. She was arranging lots of little clay figures on to a table, so they faced the door as if they expected something wonderful to come through it. Her hair was short and black, like fur. She was big and square and strong, but the clay figures were delicate: different from my fairy, but a bit the same as well. I wondered if the lady had made them. I moved closer. A label said 'Out of the Blue' and underneath it said 'Fabiola Quiggin'.

I must have accidentally read the label aloud, because the lady looked up.

'Did you make all those?' I asked.

'That's right.'

'Are you an art student?'

'In a way. I do some teaching as well.'

'My Auntie Binnie's an art student. She's got some of her paintings in this exhibition, only I haven't found them yet.'

'Your Aunt Binnie?' Fabiola Quiggin frowned. 'What's her second name?'

'Cochrane.'

Fabiola Quiggin sat back on her heels and gave me a long look. 'Binnie's a family name, right? You're part of her family?'

'I'm her niece.'

'Are you Sarah, or Jessie?'

'Jessie.'

Fabiola Quiggin nodded.

'How did you know our names?' I asked.

'Your aunt is a friend of mine.' But she kept on giving me the long look, as if being Auntie Binnie's friend didn't necessarily make her my friend at all.

'Oh. Are her – is her painting in this room?'

'Her work's through there. In the centre of the next room. You'll find her name on the label.' I felt that she was still watching me as I walked away. That long look settling itself on my shoulder blades.

But there were no paintings in the middle of the next room. Fabiola Quiggin had got it wrong. There was only a big thing made of twisted wire. It hung from the ceiling. I moved closer. There was a label on the floor under it. 'Family Cage', it read, and underneath there was the name: 'Benedicta Cochrane'.

The wire cage swung a little. Inside there were no colours at all. Against the wire bars there were photographs of a little girl, staring out. Lots and lots of photographs, so that as you walked around the cage, you saw the same little girl every time. In some of the photos she was smiling, and in others she looked sad. The wire bars made stripes across her face. From the bottom of the cage there hung plumes of colour, almost down to the floor. I stared at the colours. They were so familiar, they were—

I reached out to touch them. They were silk and satin. They were magenta, lilac, flame, crimson, rose and scarlet. They were Auntie Binnie's scarves, cut to ribbons and hanging from the base of the cage and from its bars like fountains of colour.

'Family Cage', by Benedicta Cochrane.

Fabiola Quiggin was watching me from the doorway.

'What do you think?' she asked.

'I don't know.'

'I think it's beautiful. I think your aunt is a very talented woman.'

I reached out and touched a long ribbon of magenta silk. I remembered the scarf it came from, and how I used to stroke it when it was around Auntie Binnie's neck and I was sitting on her knee. I had stopped asking Auntie Binnie if she would leave me all her scarves in her will when she died. And so here they were. I wondered if Auntie Binnie would find my fairy and put that into an exhibition as well.

'You've got a bit of a look of her,' said Fabiola Quiggin. She came across to the cage and pointed at one of the photos. 'Especially in this one. She must have been about your age when this was taken.'

I stood still, and waited until Fabiola Quiggin moved away. The girl in the photo looked out of the cage at me. Her hair was cut short and it was fairer than mine. She had freckles on her nose. I had freckles too, in summer. But surely I couldn't really look like Auntie Binnie?

The girl in the photo looked straight at me. She didn't have a big, bold smile, like Sarah's in the studio portrait. But she was smiling as if she wanted to be my friend.

'Hello, Auntie Bi—' I whispered. Then I stopped, and started again. 'Hello, Benedicta Cochrane.'

ABOUT THE FIRST WORLD WAR

⌒

'Does this young man know it's my birthday?'

'Yes,' says Barbara.

'I'm a hundred years old today.'

'I know,' says the young man.

I woke at five this morning, same as always. Barbara brought me a special birthday cup of tea.

'You're not waiting for your tea on your hundredth birthday,' she said.

It's all a lot of nonsense, having a birthday when you're a hundred. I'm the same as I was yesterday. Here they come, Mrs Darshan from the kitchen and Barbara with the pink cake and the gold-paper crown. Mrs Darshan makes a beautiful sponge. She places the cake in front of me, and I read the icing aloud.

'"Happy Hundredth Birthday, Mrs Jackson, and congratulations from all your friends at St Monica's."'

How she got all that on a cake I'll never know.

'In my country we show *respect*,' Mrs Darshan says, if any of the young girls says a word out of place.

Barbara's decorated the table with gold-edged serviettes and a flower arrangement. We didn't use to bother with all that sort of thing, years ago. You didn't make a song and dance about your birthday. I remember one day I was reading a book Miss Lambert lent me, and the children in it were getting dressed up for a birthday party. I said to Stuart, 'What's a birthday party, Stuart?' Well, I was going on seven and he must have remembered it, because when I came back from school on my birthday there was Stuart, home early from work. He'd bought a bag of iced buns for our tea, and a bottle of ginger beer.

That young man with the tape-recorder is still waiting.

'Did I tell you that it was my birthday? I'm a hundred years old today,' I tell him, in case he forgets why he's here.

'Yes.'

They put the crown on my head. It tickles and slips down. I'm afraid it's going to go over my eyes and make me look foolish in the photograph, but Barbara rescues me.

'Should I fix it for you with a hair-grip?'

'That was a very nice cup of tea, Barbara,' I say. But she thinks I mean the one I'm drinking now.

'I'll get you another in a minute. There you are, Mrs Jackson, that's fixed. It won't slip down now.'

Barbara won't have us called by our first names, not by anyone. She and Mrs Darshan think alike, for all Barbara's got her social-work qualification. It hasn't spoilt her. She lets me call her Barbara. I tell her she's welcome to call me Ivy any day of the week, but no, she says. It doesn't set the right example for the Community Care students.

'I've had a lot of birthdays,' I say. The young man leans forward.

'I know,' he says. 'How far back can you remember? Can you remember the First World War?'

They've all got the First World War on the brain. All the ones who come in here from the schools with their history projects.

'I don't want to talk about things like that on my birthday,' I tell him. He shifts his backside and fiddles with the tape-recorder. He didn't give his name, did he? No. Mumble mumble about the First World War. But if he thinks he's getting anything about Stuart, he's mistaken.

'Would you like to cut your cake, Mrs Jackson?' That's Barbara again. I told her beforehand I didn't want candles and singing. Just a nice cake, cut up so there's a piece for everyone. But this young man's terribly disappointed, you can tell.

'Aren't we going to sing Happy Birthday?'

'Not today, thank you,' I tell him.

I eat a little bit of my cake.

'Isn't he taking a picture for the newspaper, Barbara?'

'He's not from the newspaper,' she says in her gentle voice.

I thought he was. That's what happens on a hundredth birthday. We've had two in the time I've been here, so I know. They take a photograph, and they write a little piece for the paper, and it gets pinned up on the notice-board in the hall.

'Oh, he's not from the newspaper office then.'

'No,' she says. 'You remember. We talked about it this morning. He's Alice's son.'

'Oh yes, I remember,' I say. 'Lovely moist sponge, Mrs Darshan.' But when I look around, Mrs Darshan's not there any more. I'll ask Barbara who this Alice is later on, when the young man's gone.

'I was born on a day like this,' I say suddenly. 'The mock orange was out in the yard.'

'Mock orange is a lovely scent,' says Barbara.

Funny how I can see that mock-orange bush. I must have been four or five, and my mother pointed at the flowers and told me how they'd been blossoming when I was born. I used to make a little house for myself in the dust under that bush. Well, I wish I could go back to that day. Not to see myself, but all the rest of it. A whole world that's passed away.

'They're all dead now,' I say.

They always want to know about the First World War. It's the people dying that fascinates them. Millions and millions. They can't get over those millions. But I want to say, I've seen the whole world die in my time, every one of them. Out of all those who were walking about the world in the brightness of that day I was born, there'll only be a couple of dozen clinging on, eating bits of cake.

Well, I won't think of that. But no one thinks it's a tragedy, do they? They want to know about what I eat and do I smoke and do I drink, and about the First World War.

'Barbara—' I say, but then I forget what it was I wanted.

'Did you want another cup of tea, Mrs Jackson?'

'Your brother—' says the young man.

'How does he know I've got a brother?' I ask Barbara. He's got no call to go bringing up Stuart. What's Stuart to him? 'I'm tired,' I tell Barbara. 'I want to go to bed.'

'Can I take a picture of you, Mrs Jackson? For my mother?'

For his mother! He must think I'm soft in the head.

'You remember,' says Barbara. 'He's Alice's son.'

'Then why can't this Alice come herself?' I ask.

'Alice is back home. In Australia.'

This young man doesn't *look* Australian. I thought they were all big and brown out there, and this one's pale, with reddish hair. A nice-looking boy, though, when you come to look at him. Nice smile.

Stuart had the buns in a brown-paper bag. When we came home from school he fetched a bottle of ginger beer out of the larder, where he'd been keeping it wrapped in a wet cloth. The buns had currants in them as well as the icing. Dad was at work, and Mum was at Mr Zelinski's where she did the alterations. Stuart poured the ginger beer into Mum's teacups.

'Happy Birthday, Ive.'

He always called me Ive. 'Her name's Ivy,' Mum used to say. But I said, 'I like him calling me Ive, Mum.'

It was a lovely day. We still had that mock-orange bush, and the flowers were out.

'Here, Ive, I don't want all this,' said Stuart. 'You have it.'

So I had three buns. They were beautiful fresh buns from Morley's. I cut the last one in half but Stuart wouldn't touch it.

'They're for you, Ive. It's your birthday.'

That young man's still eating cake. He's got a good appetite, I'll give him that. Mrs Darshan'll be pleased.

'Give him another piece, Barbara,' I say. He blushes. 'What's your name?' I ask him.

'Alec.'

Alec. Alec and Alice. Sounds like a comedy duo. 'Have another bit of cake. Or you could take a piece for Alice.'

'She's in Australia, you remember,' says Barbara.

She's in my head somewhere, but I can't get at her. Alice. Maybe when I'm going off to sleep it'll come back.

'Do you still want to lie down?' asks Barbara.

'I'll have another cup of tea, Barbara. I'm not going to be hundred again, am I?'

Then I remember.

'I had a sister called Alice, but she died.'

Alice came after me, but she only lived for three weeks. They say it's a terrible thing to lose a child. I wouldn't know. There were children all around while we were growing up. I used to think there ought to have been a spare baby somewhere for my mother, to take Alice's place. The one thing I do remember is Stuart holding Alice. He wanted to say goodbye to her. People thought that was very strange then, him being a boy as well. When I saw the way Stuart looked down at her, I ran off and hid in the coal bunker. Well, I was only four. He said, 'It's all right, Alice,' as if she could still hear him. I wanted Stuart to hold *me*, not Alice.

My mother wasn't the holding sort.

'It's a family name with us,' says the young man. 'My mother's called Alice, after my grandmother. I was a boy, so I got called Alec.'

'It's a family name with us as well,' I say, a bit sharp.

Australia. People used to say there was money out there. Not like here, where the money was already spoken for. Nobody ever came back from Australia, once they'd gone.

'My mother'll be very glad to see these photographs,' says the young man. Alec.

I don't feel very well. That cup of tea was too strong. I've got a feeling in my chest.

'Barbara,' I say, 'Barbara, why is this young man taking photographs of me? I don't want him to take photographs of me.' The feeling in my chest swells up. 'I need to lie down.'

The teacup's out of my hand and Barbara's holding my arm as I struggle to get up. I'm trying to unpin the gold-paper crown. I don't want this birthday any more. I want my proper birthday, the one with the iced buns Stuart bought. But the young man's at my other side, holding me. I want his hands off me, but it'll upset Barbara, so I let him take my elbow and together with Barbara he shuffles me out of the room and across the hall to the lift.

They let me down on to the bed and I lie there. I turn my head and look at my new silver photograph frame. Barbara bought it for my birthday. This morning she took the photograph of Stuart out of its old frame. Now the young man's staring at it.

'My brother,' I say. I don't mind him knowing now. Stuart's in his uniform. It was taken just before his wedding day. He always said I'd be his bridesmaid, but they had to get married quick, because he was being sent out. All she had was a grey costume, and a little bunch of lily of the valley.

'Iris is going to be your sister,' Stuart said.

Iris and Ivy. Another comic duo. But she wasn't my sister for long.

Not a lot of men would take on a war widow and someone else's baby, and Iris's new man, Mr Orme, wanted a fresh start. If he was going to take on the child like his own, he didn't want Stuart's family clinging on to it, or Iris clinging on to the thought of Stuart.

That's why I've got this photograph. Iris gave it to me. Mr Orme said she'd got to leave all that behind her.

Iris and Mr Orme went to Deal, then we heard they'd gone overseas. She was Iris Orme by then. And the baby took his name as well. Iris cried when they went, and held on to me, but I was like a stone. Iris always used to say the baby came to me like no one else.

Stuart was gone, and Iris, and little Alice.

I touch Stuart's photograph.

'He was twenty-three when this was taken,' I say to Barbara. She nods. It's a black-and-white photograph, so you can't see the colour of Stuart's eyes.

They think the whole First World War happened in black and white. Stuart's eyes were brown, and he had red hair. Not bright red, not the red that gets people calling after you in the streets. Just a soft, reddish-brown colour he had, like this young man here.

A VIEW FROM THE OBSERVATORY

❧

I've kept quiet about it for a long time, partly because
I thought Manjit might get into trouble over the keys,
and partly for another reason. But I don't see how this
story could bring her down. Her opening season as
director at the Scaffold Theatre blew all the critics away.
Everyone sees the glow around Manjit's name now, but
it was always there, even when she was a skinny little
girl. Things that I thought were solid, like school and
home and growing up, were just shells to Manjit. She
was the swan who'd got to hatch out of them. That's
why Manjit got the job at the Observatory. It was all
part of her hatching. There was a theatre-directing
course that she knew she had to get on.

'It's the best. It's the only one, Zahz.'

Manjit always called me Zahz, right back from the
first year at primary, and soon everybody else was calling
me that, too. My name is ZsaZsa. My father just liked
the sound of it, he said. I've sometimes thought that if

my name had been Emily, Manjit might never have become my best friend.

So Manjit had to do this theatre-directing course. It was expensive, and you couldn't get funding for it. Manjit was back home in Bristol, and she had two jobs, one waitressing in Browns, and the other working at the Observatory, selling tickets for the Camera Obscura and the Caves. I was working in a deli in Clifton, so I saw a lot of Manjit at lunchtimes, up at the Observatory. I'd been to uni, but I didn't know what to do next and I was back at home getting some money together, like Manjit. When people asked, I said I might go travelling. But I knew, and so did everybody else probably, that I wasn't the kind of person who goes off travelling on her own.

It was a hot September day. Really hot, really beautiful. Manjit and I sat on a bench overlooking the bridge, and ate the olives and smoked cheese and flatbread I'd brought from work. There were butterflies on the ripe blackberries that were just out of reach on the other side of the fence. We didn't climb over to pick them, because the drop is over two hundred feet, sheer to the Portway below. The sun glittered on the cars crossing the bridge.

'It's a great day for the Camera,' I said.

The Camera Obscura always worked best on a clear, bright day. Manjit let me in free. I liked it when there was nobody else there; I liked the echo of my feet as I climbed the staircase that wound its way up the tower. If the door to the Camera chamber was open, that meant nobody was in there and I could take possession. Sometimes Manjit came up with me, and that was all right in a different way, because of the stories she told.

You go inside, you close the door and wait until your eyes get used to the dark. There in front of you is the wide bowl where the images fall. It's a circular screen, so big you have to edge your way around it sideways, pulling the wooden handle that alters the Camera's focus and changes the scene.

Everyone looks for the bridge first.

There it is, the bridge!

Look, you can see the cars going over the Suspension Bridge!

The Camera makes the bridge look even more fabulous than it does when you're walking across it. There it is in the bowl, slung over hundreds of feet of emptiness. The cars don't look important at all, but it's wonderful when a gull swoops under the bridge. Or even a falcon, sometimes. There's the mud, shining at low tide, and the river is as narrow as a worm.

If there are other people in the Camera chamber, you can't control the view. Somebody gets hold of the wooden handle and the bridge disappears. The view skims over the Cumberland basin, over the city houses and all the way around to the hills of Wales in the far distance. But when I'm on my own, I hardly move the handle at all. I watch the bridge.

I haven't looked into the bowl of the Camera for years. Even if I still lived in Bristol I'm not sure I'd ever go there again.

When Manjit and I went into the Camera together, and she had hold of the wooden handle, she would watch the people and tell stories about them. If a dad was fumbling over his child's inline skates, Manjit would say, 'Look, Zahz, he doesn't know how to fix the skates. It's an access visit. His wife won't even let him in the house, she hates him so much. He's always here with his boy, skating up and down.'

There was a woman in a blue suit who stared out over the Gorge for a long time and then suddenly, secretively, brought something from a bag and flung it into the deep.

'Her husband's ashes,' said Manjit. 'He hated heights.'

'Maybe it was their favourite place,' I said, but already the woman looked furtive to me.

We both liked to watch the trees. There's virgin forest on the other side of the Gorge. Right bang next to the city, land that's never been cleared, full of owls and murders and rare orchids. You look at the trees on the Camera and at first they're like a painted backdrop, then you realise that they're moving, swaying to the wind that's shut out from the Camera chamber. In real life I never notice how beautiful it is when trees move.

On that September day there wasn't enough time to visit the Camera. I had to get back to work. Manjit ate the last olive, and flicked the stone into the Gorge. We watched it tumble into nothing.

'I'm looking after the keys,' she said.

'What keys?'

'The keys to the Observatory. Just for this week, while Charlie's away. The keys to the only Camera Obscura in the whole country are in my bag,' said Manjit.

'It's not the only one, is it?'

'Pretty much.'

'You'd better look after them then. You're always losing stuff.'

'Don't you see what it means?'

'You get to lock up the Observatory at night, and unlock it in the morning.'

'Zahz. Keep up. Why just at night and in the morning? Why not at other times?'

'You're joking. You want to have a party there?'

'Not a party,' said Manjit with a flick of her hand. 'But listen, Zahz, it's full moon on Thursday. And the forecast's good. There'll be a big bright moon. Can you imagine the Camera by moonlight?'

'It won't look like anything,' I said quickly, even though I knew already that Manjit had planned it all and it was going to happen. 'There won't be enough light for the contrast.' Perhaps I was nervous about being on the Downs at night. When you grow up in Bristol you get it drummed into you that the Downs at night is not the place to be.

'How will we know unless we try?'

'What if we get caught?'

'We won't get caught. Anyway, I'm in charge of the keys. I'll say I was working overtime.'

Her face flared into laughter. I knew I wasn't being offered a choice.

Manjit borrowed her mum's car that night, the night she had chosen for us to go. We parked near the Lord Mayor's House, which meant we had to walk up to the Observatory through the woods. Manjit was right, there was so much moon that we didn't need our torches. There were one or two people about, even though it was so late, but they weren't interested in us. I didn't like it, though. There were always strange sounds in the woods at night; I knew that. It didn't mean anything, it was just birds and animals and—

'What was that, Manjit?'

'Nothing. Ssh.'

We crept on, stepping as lightly as we could, along the path that skirts the Gorge and then rises to the Observatory.

'Manjit—'

'Ssh!'

Her fingers dug into my arm. We stood frozen, listening. A woman's cry echoed, cut off as if it had been pulled out of her throat.

'It's OK,' whispered Manjit, but her voice was thin. 'You know what this place is like after dark.'

The daytime face of the Downs was peeled away like a mask. The sunbathers and kite-flyers and joggers and ice-cream vans were gone, and something else was here.

'The keys, Manjit. Have you got the keys?'

I wanted to get out of the moonlight, out of plain sight. Manjit fumbled the keys and I kept watch. There were shadows all around us. As soon as I turned, they jumped closer.

'Manjit!'

The key clicked. We were in. Manjit pointed her torch beam down, so no one would see our light. There was her chair, where she sat all day selling tickets. Manjit slipped past it, like the ghost of herself, and I followed.

I kept my hand on the wall as we climbed the stairs. It felt rough and safe. Manjit was up ahead, and darkness was behind us.

'You did lock the door again, didn't you?'

'Zahz, relax.'

The door to the Camera creaked open. Manjit's torch beam found the wooden handle. We closed the door and bent over the Camera's bowl.

I hadn't believed it could happen. You need bright sun for the Camera. But as we watched, the bridge swung into view.

'The lights are off,' I said.

'Maybe they switch them off after midnight.'

Even so, the bridge was darkly brilliant in the moonlight. The trees behind it swayed like seaweed.

'There aren't any cars,' said Manjit.

But there were people. A man and a woman. We could see them clearly now, coming over from the Leigh Woods side of the bridge.

'The fence has gone,' whispered Manjit.

'Which fence?'

'You know, the one that stops people from jumping.'

She was right. The high, incurving fence was gone, and there was only the wooden handrail, chest high. The woman was hurrying, almost running, but the man was gaining on her.

'They've had a quarrel,' said Manjit. 'She told him it was over. He's desperate, he wants to make it up with her.'

The woman was really running now. She was more than two-thirds across the bridge.

'There's always someone in the toll-booth,' said Manjit. 'She can go in there if she's upset.'

But the booth was dark. There was only the woman, running, and the man close behind her.

'There,' said Manjit, 'he's caught up with her. I told you, it's a quarrel. They know each other. Look at them.'

He'd taken her in his arms, lifting her off her feet. They were one body now, vanishing into each other. They swayed awkwardly, dancing but not dancing, him holding her off the ground. The spread of overhanging trees hid them as they came to the piers, and we couldn't see them any more.

I let out my breath.

'I want to go home,' I said.

'No, we'll see them again in a minute. I can't believe
how clear everything is in the moonlight. It's like a
stage-set.'

A few seconds later a figure came out from the
shadows. A man, walking slowly, almost strolling,
you could say. Alone. Manjit and I stared into the
bowl.

'Move the handle, Manjit. He's walking out of range.
Follow him.'

But Manjit didn't touch the handle.

'It's not the same man,' she said.

'Of course it is.'

'Maybe she ran across the road, away from him. We
wouldn't have seen her.'

I didn't answer. Moonlight lay in the bowl, washing
the bridge into glory as it hung suspended over more
than two hundred feet of nothing. Manjit's fingers dug
into my wrist as we watched until the man had disappeared.

'Manjit—'

I heard Manjit's breath sigh out of her. She turned to
me and her eyes shone.

I laid my hand on the screen and trees rippled over
it. I could touch the trees, but they couldn't touch me.
If I went out of the Camera chamber and opened the
windows of the tower, I might hear something. Maybe
footsteps, hurrying. Maybe a cry, suddenly cut off as if
it had been pulled out of a woman's throat. But I didn't
move.

We never talked about it, did we, Manjit? We never said another word about what we saw that night when the safety fence melted away, and the moonlit bridge printed itself on to the Camera's bowl.

COUNT FROM THE SPLASH

✺

'You must meet Lucie. We're all very excited about the new series.'

Fredrik had his arm around Kai's shoulder, like a bear. They were good mates, great mates, although Fredrik was the chief bear who could place the paw of success on Kai's shoulder, or not. As he chose, thought Maija. He chose to have us here and so we are here.

'You'll know pretty much everyone,' said Fredrik. Kai nodded casually, but he couldn't help it – his eagerness showed through. He wanted to know everyone. This invitation to Fredrik and Anna's Midsummer party was a first.

'But, Kai, it's Midsummer!' Maija had said.

They always went to their summer cottage for Midsummer. They had a bonfire, they cooked crayfish, and Liisa and Matti were allowed champagne. It was a family party, just the four of them. She and Kai sat up late, late, as the fire sank and the sun grew strong.

They slept for an hour or two, and then swam in the lake and went to the sauna. The next day, you knew that it had begun: the slow shortening of the days, the lopping of minutes that took you back into winter.

'*I* don't care if we don't go to the cottage,' said Liisa. 'It's boring, just us. Everybody else has parties.'

'We're always going there anyway,' said Matti. 'Why can't we ever just stay in Helsinki at weekends? There's nothing to do at the cottage.'

Nothing to do.

Sitting for hours on the smooth flat rocks of the lakeshore with Matti, while he fished. Teaching Liisa to dive.

Was that better, Mum? Were my legs straight?

Walking to the farm for milk. Deciding that the children were old enough to fetch the milk themselves. Hunting for mushrooms on mornings that already held a tang of autumn.

'You guys will love Fredrik's place,' said Kai. 'He has a home cinema.'

'A home cinema in a summer cottage!' said Maija.

Then Kai told Maija to ask the kids what they'd like to do. They betrayed her, of course they did. A home cinema and a house party – 'Fredrik's kids are teenagers; there'll be a load of their friends there.'

Liisa and Matti had gone off with the others as soon as they arrived. They were all sleeping out in the woods. They were having their own bonfire and their own music.

'Light beers, nothing too alcoholic,' said Fredrik with a grin. 'We know what kids are like.'

A tall dark boy with hair over his face loped down the path ahead of Liisa, carrying iPod speakers. They were gone.

'And what do you do, Maija?' asked Fredrik.

'I work in a rehabilitation centre. I'm a nurse,' said Maija. Sometimes it could be awkward to reveal her profession among film and TV people. They wondered if they had already met her, in another life. 'I work mostly with young people,' she added, and Fredrik nodded quickly.

'Oh, right, good. Well, Kai, let me introduce you to Lucie. Harry Vikstrøm's coming along later; I really want you to meet him. *Julia's Skirt* is in post-production now ...'

They were gone. Kai didn't look at her. But she wanted him to meet people, of course she did. Even now, with their children teenagers, Kai was younger than most of these people. 'You've got kids? *How* old? You must have been still at school when you had them!'

She was holding her bag too tightly. She must relax. Anna seemed a nice woman, and not in TV or films or anything. She'd go and chat to Anna. People always need help in the kitchen at parties.

Anna was splodging caviar on to smoked salmon blinis.

'Let me help you with that,' said Maija.

'A girl was supposed to come – I can't think what's happened to her.' But Anna didn't seem perturbed. The table was covered with food.

'It looks wonderful.'

'It's simple stuff really.'

There were sides of salmon, reindeer tongue, bowls of crayfish with lemon mayonnaise, fresh little carrots and new potatoes, salads that looked as if they had just been pulled from the earth.

'Everything's organic,' said Anna.

'My father has an organic market garden,' said Maija.

'Has he? Has he really? That's amazing. Fredrik wants us to grow all our own veg up here.'

'Oh,' said Maija, warming a little to Fredrik the bear. 'Does he like gardening then?'

Anna scraped the last beads of caviar. 'I don't think he's ever done any.'

The light changed. A woman was standing in the doorway, surveying them. Not a guest, Maija thought. A maid perhaps? No, she was too unkempt.

'Oh, hello, Birgit,' said Anna, and for a second she hesitated, as if she didn't want to introduce her to Maija. She wiped her hands on a cloth, not looking at Birgit. 'Maija, this is my sister. Are you hungry, Birgit? There's loads to eat. I don't know what we're going to do with all this food.'

'You'll throw most of it away tomorrow,' said Birgit. Her voice was harsh, as if she'd had to shout for much of her life to make herself heard. There was dirt under her nails. She came close and Maija recognised her smell. Metabolised alcohol was leaking from her pores. On top of the alcohol smell there was the smell of smoke. Her hands shook finely.

Maija put down her knife and pressed her own hands flat on the table. *Birgit*. Everything was different, but the way the hair lay flat to her beautiful skull was the same.

'Birgit,' she said. 'Don't you remember me?'

Birgit threw her head up and examined Maija. Anna looked alarmed.

'You are Birgit Lindberg, aren't you?'

She could see the words *What if I am?* trembling on Birgit's lips.

'Don't you recognise me? I'm Maija. Maija Koskinen. You moved away when we were nine.' *When your parents got divorced, and your mum dragged you off to Helsinki. We swore we'd always be best friends, but I never saw you again. I wrote you all those letters but you only wrote back twice.*

'*Maija Koskinen*,' said Birgit slowly, as if these were words in a foreign language.

'Don't you remember?'

'Of course.' But it changes nothing, her look said. I am what I am, and you are what you are. How old she looked. Perhaps I look as old as that too, thought Maija. But we are only thirty-five!

'Were you friends at school?' asks Anna, looking from one to the other. Of course, she was Anna, Birgit's big sister whose friends teased them when they were round at Birgit's house. Anna would have been sixteen or seventeen then.

'You look good, Maija,' said Birgit. 'Do you work in TV?'

'I'm a nurse. It's my husband who's in TV.'

'Or you wouldn't be here,' said Birgit. 'I can't imagine Fredrik inviting nurses to his big party, can you, Anna?'

'Birgit,' said Anna.

'But he invited *me*. Now there's a surprise,' said Birgit.

'*I* invited you. It's my house too. You are my sister and I love you,' said Anna, as if this were part of a script she had read over many times.

'Let's go outside,' said Birgit to Maija. Maija still didn't know whether or not Birgit really recognised her, but she followed her outside. There were people everywhere now. Tango was playing from the speakers; there was a tin bath full of ice and beer bottles. How had they managed to get so much ice? She saw Kai in the distance talking to an older woman dressed in black, with sharp-cut silvery hair. Fredrik was in the middle of a crowd around the bonfire, his head flung back.

'This was my father's summer cottage. Fredrik bought out the rest of the family,' said Birgit.

'It's a big place.'

'It wasn't like this. Fredrik knocked down the original cottage. All this is new. Haven't you seen the solar panels? There's a geothermal heat pump too.'

'Why did he buy it, if he only wanted to knock it down? He could have built elsewhere.'

'The lake is so beautiful. People kept on telling him that. Shall we go down there, Maija?'

'Birgit, do you remember me?'

'Of course I remember you. I remember everything,' said Birgit. 'Do you have children?'

'Two, a boy and a girl. They're already older than we were back then.'

'Mine are too.'

Birgit looked as if she might say more, but they walked on in silence, threading through the partygoers as if they were ghosts. There was a path down to the water.

'We won't bathe here,' said Birgit, 'it's too near the house. We'll walk around the lake.'

Maija remembered the tone – imperious, and coaxing too, leading Maija into trouble. They were picking their way among rows of early peas, snapping off the crisp sweet pods. They were ducking into the fruit cages. They were screaming along forest paths, Birgit the leader, bold and wild. They were swimming naked and draping themselves with waterweed, 'like mermaids'. It was always Birgit's wildness that drew them on. Her singularity; her difference.

She was quiet now. They walked past the little beach of grey sand and took the path that skirts the lakeshore. Birgit walked slowly.

'How old are your children?' asked Maija.

'I have one, a daughter. She's twelve. She lives in England,' said Birgit, turning to look Maija full in the face.

'What's her name?'

'Jessica. Her father's English.'

They walked on. Maija could hear Birgit's breathing.

'Let's stop for a minute.' Birgit leaned against a tree and closed her eyes.

'You've been ill.'

'Yes.' Birgit's face was leathery, as if she'd spent years living outdoors. That was all they wanted to do when they were eight years old. They were going to build a house in the forest and live there forever and ever.

'I got an infection. I didn't see a doctor; you know how sometimes you can't be bothered. That's why I'm staying at Anna's in Helsinki for a while. Fredrik doesn't like it, but he gets a bit of street cred out of it. *We're giving Birgit support, she's been in and out of rehab.* "Rehab", as he says it.'

Birgit caught the bear's voice, just as she had caught every voice of their childhood.

They were at the jetty.

'We'll take the boat out,' said Birgit. 'Can you row?'

'You know I can, and so can you.'

'Not any more.'

The boat moved out clumsily, as if it wasn't used to the weight of people. Maija dug the oars too deep, caught a crab, then caught her rhythm. It was neither dark nor light. The summer gloaming hung over the still water and from the distance they heard the cries and music of the party. Maija thought of her children, deep in the forest, drinking beer with strangers, but for once she wasn't afraid.

'Let's swim,' said Birgit.

Maija didn't reply. She watched the water, the dark trees, the light behind Birgit's head, shaping it.

'I can still swim,' Birgit insisted.

'Maybe it's not such a good idea,' said Maija in the mild voice of work, but she stopped rowing and shipped her oars. Birgit stood up and the boat rocked wildly as she tore off her shirt, her jeans, her pants, T-shirt and bra, and stood naked. Her poor body was seamed with scars. It looked as if someone had sharpened a knife on her, but over many years Maija had learned not to show surprise, still less revulsion, still less fear. Maija remembered how Birgit used to dive. The lake surface would open for her with barely a ripple, as if Birgit herself was made of water.

'I was in an accident,' said Birgit.

'I thought you must have been.'

An accident that had gone on for decades.

Birgit raised her arms, preparing to dive.

'I can't stop you,' said Maija.

'I know that. Close your eyes. Count how long it takes me to swim to shore.'

'But how will I know when you dive, if my eyes are shut?'

'Oh Maija, that's pimps! Count from the splash!'

There she is, laughing. She leans forward but she hasn't launched herself yet. *It's easy-squeezy, Maija! Come on, Maija, it's pimps! Maija ... Maija ... Maija ...*

The circles widen, going out, going back. Maija counts from the splash.

IN CHINA THIS WOULD
NOT HAPPEN

❦

It's that time of the year again. Students stand moon-struck in the roaring streets, clutching maps of the city. They enter banks in herds, to open accounts and find out what an overdraft is. All the time they talk loudly about what happened last night, what's happening tonight and what will happen at the weekend. There are poster sales, houseplant sales, pizza company freebies and Christian Union leaflets all over the grass. The held breath of bars, clubs and cafés, which have been half-empty since June, begins to exhale.

The girls are so lovely. There are the glossy ones and the nervous ones; hockey girls with their big rolled socks on a Wednesday afternoon; girls who know the difference between a wok and a frying pan; girls who spill over the pavement edges after too many drinks or teeter half-naked, holding on to each other; girls who smile suddenly, sweetly, at middle-aged women who remind them of their mums. Because they are homesick, of course. Everybody's homesick, as well as beside themselves with excitement to be away from home. That's what all the noise is about.

I'm not jaundiced at all, even though I've been working most of my life in what is now known as Student Recruitment. Join the student army, and see the world ...

I go to China a lot. That's the way things are these days. We were caught out in one of those Sunday newspaper exposés a few years ago. You know the kind of thing: popular university course already full and no further offers being made; journalist poses as overseas student; qualifications not quite up to mark (to put it mildly); lots of chat about 'flexibility' and 'equivalence'; offer of place more or less made on the spot. Standard approach, in fact. Our Guidelines for Telephone Procedure have altered considerably since then.

Do you believe that I am who I say I am? Fortyish, reasonably kindly, observant (as you have to be in my job) and a little world-weary? Or maybe you don't. Maybe you've noticed already that there's something which doesn't quite fit. Fortunately, texts are infinitely correctable these days. I am just about old enough to remember what it was like to fossick about with Tipp-Ex, and I thoroughly appreciate the way words, paragraphs – whole histories – can be made to melt away without trace, and re-form according to the author's desire.

I even have a parking space with my name on it. Or rather, my role. We call our jobs 'roles' these days, even in an institution as conservative as this one, as if to suggest that we are all highly trained actors who can slip in and out of character as required. My allocated parking space is in a courtyard by the rear entrance, which means that I don't need to carry an umbrella. Female members of staff prefer to park in the main car park, which is properly lit and patrolled by security. But you can't have everything.

It's 7th October. Freshers' Week is over, and the students are wanly settling down to the routine of their lives. If such it can be called. Soon some of them will be suffering from 'stress' and traipsing to the University Counselling Service. Others will be in their glory. Successfully auditioning for the Drama Department's new production of *Phaedra's Love*; running PoSoc and LitSoc; quirkily passionate about breakdance or Black Crane Kung Fu; blogging about Syria on the student website; staying up all night to present the folk/punk hour on Whizz Radio ...

The girls are so lovely, and they don't know it. I stand at my office window and watch the wind blowing them along the street. I have my phone to my ear, and if anyone looks up I'm gazing into the distance, deep in an important call to Zhengzhou or Qingdao. (It is necessary to trawl well beyond the great conurbations of China these days, given the competition.) The autumn leaves fly, and the girls' hair streams behind them as they run. They always seem late for something. I don't suppose they eat breakfast. I'd like to sit them down in front of a plate of eggs and bacon and watch their eyes widen with pleasure as they squeeze the sauce bottle.

If I had my time again ...

When I was eighteen, I worried about whether other people in my kitchen were helping themselves from my tin of Marvel. I joined Chess Soc and Orienteering. I was never overdrawn. My girlfriend from home came up every weekend, tidied my room, tried to put up a Kylie Minogue poster and made coffee for everyone I even vaguely knew, as if her life depended on it. It was the end of the second year before she realised that she didn't love me, by which time it was too late for all those other girls. My girlfriend never squeezed the sauce bottle. Fried breakfasts weren't her thing.

I like China. I feel at home there. It's an odd thing, because I don't speak the language and I stick out like a sore thumb, especially in the smaller cities where Westerners are rare. I remember a lecture I went to years ago, when our mission to attract Chinese students was just beginning. It was on 'The Concept and Function of Face in Chinese Society'. A big subject for a single lecture, you might think, but it intrigued me. I was struck immediately by a sense that the Chinese had got it right. They had found a way of negotiating around the infinite possibilities for humiliation that human life offers to us all. I felt sure that if I had been born Chinese, I would have fitted in and understood what to do and what not to do, from the very beginning.

I like to have a chat with our students from China, a week or so after their arrival, when they have begun to orientate themselves but are still eager for advice. I tell them to be themselves. I do have to mention the fact that their essays may be run through plagiarism software these days, but they appear to be more grateful for this information than offended by it.

I want them to get good degrees. I want them to be rewarded for what they have done. It's not easy – none of this is easy. I'm sorry. I'm losing the thread again. You may have noticed another small clue in the preceding paragraphs.

Our society is so disorderly. Outside my office, on the other side of the road, there is a row of cafés with Italian names, packed with young people talking and laughing or studying Facebook on their laptops. Boys leaning across tables to speak to beautiful girls. The hubbub is so joyous that you could close your eyes and imagine that you were at a children's Christmas party.

In between two of the cafés there is an alley, and there sits a man so shrunken by addiction that I doubt if he would be more than five foot tall if he stood up. He has been there for years. He told me his name once, although I hadn't asked: he said he was called Trevor. He holds a paper cup and into it these tall, stooping students, from time to time, drop cash. I see them straighten up afterwards and the look on their faces is warm, as if they have felt the glow of a fire.

He may not be an addict at all. We are all too quick to jump to conclusions about other people. But he has lost face. I have the feeling that in China this would not happen. Not opposite the administrative buildings of a prestigious university, at least.

My girlfriend from home got married, not long after finding out that she didn't love me. Her name was Anthea, and she never liked it. When we were together, she once said she would give her children plain English names. As she said it, she glanced at my face. I've had other relationships, of course, but never anything that looked like becoming permanent.

It is 4th December. Apparently the intense cold we've had these past few winters has something to do with the sun. Low solar activity. You can hardly see the girls' faces, they are so swathed in scarves and hats. Just a strip of rosy skin, and their eyes. They stamp their feet in fleecy boots. Term finishes this weekend.

Last night I worked late and then went for a long walk, towards the Common. The snow has lain since last weekend and it's frozen hard. There was a moon. I had my walking boots on, and so the ice was no problem. It was very quiet. The roads and pavements were ridged with ice; the council doesn't seem to clear them. There were only a few students about. By this stage of term they've spent most of their money and are frantically finishing off their final essays. It felt as if the city belonged to me. I walked away from the street lights, where the Common lay dark. I went over snow that no one else had touched, through trees and then out into the open. I stared up into the hard, black sky where stars flashed, and tried to identify the constellations. But I didn't know what to look for, and the cold was working its way into me, so I turned and walked back again, all the way back into the city centre.

Soon I was standing opposite the admin building. I said in my head, in the humorously self-deprecating voice one might use to a colleague: *Can't keep away from the place!* Trevor's nest of dirty blankets was empty, and he'd taken his sleeping bag. He must have gone into a hostel, for fear of freezing to death.

I was very, very tired. I went into my office and sat at my desk, but I didn't do any work. I keep getting these flashy headaches. It's a worry, because it makes it difficult to focus. I thought: I can't. I can't.

I'm feeling a lot better today. No headache, and the cold was quite invigorating as I walked into work. I had to prepare for the interviews I'd arranged. It's perfectly clear to me now that the reason I'm getting these headaches is that I need an eye test. My prescription will have to be changed. In China, 80 per cent of college students are myopic.

Trevor is back at his post, inside his sleeping bag, huddled against the wall. I break all my own rules, go into the café and order a large latte. I put in three sugars. As I lean down to give Trevor the coffee I catch the stench of him. He wraps his hands around the paper cup and folds himself over the hot drink as if there's nothing else in the world. I cross the road, back to my office.

Most of the students whom I invited for interview have emailed to say that they can't make it. The timing is awkward, because I've had to arrange the interviews after office hours. But it doesn't matter. I have three students coming in, at carefully spaced intervals.

My windows are full of darkness. I pull down the blind. It's still only half past four: an hour and a half to wait until my first student. I'm restless, and although the pain has gone there is still a tight feeling inside my head.

For some reason I keep thinking about Anthea. I wonder what my life at university would have been like without her there every weekend, arriving with her things in the blue Pan Am flight bag that her father got when he went to New York.

I see her making coffee for people she doesn't know and whom I'd never know either, not really, because I was the guy with the slightly weird girlfriend who didn't belong. Suddenly I want to reach back through time and slap Anthea's smiling face to the left, to the right, to the left again, until there is nothing left of her smile and she will never come near me again.

I blink, and look at the clock. I must have been thinking for a long time, because it's ten to six. Quickly, I put my jacket on and sit at my desk, ready to swivel round at the knock on the door.

The first one is a tall, rangy boy from Weihai. He's very much at home, with a relaxed smile that I remember from the student welcome party at the start of term. He's had a good term; of course he has. He's staying with friends in London over the Christmas vacation. I hadn't noticed the American twang in his voice before. He talks about London with a casual familiarity which makes me angry. We chat for a few minutes, and he's clearly wondering why I've bothered to call this meeting. I give him a couple of questionnaires about the student experience to return to me at the beginning of next term, and ask if he'd be willing to write something for the website. He's flattered, and agrees. Will I need a photo?

When he's gone I realise I'm sweating. I open the window, then quickly close it again. The next student arrives a little before I expect her. She's a puddingy girl whose spoken English was so hesitant at the beginning of term that I had a concerned email from her personal tutor. Fortunately, her written language turned out to be much better. She sits down squarely in the chair opposite me and tells me at length about the difficulties she has had with the other students on her corridor, and how much she would have preferred completely self-contained accommodation. I take notes, nodding, and thank her for this valuable feedback, which will be passed on to the accommodation office for future reference. My heart beats hard.

At last I usher her out. She is still talking and making small, stiff movements of protest with her hands over the behaviour of her fellow students. I tell her again that I am grateful to her for coming along and sharing her experiences. She does not smile, but she nods in acknowledgement and I know that we have both emerged from the encounter without embarrassment.

I sit down, and rub my eyes. Outside the ground is frozen hard. Trevor will have gone wherever he goes. All those lovely girls have dissolved as if they never existed. I say that they are lovely, in the indulgent way that a man who has found happiness in his life might say it. Fortyish, reasonably kindly, observant (as you have to be in my job) and a little world-weary. I am a better actor now than I was when I was eighteen. If I could have my time again, I wouldn't start from here.

I make a cup of instant coffee, and stir in sugar. It is quarter past seven. The admin building is empty at this hour, apart from security. They patrol at predictable times. They much prefer driving around in luridly striped vehicles which, if you don't look closely, bear a passing resemblance to police cars. Day and night, they wear high-visibility jackets.

Security is far better organised in China. On campus, there will be a control room where security staff scan the video feeds from cameras placed to cover all angles. They look calm, even serene, but if they see something out of place they react immediately, picking up a telephone and issuing instructions. You don't see them stopping for cups of tea or banter with the students.

I can smell myself. Quickly, I go to the sink and run my wrists under the cold tap.

The third student is late and I'm beginning to think she's not coming, when she taps at the door. She is muffled up against the cold, and she unwraps her long scarf carefully before she sits down. It's a beautiful scarf. Cashmere, I think. Her hands are small and delicate as they fold up the scarf. She looks at me, and smiles. Her smile is exactly as I remember it.

I take a questionnaire out of my desk, and am about to give it to her when I realise that my hands are trembling. I lay it on the desk, hoping that she hasn't noticed. She is a polite girl, and keeps her eyes on my face, waiting for me to begin. I first noticed her when she offered to help clear away after the student welcome party. *Please, it is a pleasure.*

I ask her if she has enjoyed the term. Have there been any problems? The slightest of frowns creases her forehead. She looks as if she is trying to find some little problem, in order to please me. Finally she says, 'Everyone has been very friendly.'

'And you like your family?' I ask her. This is a pet scheme of mine. I match students to local families who offer Sunday lunch a couple of times a term. A sense of welcome is so important.

Yes, she likes her family. They have taken her on a visit to an English country house.

'Good,' I say. 'So everything's going well. The first term isn't always easy, but you've clearly made an excellent beginning. Would you like some tea?'

She shakes her head. 'No thank you, no tea.' She says it in a small, polite but absolutely firm voice. She is refusing me.

I smile at her indulgently as I get up to fill the kettle at my little sink.

'Please,' she says, more insistently. 'No tea, thank you. I must be at home.'

Her English is breaking up slightly, under pressure. I swing round with a kindly, disbelieving smile. 'I have Silver Needle!' I say. She thinks that I am offering her ordinary English tea. But she shakes her head again.

'No thank you. It is very kind, but no thank you.'

I stare at her, confounded. What am I going to do now? In China this would never happen. She looks back, still polite but embarrassed too, because I'm insisting and I'm a senior official in her university. So why has she refused me? Doesn't she understand that it's polite to accept what you are offered? I flick down the kettle switch and lift the little teapot, just big enough for two, ready to warm it when the water boils.

She has got to her feet. She has picked up her scarf and is holding it close to her body as she looks at me. 'Please,' she says again, 'I must be at home.'

I open the packet of Silver Needle with shaking fingers. It is awkwardly sealed. She is edging towards the door, but I am in her way. I have a little chased-silver scoop for the tea. It's important to do these things with a degree of ceremony, otherwise we live like beasts.

'It won't take long,' I tell her. Her fingers clutch the scarf. A drop of sweat runs down my forehead, tickling like an insect. She won't stop staring. The kettle is coming to the boil.

'Sit down,' I tell her. 'Please.'

I think that she's going to obey me, but at the last moment she dodges under my arm and rushes for the door. Her fingers scrabble for the handle but it's too late. I take hold of her, turn her round and point her towards the chair where she was sitting.

'All I want is to drink tea with you,' I tell her.

She stumbles to the chair and sits down with her arms wrapped around her body. The kettle switches itself off.

I am tired, so tired. My headache has come back, worse than ever. I just want this to be over. Anthea used to make coffee all the time. Why did she do that? This girl is crying, but all I want to do is make her welcome.

'My mother,' she says. She looks at me but her eyes keep flickering to the door.

'Your mother?'

'My mother – does not make me drink tea.' She is crying but she still manages to speak quite clearly. 'I never like it.'

My hand goes slack. Slowly, the Silver Needle tea pours from the scoop on to the floor. I watch it go. I will need to clean it up. I move closer to her, and she shrinks back in her chair. There is a smell of sweat and I'm not sure if it is hers or my own. My room is brightly lit and much too hot. I think of the snow outside.

I step back and make a movement with my arms, as if I'm shooing a cat. 'Go,' I say, 'go, go, go—' I can't seem to stop saying it. She edges out of her chair and retreats backwards, her eyes on me, fumbling for the door behind her. She has dropped her scarf. She makes a sound in her throat, wrenches the door handle, and then she's gone. I hear her feet clatter down the empty corridor, and then a door bangs.

I put the chair back in its place. I am sweating and trembling. Everything is over; I know that. I cannot come back here. I have lost face.

For a moment I don't know what to do. I even start scooping the tea up from the floor. If I make tea, and sit down, and drink it, then maybe everything will be all right. But I know it won't. I go to the shelf above the sink, where I keep pound coins in a mustard tin. It is heavy. I put the tin in my pocket, and without bothering to put on my coat or switch off the lights, I leave my office, stepping over the cashmere scarf.

The cold strikes through my jacket. The cafés are still open; it's only eight o'clock. For some reason I think that Trevor will have come back, but his corner is empty. I lean down and empty the mustard tin into the folds of the blankets he sits on; then I fold them over again so that the coins are hidden. After a moment's thought, I also take off my jacket and leave it there.

Oddly enough, I feel warmer in just my shirt than I did with the jacket on. It's quiet again. My feet slither on the packed ice, but I've a good sense of balance, and I don't fall. Soon I'm beyond the shops, bars and cafés, taking side streets, going uphill towards the Common. It's beautiful there in summer. My hands hurt but they've stopped shaking; at least, I think they have. On my first recruitment trip to the Far East I went to Hong Kong; that was before we got going in mainland China. I couldn't sleep on the flight. I went to stand at the back of the plane, and there below us, in the dawn light, were the mountains of Mongolia. At least, that's what the steward told me they were called. I gazed down at them for a long time. They were huge red mountains, deeply ridged, ancient, folded into themselves. There wasn't a mark of human existence. They looked like a dream as our plane throbbed over them, on and on. The light grew strong and the shadows between the ridges grew deeper. We passed over them like gods, but

I knew that if the engine note changed and failed we would be down there, and the red mountains would be real.

Soon I'm in the middle of the Common. There are no street lights here, and so you can see the stars. I can't see them tonight. Her face gets in the way. All I wanted was to drink tea with her.

I lied to you about the scarf. I brought it with me. It's very soft. Probably from the Qinghai area. I'm still holding it as I walk towards the darkness under the trees.

A VERY FINE HOUSE

❧

I'm home at last. It's taken all my life to get here. Home.

I can hear the children, two floors down. The sound's muffled by closed doors. It's only because I'm listening so carefully that I can pick it up at all. I'm on the first floor, and they are deep down in the Lower Ground Floor Accommodation: that is, the basement. I'm upstairs, in the elegant First Floor Drawing Room, which looks out over the recently landscaped south-facing garden. There are four floors: basement, ground floor with kitchen and family room, first floor with drawing room and bedroom suite, and the children's bedrooms on the top floor. I could tell you the dimensions of every room. I know them all by heart, even though this is my first day here. My first hour, almost.

Of course I won't call this room the drawing room. That's so pretentious, don't you think? Drawing rooms and master suites and cloakrooms and mature trees and original features. All very well for estate agents' particulars: in fact, it is expected from them. My home is 'a fine Gentleman's Residence in a prime position with charming lower-ground-floor accommodation, which could easily be converted to form a separate apartment'.

Or, in other words, a basement which houses the remains of a kitchen range, a servants' toilet, and a warren of cellars where people have been burying bodies for two hundred years.

Children love secret passages and hidey-holes. They'll be fascinated by the bell-board, and the thought that someone upstairs could press a bell and a tired girl in the kitchens would have to put on a clean apron and toil upstairs to find out what was wanted this time. *You rang, ma'am?* The basement's going to be converted into a huge playroom, with white paint and spotlights everywhere. Even though it's dark and dusty now, you can see the potential.

Seeing the potential is very much my thing. I do read all the magazines – *Your Period Home, Converting Period Property, Foraging for Features, Victorian Interiors* – but I like to have my own vision. Without vision, a house is nothing. Just a doll dressed in whatever was closest to hand.

This house has got everything. I knew it was for me as soon as I saw it. It wasn't on any of the agents' websites, and there wasn't a For Sale board outside. You can afford to be discreet, with a house of this quality. I was new to the city, and the agents didn't know me yet. I saw the photograph go into the window of Gibbet and Glyde. Yes, literally, just as I was passing. I glanced, and stopped dead.

The house is Grade II listed. The agent explained the implications to me, because a listed building can be a stumbling block for some purchasers. You can't touch the exterior. I nodded, as if I didn't know it all. I explained to him that my husband worked in London during the week, so I was doing the preliminary viewings. The glossy brochure wasn't ready yet, but the agent gave me draft particulars. I put on my reading glasses, although I didn't need to. I knew already, you see. It was like falling in love, only better. We were a match. But I didn't want the agent to guess that I'd made my mind up, because then they start to get silly. You have to be a bit cunning, a bit of an actor.

'Oh,' I said, letting a shade of disappointment into my voice. 'Only four bedrooms ...'

'The fifth bedroom is in the base— in the lower-ground-floor accommodation,' he corrected me eagerly.

I love times like these, when it's a buyers' market. Prices are flat, and people are staying put. Then the estate agents start to jump. The very ones who've been so snotty, so sure they've got nothing to show you ... suddenly they're returning your calls twice over.

I read through the particulars slowly, keeping my head down. I could feel the agent taking me in. Mid-forties, expensive jeans, buttery leather jacket, hair blunt-cut and skilfully highlighted, crocodile loafers. Husband sweating it in a bank somewhere, wife left to make the lifestyle decisions.

The house had everything I wanted. I'd known as soon as I saw it. You can tell a house from its face. And this one wasn't just a face, it was a voice too, a beautiful voice that no one else could hear. Home, it said. *Home.*

'The drawing room is particularly elegant,' the agent encouraged me. 'There are the original French-style doors to the terrace, and working shutters.'

'Cornices? Coving?' I murmured.

'Of course. All original. And a very nice marble fireplace, *not* in fact original to the house, but absolutely of the period.'

'And the bedroom balcony is sweet,' I let myself observe. 'It *does* seem as if it might be the kind of thing we're looking for … Now that the boys are away at school, we ought to be able to manage with four bedrooms—'

'If I might just correct you: *five* bedrooms.'

'But I suppose it needs work.'

'An opportunity to put your own stamp on the property – your personal touch—'

'Damp?'

'Dry as a …' He floundered, as if for a moment he'd lost sight of cliché, then he brought it out triumphantly. 'Bone!'

'Bone. Lovely.'

'Shall I arrange an early viewing? If I might advise you, houses of this quality rarely remain on the market for long.'

No, they don't, do they? Not even now, in a buyers' market. I knew that, and so I put in an offer the day I saw you. Of course I had to telephone my husband first to discuss it, but that was all right. He trusts my judgement.

The vendor accepted my offer. I knew he would. I know exactly how to pitch these things. Now, at last, I allowed the agent to hear the excitement in my voice as I told him I would arrange a survey as soon as possible, get my solicitor to write to the vendor's solicitor, get everything under way. I smiled at him, really smiled at him for the first time.

'It's a lovely house, Edward,' I said. 'I'm very happy.'

And I meant it, every word. Happiness, oh happiness. You don't often feel it, do you? Not really. Not on those occasions when happiness is called for and expected. Weddings, engagements, christenings, new jobs, exam passes. I try to feel it, but I just can't. But at that moment, sitting opposite Edward on one of the agency's dark brown squashy leather armchairs, I was flooded with pure happiness, until every cell in me was radiant with it. Impressive, original, integral, magnificent, full-height, double-panelled happiness.

'I can't wait to tell my husband,' I said.

Was that my mistake? Shouldn't I have smiled? Maybe if I'd kept my poker face all the way through, allowing myself only the mildest expression of satisfaction, maybe then none of it would have happened. Did I tempt fate? Did I betray you by betraying my feelings? We were made for each other. I knew it, and you knew it. Your lovely quiet façade was like a smile when I watched you from the other side of the road. I was always calling to see you. Discreetly, on foot, never stopping long. The vendors were away, visiting a daughter in Italy. Imagine going to Italy, when they had you. They didn't deserve you.

It's quite normal to visit a house you're going to live in. People want to see how the light falls, morning and evening. What noise there is, what the parking is like. But you didn't reveal a single flaw.

Edward kept in close touch. He knew we had a buyer for our flat in London, and the mortgage for the balance was arranged. My solicitor's letter was slow in arriving, but that didn't matter. Everything was going forward.

And then the blow fell. It was Edward, on my mobile.

'Hello?' I sang. I was still so happy, you see. Every day and in every way.

'It's Edward,' said Edward.

I knew straight away that something was wrong. I started to gabble about the weather, which I never do. He was unresponsive. It's happened, I thought. He knows.

Edward cleared his throat. 'I'm sorry, Mrs Howard. I'm afraid something's come up with regard to the house.'

'What?' I said.

'I'm awfully sorry.' But he said it smoothly, professionally. He wasn't sorry – why should he be? 'But I'm afraid we've had a cash offer on the house. And of course we are obliged to pass on such an offer to the vendor. And I'm afraid, naturally ...'

'He's accepted it,' I said.

'Yes.'

'How much?'

'I'm afraid I'm not at liberty to discuss the detail—' Yes, he actually dared to say that. Not at liberty, in the drawing room with the brass candlestick.

'I'll match it,' I said. 'Whatever he's offered, I'll match it.'

'Mrs Howard, I'll be frank with you. His offer is only very slightly higher than yours. But it is a genuine cash offer, the purchaser was able to give us documentary proof of that.'

I held my mobile away from me for a few seconds, and stared at the tiny hole from which Edward's voice quacked. Words boiled in my mouth but I wasn't going to let any of them out. It wouldn't do any of us any good.

'I see,' I said at last, nearly as smoothly as Edward. 'I understand. It's very ...'

'Disappointing.'

'Yes. My husband will be—' But for once, I couldn't go on with it. Edward heard it in my voice.

'I'm sorry, Mrs Howard. We'll keep in touch. There are a lot of properties coming on to the market.'

You're mad, I thought. I said goodbye politely, and ended the call. People know nothing. They don't understand reality. The house was mine.

I don't usually wait around after a disappointment. There are other cities, other conservation areas, other houses. But not this time. No, this time I stayed. I was going to be faithful. I kept on visiting you. Not so often, not in the daytime. But often enough. The owners came back from Italy and packed up their wretched possessions. They got careless, left the shutters open and the lights on so I could see everything. They didn't feel it was their house any more. They stopped looking after it. And they were right. It wasn't theirs now. No. It had passed to someone else.

The day the vans came was hard. I hired a car, wore dark glasses and a headscarf. I drove past the house a few times, and saw it all. A huge van slid into place just after midday, then a Mercedes estate. Out they all jumped. Mother, father, two little girls. My God, the woman couldn't have been more than thirty. Fair hair, tiny body, little piping voice. I parked down the road for a while and watched, and listened.

Inheritance, that's what it was. They'd never earned all that money themselves. They stretched out their hands and grabbed my house. That silly, high, piping voice.

'Lettie, sweetheart, why don't you and Cincie go and explore the garden?'

They left the shutters open, too, and lights blazed until late at night. I saw them going from room to room, taking possession.

But even with all that inheritance, the husband still had to go to work. *Bye bye, darling, remember I'll be home late tonight!* And the little girls had to go to school. Back she came in the Mercedes estate. Just her. I was tucked in at the end of the road. After a while, I walked briskly down the pavement and knocked on the door. I had a bunch of keys in my hand.

'Good morning, I'm from Gibbet and Glyde. We like to call round for a chat after a move, just to check everything's gone smoothly. If you could spare a few minutes?'

Of course she could. Would I like a cup of coffee? Terribly sorry, everything's such a tip, but the house is *wonderful* – and she actually invited me into my own kitchen.

'Coffee would be lovely,' I said, 'but first of all, my colleague forgot to hand over the cellar keys. Could we just check that these are the right ones?'

Of course we could. She'd lead the way. Careful, these stairs are rather steep, she said, as if I didn't know my own house.

I love my drawing room. It's not really a pretentious word, when a room is so beautiful. And so peaceful, in the middle of the city. All you can hear are the birds.

But if you listen carefully, you might hear something else. A scuffling noise, far away, very faint. Perhaps a tiny cry. It's the boys, back from boarding school, playing in the basement. I listen with a smile. They're having a wonderful time; there's no need to worry about them at all. In a minute I'll make myself another cup of coffee, bring it back in here and close the doors. I don't want any distractions now. My house is waiting for me.

DUTY-FREE

❧

They were the cleanest airport floors I've ever seen. Even so, a man was buffing up sparkles in a corner of the duty-free, beside a display of pixies and lucky charms. I was not quite the only customer in the half-acre of perfumes, whisky and cosmetics. Two or three of us drifted, desultory, fingering but failing to buy. The goods that shone inside the cabinets seemed to have nothing to do with us. A sound system played music that broke on our ears as waves break on the shore. The staff were so attentive, so knowledgeably eager to carry out the tasks which could not be completed without the absent passengers. Even as you quaked for their jobs, you couldn't help warming to their unfounded optimism.

Friendly were the security staff, gassing to one another about a football match. No one mentioned the result. Perhaps they'd all stopped watching at the same moment, to keep up the suspense for yet another working day. Warm and tasty drifted the smells of chilli con carne

and mushroom lasagne in the restaurant. I ordered a
cup of coffee.

'Will there be anything to eat with that?' sang the
young man behind the counter, and I had to fight not
to ask for the whole sweep of it, piping hot, just so that
his face would light up. But he flourished the coffee on
to the counter before me and smiled as if mine were
just the order he'd been hoping for.

The silicate-glitter of the floors was getting to me.
I'm easily disorientated, and on my way back through
duty-free I was busy counting the small airport tasks
that I had yet to carry out: buying a bottle of water
and the newspaper if they had it, checking my email
and the price of Chanel No 5 ... So I organise even my
empty hours. There was a recycling bin handy, and there
I sorted and threw away the papers from the conference
I'd just attended. I held on to the timetable for a moment.
It was marked out with notes, and the couple of sessions
I'd presented were highlighted in green, the colour of a
knot in the stomach. Strange how things could be so
important, and then not important at all.

When I looked up, the desert had flowered. The duty-
free was packed. Scores of soldiers, men and women
both, a hundred of them, no, many more than a hundred,
milled purposefully around the displays or lined up in
front of the tills. They had big boots and pale sandy
uniforms. They were large, eager, polite, weary. You could
see their health and youth in their springing hair and
quick, observant glance. Their skins, however, were poor.

They all wanted to buy something in the short time that they had. Packed into bulky trousers, women soldiers compared lipsticks. Men queued for cologne. Names were murmured like prayers: L'Oréal, Shiseido, Versace, Prada, Paco Rabanne ...

The assistants had risen to great heights and were changing dollars into euros in their heads as they advised on a set of headphones while clicking up a fragrance purchase. Politeness flowed over us all, ample as a river.

'This one is seventy-three euro, or would you prefer the larger size?'

We were at home again, in the kingdom of our preferences. The cabinets opened and disclosed their contents to eager hands. White glossy packages were fetched down from the highest shelves. Pixies tinkled against one another. I fell into the swing of it and began to search among the lipsticks for number 719, the one I always wear. A young woman soldier alongside me waved a perfume tester strip under her nostrils. She had stains of fatigue under her eyes. Maybe this one wasn't right for her, she said. All she could smell was aeroplane.

'You can't go wrong with Chanel No 5. It's a classic,' I said, as I say to my daughter.

The soldier's face lightened. 'I guess it is, but I don't know that it works on me,' she said. She sprayed again, on her wrist this time, and turned it this way and that. She had a Southern voice. Her skin was pitted, not beautiful.

'Where are you all going?' I asked her.

'Afghanistan.'

'I think it works on you,' I said, breathing in the wrist she held out to me. There was her body smell under the perfume. It was dry, powdery and somewhat metallic. She was correct. She smelled of aeroplane.

Theirs was a short stopover, for refuelling. I thought that these soldiers must be the lifeblood of the duty-free. They would have spent thousands of dollars in their short time off the plane. After they'd made their purchases, they sat quietly on banks of plastic seats in the hall outside the duty-free, waiting for the tannoy. The bulk of their uniforms made them sprawl somewhat, legs apart, but not as students sprawl, ostentatiously at leisure, infantry of the gap-year dream that other travellers can only envy. These soldiers rested. The group beside me talked about mobile phones, as if there were nothing else in the world.

How vast the airport was, and how bare of purpose. The life in it, for which it had been built, had sunk down to barely a murmur. Cafés, departure gates, transit lounges and scanners were becalmed. A coffee machine hissed to itself. Only, everywhere, as far as the eye could see, there were these soldiers.

Afghanistan. They were not even born in the days when the boldest of my generation took the Magic Bus to Kabul in search of Afghan gold. Here they sat, composed, under orders, touching Irish soil; or, at least, their boots touched silicate particles in the flooring that caught the light as far as the eye could see. They were not unhandsome, some of the men. The girls, too, rested utterly, closing their eyes so that the harsh overhead light exposed the pure cut of the lids, and every blackhead on their overworked skins. All the same, they were not unbeautiful.

There was one low-key call for their flight. Immediately, they were on the move, down the long hall, through an exit which had nothing to do with the civilian airport. There was no gathering of hand luggage, mustering of children, wheelchairs, pushchairs. The soldiers were there one minute, filling the lounge, and then they were gone through a flap that had appeared somewhere in the wall of the airport, revealing it to be no more than a transit shed which had served its purpose. On my left the duty-free still glittered. Now there came four or five stragglers who had just succeeded in making their purchases. They loped past me, and for the first time I saw that they were fit and fast for all their heaviness. They quickened almost to a canter, laughing for the first time, then they too disappeared. The tin shed turned back into an airport. The soldiers' big-bellied plane was already receiving them into itself.

An incident, I thought. A notable moment, equal to the sighting of rare passerines. But I was mistaken, because at that time they came in almost daily. A quarter of a million US military personnel, it seems, went through that airport in one year alone.

Backwards and forwards the planes go, settling briefly on this small space of Irish soil, releasing, briefly, their uniformed passengers. The duty-free must live for them, now that the Celtic Tiger is dead and the acres of car park around the airport stand empty. The US military has come to its aid for sure.

They go up slowly, those big-bellied planes. They are far from new, and they labour sometimes under the weight of what they carry. The youth inside them, packed into flesh, packed into uniform, and then filling the metal skin of the DC-10. The youth that comes once, and doesn't come again.

As your plane rises you see the land, the water, and then the wing tilts and the sky is there instead, reeling away from you, all that greyness thickening to muffle your eyes, your ears, your lips. You will never see earth again. You say goodbye to it without emotion, among the whiteness, as if this is the death you have always expected; but as it happens this time the plane keeps climbing, and you punch through the clouds and out into the blue.

CHOCOLATE FOR LATER

❧

'**W**ill there be port wine with the cheese, Mrs Marion?'

I've never tasted port. I consider. There are five cheeses, a slice of quince paste, a branch of raisins. I'm not hungry, but Aimée is so sweet, so eager.

'They are very good, the cheeses, Mrs Marion!'

Her eyes are soft and dark, and she is graceful. There was a tiny misfortune as she removed the empty dish which had held my mango fool: slices of fresh, glistening mango, flakes of coconut, luscious cream with a thread of mango coulis running through it. The descriptions on the menu are so appetising. It makes you appreciate things even more. So, Aimée lifted the dish and began carefully to place the cheese plate on the thick white cloth in front of me. But something caught as she lowered it. The knife clattered, and fell. She was mortified, bless her.

'Oh, Mrs Marion, I am so sorry. It did not touch you?'

The raisins are plump, and they fan out from their stalks like fresh grapes. I pick one off, and put it in my mouth with a corner of artisan sheep's cheese from the Wallambura Hills.

'Just a taste, please, Aimée,' I say, and she pours a careful inch of port into my glass. I lift it, and smile at her.

'What do you think, Mrs Marion?'

'Delicious. Thank you, dear.'

She moves off to attend to another passenger, and I press the button to adjust my seat just a little. I never lie flat while food is being served. It seems disrespectful. After they've finished serving coffee and have taken away the trays, the big white napkins and the tablecloths, I'll have a little nap. It's important to arrive fresh.

I'm used to this journey. I make it three times a year. Not at Christmas or Easter, or the big holiday times: they are too expensive. You have to plan these things carefully. I explained that to Aimée when she came round with the hot towels, before dinner.

'You are going on holiday, Mrs Marion? Or you are visiting family?'

The hot towel is such a good idea. I find myself thinking that perhaps I should do this at home. Damp a towel and put it in the oven, perhaps – would that work? It is so soothing, so refreshing. All your worries disappear and you're ready to enjoy the journey. There is a glass of champagne in front of me, and a dish of warm nuts. Aimée makes quite a point of these nuts being warm, and she entirely understands why I only take half a glass of champagne. She approves of it.

'I'm going out to see my son and his family. My grandchildren.'

'How old are they?'

'Jess is seven, Rory is four and the baby – Clara – she's eight weeks. It'll be the first time I've seen the baby – apart from on Skype, of course.'

'What a happy time it will be,' says Aimée, and she smiles with gentle, sympathetic excitement for me.

'Yes,' I say. I am entirely happy as I smile up at her, my mind full of Jess, Rory and Clara. Champagne bubbles break on my tongue. I won't drink much; I never do. Otherwise, I might fall asleep and miss the whole experience.

There's a woman at the front of the cabin with a little baby. Four months old, I heard her say. She is well off, you can tell. Smooth tanned skin, casual, lovely clothes, confidence. As I walked past I heard her say to Aimée, 'I shan't bother with dinner. He'll sleep, and I'll sleep. Heaven.'

She just wants to get there. Her husband will be waiting. They'll settle the baby into his car seat and whirl off to their own life.

Aimée stood by the woman's seat, holding the baby. She held him so tenderly, her sweet, gentle face bent over him so that her cheek almost touched his downy head. I wanted to press my bell. I wanted to bring Aimée back to me.

This cheese is delicious. I wish I hadn't eaten so much of the mango fool. The beef dish was unusual, too. I'd like to know how they made it. Of course you need top-quality beef to get the flavour. Not undercooked or overcooked: just perfect. The menu said that it was an oyster mushroom sauce. I wish I had more of these raisins. We used to buy raisins in triangular boxes, at Christmas time. You peeled off the cellophane and there they were, still on their branch. They were called Muscatel raisins, but they weren't as nice as these. These are so fresh.

I don't want dinner to end. Everyone will go to sleep then, while the plane bumps its way through the dark. There's always turbulence over Australia. I suppose it's because of the desert. I like it when I hear all the cabin staff stirring again behind their curtain, getting ready with the breakfast. But they'll come in the night if you want them. They're very good like that.

I wasn't sure which to choose, between the soup and the meze. The soup was a fragrant Thai seafood broth, which I've never had. In the end I chose the meze. One of the dishes was covered with fresh chopped coriander. That's something I could do.

I doze and dream. Aimée has made up my bed for me, and brought me an extra pillow. She wants to make sure that I am comfortable. In her culture, I think older people are respected. She brings me a fresh bottle of water, and pours it into my glass.

These flights are very expensive, but they are worth it. Three times a year, there and back again. Seven days in the air.

'Now you will sleep, Mrs Marion, and you will be ready for your grandchildren. Your son, he will be coming to meet you?'

'Yes,' I say. 'Robert always meets me.'

I sleep a little, and wake to the sound of them getting breakfast ready. I can smell coffee, and warm bread. I comb my hair, move my seat to a more upright position and look at the menu. I'll have a dish of fresh tropical fruits to start. Three different kinds of melon, with pineapple and mango. There's granola, yoghurt, a variety of breads and pastries. I never bother with the cooked breakfast. It's too early – or perhaps too late. The best thing at breakfast is the fresh orange juice, and the silver pots of coffee with their curving spouts. They are wonderful at pouring coffee, even when there's turbulence.

There's turbulence now. The seatbelt sign goes on and suddenly you can sense the rush of the plane, the speed at which it's going. It's not a very nice feeling. Things begin to bump and rattle.

'Cabin crew, take your seats,' says the calm voice of the captain. I can't see Aimée. I know she will be troubled that the service has been interrupted. Everything is so carefully timed on board.

The plane rushes, jolts, and then, sickeningly, it drops with a bang. The engines roar. We are going steeply downwards. No one says a word. I grip the sides of my seat and think of Aimée.

The plane levels out, and the captain's voice comes back on to the intercom, unruffled. 'Sorry about that, folks. We hit some rough air so we needed to lose some altitude to get out of it. We should be fine now.'

The cabin relaxes. We are still rushing forwards, but the plane is steady again. After a few more minutes the cabin crew leave their seats and begin to move around, although the seatbelt sign stays on for us. There is Aimée. I catch her eye and smile. She pauses for a second.

'Are you all right, Mrs Marion?'

'Yes, dear, thank you.'

I spread butter on a poppy-seed roll. It comes in little curls on a white dish. I'm thirsty, in spite of the water I drank in the night, and very hungry. I try half the roll with eucalyptus honey, and decide that I prefer it without. A young man stops with his coffee pot and pours a long, dark, fragrant stream into my cup. Aimée is busy with that woman's baby again.

There's a sense of expectation now. It won't be long before we land. People are tidying things away, going to the toilet, scrutinising themselves in tiny mirrors to see what those who come to meet them will see.

I'm quite ready. The young man whisks away my tray. That's the last meal of all. Suddenly he turns and with a smile places a small white box on my table.

'Chocolate,' he says. 'For later.'

I put it carefully into my bag.

As we leave the plane, the cabin staff flank the exit, smiling and wishing us well. I give Aimée a special smile. She is such a lovely girl.

'Goodbye, Mrs Marion,' she says.

'See you again, I hope,' I say, because it's always possible. Now we are out of the plane, walking along the steel tube to our destination. Soon we won't be passengers any more. We'll be back in our own lives, the lives we've made. I take a deep breath. My journey is over. I think of Robert, Melanie, Jess, Rory and little Clara. They smile in my mind's eye, and for some reason their smiles are mixed up with the gentle smiles of Aimée. Everyone is impatient at the carousel because the bags are a little slow. A young customs officer questions me about my immigration card, and asks if I'm sure I have no fruit, plants or seeds with me. I smile at her and say no, and she smiles back, just a little. She is quite a burly girl, in shorts. Full of purpose, she moves off to the next passenger. So different from Aimée, but professional too, in her way.

There's my bag, with the green ribbon around its handle. I grasp it, lift it and heave it down beside me. I walk through Customs and suddenly there is the Arrivals Hall, glaring bright, milling with people and placards. Faces bulge, smiling past me. There are two little girls jumping up and down, clapping. A woman runs into their embrace. I calm myself. Take a deep breath, Marion. Look carefully. Don't panic. He's bound to be here.

The faces steady. I scan each one as the placards joggle. And there he is. He was there all the time, standing close to the rope in the same poorly fitting jacket that all the drivers seem to wear.

On his placard is written: 'Mrs M. W. Buchanan'. I go up to him.

'Mrs Buchanan?' he says.

'Yes.'

'Just the one bag?'

'Yes.'

It is expensive to hire a car with a driver from the airport out to Kilmora Park, but worth it. I sit back and fold my hands in my lap. The journey takes about twenty-five minutes, if the traffic isn't too bad. The city streets give way to broader suburbs. The kind of area where families live. Quiet, green, inexpensive. The driver knows the way.

We are there almost too soon. Uneasiness clutches at my stomach as I get out of the car. I'm no one's passenger now. I pay the driver. He offers to help me with my bag but I tell him I am fine. I go up the path to the front door.

It's a nice little guesthouse. I found it three years ago, on my second trip. I always have the same room, facing over the garden. They don't do meals, apart from break-fast, but there's a kitchenette where you can cook. I'm used to the routine. There's a mini-market nearby which has a good selection of ready meals, and I buy cold meats and cheeses too, to make up my packed lunches. And I've got the chocolate, for later. I'm always quite all right on my own.

I press the bell, drop my shoulders, relax. Mrs Carmody is a nice woman. She'll be expecting me.

THE MEDINA

❧

'The medina is like a dream. You never know what you will find here. All the things you have lost.' Najia smiles. 'That's what I think, anyway.'

Najia's English is perfect. She spent four years in Manchester, writing her PhD, while Jamal was a senior registrar there. Jamal's ahead of us now, his broad back solid in the crowded, glinting medina shadows. The two little girls, Amina and Khadija, swing on his hands and coax him from embroidered purses to glittery red slippers. I stop by a date stall. The date-seller springs to life, plucking fruit from different piles, amber, chestnut or sticky black.

'Taste,' says Najia. 'Which do you like? How many?'

'Those, the pale yellow ones.'

Najia settles a price with the date-seller.

'It's a good place,' she says.

'I'm glad I'm with you,' I say.

'You'll soon learn enough Arabic to manage,' she says.

I've been here a month now. New job, new flat, a dazzle of words and faces. Everything's new, even me. I feel bare and tender, and sometimes I feel afraid.

We wander deep into the warm, pungent maze of the medina. High above, the sun struggles to squeeze through the matting that protects us. But it won't get in. For centuries, the sun's rage has been kept at bay here.

'I don't come here often enough,' says Najia. 'We've got into a faster way of living. The medina is so different. Sometimes I think you could find anything in the world here.'

The little boy who's been following in the hope of being my guide bobs up again at my elbow. His eyes are a startling faded blue. Najia bends down and talks to him. He listens, then skips off, like one of her own children.

'What were you saying?'

'I was telling him that he must go to school, or he will always be poor. Look, Jamal's stopped. We'll have tea now.'

We duck into a stone doorway and down a flight of steps into a large, cool tiled room.

'Coca-Cola!' the children say. We settle on divans and Najia props the cushions behind my back.

'Like this. Now what will you have? Coffee? Lipton's?'

'Mint tea.'

Khadija bites off the tip of a pastry shaped like a crescent moon. Dreamily, Amina blows down the straw into her Coca-Cola. Outside, the web of buying and selling spins endlessly. Donkeys struggle with their loads, bare-legged boys wade in dye at the tannery, children carry dough to the bakers' ovens and return with trays of bread. Through the bustle the pulse of the medina beats steadily, as it has beaten for hundreds of years.

'I want to stay here forever,' I say.

'No more teaching,' agrees Najia. But Khadija joggles her mother's arm.

'Can we buy mint?'

'Can we buy the mint? Yes, soon, Khadija.'

'For tea?' I ask.

'No. A big bunch to hold under our noses when we go to the tannery. It smells terrible there, but we thought you would like to see it.'

Jamal's still talking to the café owner.

'A former patient,' explains Najia. 'Amina, don't blow bubbles. Frances will think you don't know how to drink Coca-Cola.'

I remember my Louise, sucking bright-blue Slush Puppie through a straw. And now she grabs a cup of coffee from the hospital machine at 2 a.m., to keep herself awake. Louise said I should take the job here. *Morocco's only a few hours away, Mum. It's not China.*

And it's not as if I need you any more. Louise would never say it, but it's true. She is twenty-five years old, and qualified. My daughter, the doctor. I must be very proud of her, and I am.

'Well,' says Jamal. 'Shall we move on?'

When he was twenty-one, before I met him, Joe spent a year in Morocco as a tutor in an English family. He talked about it sometimes, after a few drinks. Picking warm oranges off trees. Talking all night on a roof-top terrace in the moonlight. The sound of fountains, and the call to prayer. But he never went back. I don't think he wanted to be a tourist in a place where he'd felt he belonged.

Joe kept a pair of battered Moroccan slippers, and a photograph of the three little boys he'd taught. He still had the slippers with him in that hotel in Bradford, two years ago. The hotel people packed them up with the rest of his things. Joe was at a sales conference, sweating through presentations, staying up drinking so he wouldn't look like an old man. They don't like old men in sales.

Joe hated hotels. His idea of hell was turning on the TV to find a computerised welcome and a discreet mention of the adult channel.

Why did I let him go on with it? Why didn't I hold him close and say, 'Joe, give it up. We'll go travelling. You can learn Arabic. What does money matter? You've only got one life.' But we weren't the sort of couple who could say such things.

He lay on that hotel floor all night, and I knew nothing until the phone rang. I was taking the rubbish out. While the hotel manager went on talking, the black bag slowly settled and tipped over, and the air sighed out of it.

We're back in the narrow medina lanes.

'Yes, Khadija, we'll get the mint now,' promises Najia. But as we go past a jewellery stall my eye is caught by a necklace of turquoise beads. They would be perfect against Louise's clear brown skin. I pick up the necklace, to judge the size. Yes, it'll fit. I'll ask Najia to bargain for me.

She's disappeared. I can't see Jamal or the children either. They were here a second ago; they can't have gone far. But Najia's often said how easy it is to get lost here in the medina. You only have to take a wrong turning. This place is a maze.

I put down the necklace, and hurry on. The stall-keeper shouts after me, and a donkey's sharp hooves clatter a few inches from my sandalled feet. That child's at my elbow again, the same boy, the blue-eyed one. Has he been waiting for me?

'Guide, guide, speak good English, very good guide.' He presses up against me. He's pushing me against the wall and suddenly I'm afraid for my bag, my ring, my English possessions that hang off me like keys to open up a life this child won't ever have.

But he's just a little boy. Najia talked to him as if he were one of her own. I squat so my face is level with his.

'No,' I say. 'No guide.' I try to hold his quick glance. 'You go to school. You have a future. But no guide, thank you.'

He stares back. Does he understand? His face is stubborn, lower lip thrust out, eyes tense on mine. Then another child calls, and my little boy darts across the lane. He squats in the doorway with his friend, and suddenly he's a child like any other child, playing marbles.

And this is when I find you, Joe. You were here all the time. As I search for Najia through the brown and gold dapple your shape appears, leaning against the wall where the lane forks two ways. You're looking back at me, waiting for me to notice you.

'Joe,' I say, but my voice is trapped. You swing away from the wall in a youthful, supple movement. You're going left. I stumble after you, and when I reach the corner there you are, walking away, but not too fast. You're letting me catch up. And how strange that you're wearing Moroccan clothes: a pair of loose, creamy-white trousers, and a long shirt. Your hair's longer, too, and there's no grey in it.

'Come on, Frances. Why are you so slow?'

Was that your voice, alive with laughter? You turn to me again and smile, but you don't stop. You step under an arch, and disappear. A few more yards and I'll see you again, just ahead of me – Joe, wait, I'm coming—

My arms are out and I'm full of joy, running towards you, my Joe, young and new and tender, both of us back again where we were before the years and the presentations and the mortgages and the slow separation of our lives.

I step into a wall of light. I am out of the medina, blinking in the glare.

'Frances!'

It's Najia.

'I'm so sorry. We thought you were following, then we realised you'd missed the entrance.'

Jamal and the children come up, holding bunches of mint.

'But you didn't get lost,' says Jamal. 'You found your own way.' He smiles. 'You are at home here, Frances.'

I say nothing. I know you're still here somewhere, Joe, enfolded in the maze of lanes. You lean against a wall, watching the leather-workers. You are wearing cool, loose clothes and you are happy. You've slipped out of time and found yourself here.

'Did you like the medina, Frances?' asks Najia. 'Do you want to come here again?'

WOLVES OF MEMORY

❧

Jay was waiting for her by the steps. Together they ran down them two at a time, because already the ferry had swung round from the other side of the harbour. Its light showed dim through the falling snow. Lizzie slipped, caught the rail and felt Jay grab her arm on the other side. They were at the bottom of the steps, across the road and down to the wharf. The ferry turned and backed towards them.

How heavy the snow was now. Lizzie's heart banged from taking the steps too fast and nearly falling. The ferryman steadied her as she stepped aboard, but he didn't look at her. She'd never seen him before. She blinked snow out of her eyes and saw that this wasn't the usual ferry. It was far smaller, just an open boat with seating down its sides for half a dozen passengers.

'Jay, this isn't our ferry,' she said, and was about to get off when the ferryman said:

'There's too much ice now for the regular ferry. It's this or nothing.'

Every day that week they'd been talking about the ice. No one had ever seen anything like it. Each night the ice thickened and spread, so that ferries had to run in the narrow channel left open by the flow of the river.

'Do you go to Castle Wharf?' asked Jay.

'We go everywhere,' said the ferryman. He cast off, and then he was at the wheel and they were turning out into the water.

At once they were in a world of snow. Wharf, road, cranes, warehouses all disappeared. Even the noise of the traffic was muffled. For a long time the boat chugged on. Too long, Lizzie thought. They should have reached Castle Wharf by now. It was only ten minutes to school from there, but they were still going to be late. The ferry's light showed nothing ahead of them but falling snow. How could the ferryman know where he was going? What if they crashed into the ice, or into another boat?

'Did you finish the maths?' Jay asked her.

'I couldn't do it,' she said. Her stomach hurt. She would never have got into a car driven by a strange man, and yet because it was a boat she'd let herself do it.

'You're great at art, though, Lizzie,' said Jay.

The noise of the engine sank to a putter. The boat was barely moving, or maybe it was going round in a circle and that was why they weren't getting anywhere. They should ask him to put them ashore, never mind where. As she was thinking this, the ferryman left the wheel and came nimbly to where they sat.

'No chance of making Castle Wharf,' he said, 'but I can take you downriver.'

'Downriver?'

'Tide's high,' he explained, as if that was all they needed to know. 'We'll go out through the Basin.'

Lizzie knew what he intended. The river snaked around the city, bringing huge tides with it. You could get out of the Floating Harbour through the Basin, but ferries did not go there. The ferryman meant to take them through the deep, dark-sided Gorge where water bubbled on the mudflats at low tide, and hot springs sent up steam in the cold mornings.

He meant to take them into a blind world of snow and seething water, instead of to school.

'Jay,' she said, but he was staring at the ferryman with his lips parted and an unfamiliar look on his face.

'Let's do it,' he said.

'But we'll have to sign the Late Book!'

'We won't go to school at all,' said Jay boldly, and he took her hand.

She thought of the noise the classes made as they ranged from room to room. She thought of explaining yet again her undone homework and her too-short skirt; of a whole day running late; of the tired, angry faces of the teachers and the lonely quiet in the detention room. The way they said 'E-*liz*-a-beth' when she'd been

Lizzie from the day she was born. The only good thing about school was going there with Jay, and coming home with him again.

'We won't go, then,' she agreed, and the ferryman opened the throttle.

They were way down the river by the time the snow cleared enough to show the forest close to them. The noise of the boat's engine was fading again.

'Bit of a problem,' said the ferryman. 'I'll have to bring her in.'

The engine was missing beats as they reached the river's shore. They came alongside a rickety landing stage and the ferryman threw his rope expertly to lasso the post. When the boat was tied fast, he held out his hand to Lizzie. The gap between boat and landing stage was full of fast-moving, greasy water and the boat wobbled as she stepped up on the plank seat, but she got her balance, and jumped ashore. Then it was Jay's turn and they were together.

The ferryman had not left the boat. For the first time Lizzie saw his eyes, watching them.

'Tide's turned,' he said. 'I must be on my way.'

'On your way?' echoed Lizzie.

'Come back with me if you choose,' he said. 'Or stay here. Follow that path and you'll find shelter.'

Lizzie looked at Jay. Two spots of colour flared in his cheeks. 'We shall need fire, if we're to stay here,' he said boldly. The ferryman nodded, dug in his pocket and threw a box of matches to them.

'We shall need food, if we're to stay here,' said Lizzie, and again the ferryman nodded and this time he slung a bundle to them, wrapped up in chequered cloth.

'And—' said Jay, and then he stopped, as if he'd forgotten. The ferryman stooped to the bottom of the boat and lifted out something that had been hidden there: 'A spear,' breathed Jay, and he took its shaft in his hand.

The ferryman lifted his hand in farewell. 'Take that path and you'll find shelter,' he repeated, and then he pushed off from the landing stage. In a minute the boat had vanished into the thickening snow.

How huge the forest was, and how dark. Their skin prickled all over. They needed a wall at their back and fire in front of them. All animals are afraid of fire, except us, thought Lizzie as she walked swiftly, lightly down the path. Their footprints would soon be hidden from predators.

Their shelter was a cave. What else could it be? Wood was heaped at the back, enough to last for days, and there was dry bracken beside it. They must make fire. Lizzie piled up bracken, then built a dome of the thinnest, driest sticks. Jay squatted beside her and passed her the box of matches. Somewhere in her mind she knew there was another way of making fire, which didn't need matches. She struck one, held it to her tinder and watched the flames lick and run, blue at first and then flaring into yellow. She laid on more sticks, lightly, so as not to crush the flame, and she blew softly where she wanted fire to grow. Jay stood and drew his arm back to test the weight and balance of his spear.

The fire filled the cave's entrance. They had curving walls of stone behind them and a wall of fire in front of them. Soon they would cook the food the ferryman had given them. Already the chequered cloth looked strange. Tomorrow they would find better food: their own food. In her mind she saw sharp, sweet berries, hidden under snow.

A new sound rose keening through the dark forest. They knew at once what it was, and sat back on their heels, listening, alert. The wolves were out hunting. One called, and another answered.

'Wolf,' said Jay, and he felt the edge of his spear.

'Wolf,' said Lizzie, and she thought of how she would skin the wolf, and scrape every morsel of flesh from the wolfskin, and spread it out by the fire to cure. It would keep them warm all winter.

A cloud of things rose in her mind. She saw radiators and file paper; she saw light switches, sewing machines, whiteboards and fridges. They whirled and spun in front of her eyes like a snowstorm, but she no longer knew what any of them were. They settled on the floor of her mind and melted to nothing.

Lizzie rose and took a blackened stick from the fire. She examined it carefully and then she turned to the cave walls, while Jay watched her. She swept her charred stick down the wall, this way and that. As Lizzie drew, a figure sprang to life and became a boy, running forward, spear poised to strike. She drew again, and a wolf leaped out of the forest, on to Jay's spear.

THE MUSICIANS OF INGO

❧

O ur island is joined to the mainland by a mile of cobbled causeway. For a couple of hours at low tide you can walk out to it along the causeway, but the rest of the time visitors have to come by boat. They come to see the ruins, because they think King Arthur used to live there. We make cream teas for the visitors and I help by carrying trays of scones and jam and clotted cream. The visitors give me tips, especially when I tell them stories about King Arthur. I don't believe in them, though. There are other stories about our island which I do believe, but we don't tell these to visitors.

For centuries our island was part of the mainland, and then one night a huge storm came, and a sea surge, and miles of land were swallowed up. Many people were drowned, but a few escaped. They saw the sea rushing in and they raced for the highest point, with their children in their arms. Those people who survived are my ancestors, and since then my family has always lived on the island. We have to go to school on the mainland, but in winter when the storms blow we say it's too dangerous to take a boat out, and we stay at home.

One of the men who escaped from the flood carried his fiddle high above his head, and another carried a set of bagpipes. These were the only things they saved out of all their possessions. My father plays the violin and the bagpipes, my mother plays the harp and she can also play the bodhrán and the penny whistle.

Until I was eight I thought I played the violin well. People would say, 'Go on, Jenna, give us another tune,' and they'd clap when I'd finished. My twin sister Morveren played the harp and the penny whistle, like Mum. But then Digory started to play. He was four years old, and he picked up the quarter-sized violin I'd grown out of. He listened to the song Mum was practising and he played it through perfectly, even though he'd never had a lesson.

Most people on the island play an instrument but no one had ever heard anything like Digory's playing. Some said Digory ought to play for the visitors while they had their cream teas. If we put a hat on the ground in front of him it would be full of coins by the time the boat left. But Mum said no one was going to make a performing monkey out of Digory.

Maybe I was jealous of Digory. No, tell the truth, Jenna: I *was* jealous of Digory, for a whole year at least, while he learned to play as easily as he'd learned to breathe. But then I stopped worrying. I knew I'd never be a tenth as good as him, but it didn't matter. I was Jenna, and Digory was Digory. Sometimes he would show me little things which made my playing better, but he never criticised. In fact he would say, 'I like the way you play, Jenna. It has a nice feeling.'

Digory didn't boast or ask for anybody's attention, he just played and played and played. He liked fishing with Dad and he liked messing about on the shore, but nothing could keep him away from the violin for more than a couple of hours. By the time he was seven he had learned everything Dad could teach him, and our school said he should go to a specialist music school up in London. But Mum and Dad said he was too young. Digory said, 'Is there sea in London?' and Morveren and I laughed and said of course there wasn't. Digory said, 'I don't want to play if the sea isn't there to listen.'

'The sea doesn't listen to you, you baby,' said Morveren, but I wasn't so sure. I'd seen Digory down by the water, playing his violin on a calm day with the waves lapping, and he played as if there were hundreds of people gathered there to hear him. Mum and Dad were pleased that Digory didn't want to go away from home yet. They found him a piano teacher on the mainland, because Digory was starting to compose.

'He'll have to go away one day,' said Mum to me, when Digory wasn't there. 'With a gift like his, this island won't be big enough for him.'

I didn't want that ever to happen. I wanted things to stay just as they were. I warned Digory not to play with the window open when the visitors were on the island, because there was always someone who got excited about his playing, and used words like 'genius' and 'prodigy', which made him sound not like our Digory at all.

I told you that we have our own stories about the island, which the visitors never hear.

Before the land all around us was drowned, there was a city where the sea is now. It had churches and beautiful houses and cobbled streets. All the people there loved music. When the storm came and the sea surged they were gathered at a concert, listening to the music with such devotion that they never heard the howl of the wind and the thunder of the rising waves. That's why so few escaped. The ruins on our island are not the ruins of King Arthur's palace. They are what remains of the drowned city's castle. They built it on the highest ground, so that they could see their enemies coming from far away. If you look carefully, you can see that there are arrow slits in the ruined walls. Sometimes people who go up there at night say that they have seen ghosts.

It was the middle of September when Digory began to slip away in the evenings.

Mum never worried about where we went, because everybody knew us and we could all swim like seals. But we had to be home by dark, or she would keep us in the following evening. Digory would come back just in time, and I remember noticing that his face was flushed and his eyes were sparkling. I thought he'd been playing hide-and-seek with the other little ones.

It was a Wednesday night, 21st September. I know that because Morveren and I had a big maths test the next day, on the 22nd, which our teacher had been scaring us about since the start of term. We were revising at the kitchen table, and Mum was at the village hall with Dad, practising with the others in Ynys Musyk. (That's our island orchestra, and usually Morveren and I would be there too, if we hadn't got a maths test.)

Suddenly Morveren said, 'Put the light on, Jenna, I can't see the page.' I switched the light on, and as I did so I realised Digory wasn't home yet. I looked on the shelf and his violin was gone too.

'We'd better find him,' said Morveren. 'Mum'll get really cross with him. It's the second time he's disappeared this week.'

We were annoyed with Digory, because we wanted to work for our test, but we were worried too. Digory shouldn't be out alone after dark. Morveren got the torch and we decided we'd look for him before telling Mum and Dad.

We went all round the cottages, round the back of the village hall, and into all the likely and unlikely places where Digory might be. Morveren thought we should go up and look in the ruins, in case he'd fallen there, but I thought there was more chance he'd be down at the shore.

'If he isn't there, we'll have to get Mum and Dad. It's really dark.'

The moon hadn't risen yet, although the stars were already coming out. We took the shore path and our torchlight bobbed and flickered in front of us. The furze grew high on either side, so we couldn't see much. We kept calling Digory's name, but there was no answer except the gulls in the night sky and the sound of the sea breathing. We came out on to the shore. Usually there's a big beach of white sand, but not tonight. The sea was lapping up to the marram grass that grows on the dunes. The water gleamed in the starlight.

'Listen!' said Morveren suddenly, and she clutched my hand.

I listened and the hairs along my arms stood up. A violin was playing. It could only be Digory, because no one else on the island could play like that. But he wasn't playing alone. Behind the sound of the violin there were the sweet notes of the harp, and the drone of the bagpipes, and the sound of the bodhrán. It sounded as if there were hundreds of instruments playing.

'Do you think Ynys Musyk has come out here to play?' I asked Morveren, but I knew that they hadn't, because we'd heard them playing when we passed the village hall. Besides, the sound was too rich for Ynys Musyk.

Slowly, we crept forward. The moon was rising behind us and we were afraid Digory would see us before we saw him. We both had the feeling it might not be safe if he did. All at once I saw him, sitting on a rock with his violin under his chin and his bow in his hand, playing. When he saw us he didn't try to run away, as I'd feared. He lifted his bow and the music faded away. Not just the music of his violin, but the sound of harps and bagpipes and bodhrán too.

'Digory, what are you doing out here?'

'Just playing with my friends,' said Digory.

'What friends?' asked Morveren in a voice that would scare the life out of the little ones at school.

'Didn't you hear them?' asked Digory. 'Jenna, you've got to fetch Ynys Musyk. My friends want us all to play with them. This is the last night they can play with us, because the moon and the tide won't be right like this for another hundred years.'

Morveren and I stared at each other. Should we grab him and run home as fast as we could? But looking at Digory, I thought we'd better not.

'Digory,' I asked, 'where are these friends?'

'They're in Ingo,' said Digory. 'That's why they can't come to us. But they can hear us and we can hear them. Fetch Ynys Musyk, Jenna. They really want to play with us.'

'But, Digory, where's Ingo?' asked Morveren, and although I'd never heard the word before, a shiver went through me as if I'd known it in another life.

'There,' said Digory, pointing at the moonlit sea lapping up the beach. 'It's under the water. That's where they live. Hurry, Jenna. They can't stay long. They have to leave when the tide turns.'

Morveren and I stared at each other. We are twins and sometimes we know what each other is thinking. I knew she believed Digory, because I did too.

'You stay with him, I'll get the others,' I said, and I ran.

I could barely breathe by the time I burst through the door of the village hall. Mum saw my face and broke off in the middle of a note. Dad put down his violin. Everyone was looking at me.

'You've got – to come. All of you. Digory needs us. Bring – bring the instruments.'

I never thought they would believe me, but Dad listened while I stammered out the story and then he picked up his violin, and then all the rest of Ynys Musyk were picking up their instruments too. Mum's harp was too big, so she grabbed her penny whistle.

It was the strangest procession. As we passed our cottage I ran in and got my violin and another penny whistle for Morveren, and then we were on our way. We hurried through the village and across the rough grass until we came to the path through the furze to the shore. I led the way, and Ynys Musyk followed. The moon was bright now and as soon as we came out on the shore we saw that the tide was full, higher than I'd ever seen it, touching the rock where Morveren and Digory sat waiting for us.

'There they are!' whispered Mum.

We streamed towards the rock, skirting the water. It was all so quiet, just the moonlight and the lap of the waves. Suddenly, far above our heads, a gull cried. I was close to Digory by now, and I saw him lift his violin and place it under his chin.

'My friends are waiting for us,' he said.

Everybody looked around at the quiet shore and the still water.

'Who are they?' asked Mum, bending down to Digory.

'They're musicians, like us. They want Ynys Musyk to play with them. I'll lead, because I know the song.'

He looked out at the water as if he were waiting for a signal, then he nodded, raised his bow and the first note shivered the silence. It was a song I'd never heard before. I held my own violin, waiting, listening to Digory's music flow out until it filled the bay like a tide.

Quietly at first and then more and more strongly, there came back something which wasn't an echo, but an answer in music. It was coming from the water. There were horns and bagpipes, flutes and violins, a bodhrán and the sweet notes of a harp. The sound swelled louder and louder, more and more urgent. For a second Digory stopped his fiddling and held his bow like a baton, bringing us all in, and then he was playing again, his music high above all the other music and leading it.

I followed the second violins; I could hear them out of all the other instruments. Dad was following Digory, and Mum and Morveren shrilled out the melody. Everybody was joining in now and the moon grew so bright that it made the water transparent, just as the sun does at midday. That's when I saw them. They were just shapes and shadows at first. I saw a fiddler's elbow, and then an arm plucking a harp string. The more I played, the more I saw. There were a hundred of them, maybe more, keeping in the deep water where the white sand falls away to rock. A whole orchestra, many times larger than Ynys Musyk. Their long hair floated like seaweed. They rose until we could almost see them clearly, and then sank again beyond the reach of the moonlight.

They played as long as slack water lasted, and we played with them. I don't know how long it was. I didn't want it to end, but suddenly the music changed. The tide was on the turn, and the musicians knew it. They played faster and faster, until the sea and the island echoed to it, and then Digory threw back his head and played a long, last chord like a farewell.

The musicians of Ingo dived, holding their instruments. Their bodies glistened and their hair streamed away behind them. They didn't look as if they belonged to the human world. In another moment they were just shadows, fleeing into the deepest water, and then they were gone.

I heard Morveren sigh. Digory sat on the rock with his head bowed, looking much younger than seven.

Mum took Dad's violin, and Dad lifted Digory high on his shoulders, and that's how we walked back to the village, all of us in Ynys Musyk together.

There are a lot of stories that we never tell to the visitors, and this is one of them. Sometimes Morveren and I talk about it in whispers. We try to decide who those musicians were. Maybe they were our ancestors from the old drowned city, come back to play with us. Maybe they were the Mer, who always live in Ingo. We can never decide.

Nobody else ever talks about that night, not even Mum and Dad. But I told you that Digory is starting to write music. He wrote a piece for our school Christmas concert and after it was played, Morveren and I looked at each other and smiled. We could hear the music of Ingo woven into it, very faintly, so only those who were there that night would ever guess what it was.

FROST AT MIDNIGHT

Dear Babe, that sleepest cradled by my side,
Whose gentle breathings, heard in this deep calm,
Fill up the interspersèd vacancies
And momentary pauses of the thought!

'Frost at Midnight', Samuel Taylor Coleridge

Sam has been walking the baby up and down, up and down, for what seems like hours.

Now at last she has given way, and become heavy against him, curled into the angle of his shoulder and neck. Her eyelids are sealed shut. Their smooth, glistening line does not quiver as he lays her down in the cradle which he and Lucy bought second-hand in Newton Bere market. He stripped off the thick black varnish that overlaid it like treacle, and underneath, just as they'd thought, was the grain of oak. He fed the wood with wax and rubbed it back to lustre. Lucy bought a bundle of soft, washed linen from another stall and made cot sheets, hemming them by hand as she sat by the stove. That was the way Sam and Lucy did things. No wagging of credit cards in out-of-town babycare hypermarkets for them. Their baby would have a cradle like no other baby's, and it would cost the earth nothing.

Like the cradle, their cottage has been restored. They didn't want big changes. It is shabby but solid, shaped by generations rather than by design. The flagstone floor is uneven, and scattered with rag rugs. Two steps lead down from the kitchen to the bathroom. In summer it was full of green, swimming light. Now, in winter, there are red serge curtains with brass rings, from yet another market stall. There's a hip bath, a solid square basin, a cistern with a long chain. When they first looked around the place, the agent was embarrassed by the bare trickle of rusty water when Lucy turned on the tap. The well, it seemed, sometimes ran dry in summer.

They sunk a borehole, and now their water runs clear and plentiful. They installed a wood-burning stove. Sam built seven raised beds in the vegetable garden. They pruned their apple trees, and researched the keeping of chickens. Lucy was thinking about a goat. Sam never tired of watching Lucy, her body upright and sturdy, rounding with pregnancy until it was unbalanced and yet at the same time more beautifully balanced than it had ever been.

Now Sam rocks the cradle with his foot. The baby's fists are up at either side of her face, as if sleep has surprised her. She lies with her head turned sideways, sunk fathoms deep in her own country where he cannot follow her. In a minute he must put more wood on the stove, and get her bottles ready for the night. He rocks the cradle again, gently, although she doesn't need it. The night is so quiet that he hears the swell thudding against the base of the cliffs, half a mile away. There's no wind. He knows that the sea is flat – he walked down to the cliff path with the baby in her sling that afternoon – but there is always the swell, the muscle of it pulling from the deep Atlantic, the concussion when it runs in against granite.

He gets up, opens the stove door and settles a knot of apple wood on the fire's red core. The stove door clangs but the baby doesn't stir. Sam is restless. He ought to phone Lucy; she has left messages on his mobile. However, she knows as well as he does that there is no reception in the cottage and he will have to go to the top of the track to get a signal. Her messages are brief, and bleak. He would like to erase them, but doesn't quite dare.

He opens the door, steps out, and draws it almost shut behind him so that cold air won't reach the baby. As always, it shocks him to look up and see the night pulsing with stars. They come so close; surely they were never this close in London. Also, before he came here he never realised that starlight was a real thing. But these thickets of stars are making him a shadow. There's no moon – or almost none: it's the palest and thinnest rind.

Perhaps the baby will sleep through tonight. He lets himself think about it, even though he knows it can't possibly happen. She has never slept through the night. Sometimes he wakes just before she cries. More often, he lurches out of deep sleep, not knowing where he is, the baby's cries sawing into his head. His eyes burn as if there's sand in them. Sometimes he is afraid that one night he will fail to wake. Who is there to hear her, except for him? A fox might answer her, or an owl. The nearest human habitation is the farm, half a mile up the track. A couple of days ago he'd frozen at the thought of what might happen to her if he fell, say, and could not get to her. Now he isn't afraid of that any more. He knows that he would drag himself to the cradle, come what may. She has only him. When she cries he works steadily to comfort her. He knows that when she draws up her legs she has wind, and when she rolls her head and thrashes against him it is because she is exhausted but cannot find her way into sleep.

Lucy is at her mother's. That is what he said to them at the farm, and they accepted it, as if it were perfectly usual for a woman to leave her baby and go back to her mother. Lucy has been ill. She's had a bad time, he found himself explaining. She needed a rest. They nodded again, accepting his explanations even though there'd been no need for them. They knew enough. They had heard the ambulance blaring at the shut gate, then hurtling down the track to the cottage, on the night the baby was born.

It was his mistake. It was Lucy's. It was the terrible, almost unpardonable error that they'd committed between them, going from one of their ideas to the next without ever dreaming of what the consequences might be. They had the complaisant midwife. They had Lucy's wonderful health, her exceptionally low blood pressure, the millennia-long normality of birth at home.

Home being a cottage down a rutted track, in winter, thirty miles from the nearest hospital. But they had everything on their side. The hip bath, full of warm scented water, in which Lucy could relax. Their own prepared soundtrack, and behind it the deep shock of the swell hitting the base of the cliffs, as it had done forever.

Lucy can't get over what happened. The truth is that neither of them can get over their own stupidity: that moment when blood bloomed on the old sides-to-middled sheets, and wouldn't stop. He thought Lucy would die, and the baby too. He thought: What have I done to you? He had to run up the track, leaving them, because there was no signal down at the cottage. He heard his own blood pounding in his ears and he cursed himself because he could not run faster.

But the baby lies in her cradle. She is real, solid, alive. She is thriving; everyone says that. Only Lucy can't see it. She has lost faith. She would like them to live

permanently in a hospital ward, on alert for something
to go wrong with the baby. Failing that, she would like
them to live within two or three minutes of the best-
equipped, highest-rated teaching hospital in London.

Farewell to owls, the moon, the carefully constructed
raised vegetable beds and the prospective goat. Lucy no
longer cared about any of it. She faced him across the
kitchen table, and words of fury spewed from her mouth
as if he were an invader come to toss her child on to
the point of his bayonet.

'How can we throw all this away?' he asked her. 'Go
back to London, find some crappy rented flat – we'll
never be able to buy there – bring her up with no garden
and a park full of alkies and needles. Is that what you
want for her?'

'If you got a proper job,' she said, 'we would have
enough money to live somewhere decent.' Her eyes were
black with anger, her skin stretched and paper-white.

'But would it help, if we left here?' he'd asked her.
'Would you really feel safe in London?'

At the bare thought of London, an intolerable dreari-
ness swept through him. His Kilburn childhood had been
lightened by dreams of elsewhere. He'd been brought up
in a basement flat in Iverson Road – lucky boy, everybody
would be glad to get a flat there now. But it hadn't been
like that then. He'd joined the Royal Society for the
Protection of Birds, and known every blade that grew in
the *Blue Peter* garden, but his native air was the hot,
dusty swirl from the ventilators in the Tube.

A proper job. They had worked it out so carefully – they weren't impulsive, it wasn't some city-dweller's fantasy. With his savings, and hers, they had enough for a deposit on the cottage. He would go freelance. They would be all but self-sufficient. As long as the mortgage was covered, they could live on very little. Their children would have sea, sky, air, vegetables from the garden, eggs from their own hens, fields to run in, trees to climb, and a bus from the top of the track to the village school three miles distant.

She wasn't eating. He would wake in the night and see her watching over the baby with such ferocity that he was afraid. Lucy could not bear to feed the baby, in case she choked on the milk.

'You do it,' she said to him every time, thrusting the bottle into his hand.

Soon Lucy could neither do anything for the baby nor leave her. So it went on, until one day, in an impulse as strong as a convulsion, she took the train to Derby where her mother lived. Sam knew nothing of it until the ordered taxi bounced down the track to the cottage door.

How loud the sea sounds. He feels as if he is the only person awake in the world. The scattered lights that shine from distant cottages on the flank of the hill are all extinguished. Only the slow, breathing silence, the beat of the sea, the immensity of stars in the night that is so still he barely feels its cold. He has an instant's dread that he will walk away, letting the cottage door swing shut behind him, down the track that dwindles to a narrow footpath through the bracken. He will go all the way down the cliffs to the sea, and then out along the lane of starlight until the waves swallow him.

But of course he will not. He goes back inside, closing the door softly even though he knows that it isn't noise that wakes the baby. She lies in the same position. As always, he leans into the cradle to check her breathing. Her warmth enfolds him. All is well. He knows, suddenly, that there won't be many more nights like this. His babe is not going to wander like a breeze by lakes and sandy shores. She, like her father, is going to be reared in the great city. He knows it as if there isn't any choice involved: as if he's simply looked into the future and seen himself there with her, holding her hand as a number 16 sweeps down Shoot Up Hill. Lucy is there too, blinking the grit from her eyes. Everything else has fallen away: the cottage, the farmer's brief, acknowledging nod which might one day have turned into friendship, the cove to which they would have climbed down with the children on summer days.

Sam measures milk powder into the jug and makes up the night feeds. After a moment's thought, he reaches into the cradle and lifts out the sleeping baby. She hangs loose, like a puppy. He wraps her carefully against the cold, swaddling her as he and Lucy were taught at their parenthood class.

As he steps out of the cottage the cold hits her face and she gives a small, sharp intake of breath: a creak, almost. He holds her against him, shielding her. He has the feeling that he doesn't want that crowd of stars to see her face. He sets off up the track. It is dark enough, but he can see his way. He slips the knot of baling twine off the gate, and it squeaks as he passes through it. He almost wishes that the baby were awake, even though he knows she will never be able to remember any of this. A dog barks, far off. He can smell the sea. He stands there, snuffing it, not looking up for fear that the stars will make him dizzy. It is colder, surely. He opens his coat and tucks the baby inside, so that she will be perfectly warm. Only a little farther to go now. He takes his mobile out of his pocket and wakes it up. The signal indicator shows one bar, then two, then three. Almost full signal. He turns and looks downhill, towards the sea. Lucy's number is the first one on speed dial. He presses it. As he lifts the phone to his ear he sees that it is two thirty-four. Lucy will be asleep. But it's all right. She never puts her phone on silent.

The baby stirs, as if she can hear the phone ringing. He joggles her gently, inside his coat. She mustn't cry, not now, not when Lucy is about to answer. The phone keeps ringing. Five rings, seven, nine. But she will answer, he knows she will, and then he'll tell her that all places and all seasons shall be sweet to him, so long as she is there.

THE PAST

ROSE, 1944

❧

If she shuts her eyes and counts to twenty she'll feel him before she sees him. His hand on her bare neck.

'I been everywhere lookin' for you, Rose.'

He likes her name. He likes to say it and hold it in his mouth. She has never felt that her name truly belonged to her before, until his voice made her as beautiful as a rose.

He'll come soon. If she holds her breath till it hurts. Count to a hundred. *I'm coming.* She clenches her fists, breathes in a deep breath and holds it until the darkness fizzes. But when she opens her eyes it's the same blackout. The rain splashes. If he doesn't come, if he can't come, if he's tried to get a message to her—

Or if he's somewhere else. Someplace else, he'd say. Stepping into step with someone else, someone else's body going soft and shivery against his.

'What'd you say your name was?'

'Frederick. Frederick Lafayette.'

'That's a funny name.'

'It ain't funny where I come from, ma'am.'

And the milky smile shows, like a baby's. And the way he calls a girl ma'am when he doesn't know her name. Maybe he already knows that people like to hear words they would never put in their own mouths; maybe he already knows how the sweet formality of it marries with that smile. At first she thought he was one of those men who mean nothing by their talk. Later she understood that he was reserved, like her, but living in a crowd had taught him ways of getting along without getting close.

'Hey, how you doing?'

Is he doing all of that with someone else? Lucky it's dark so no one can see her face. Nobody's ever going to guess how much she wants him. She's had him now, hundreds and hundreds and hundreds of times, in parks and bus shelters and in her mind. Most of all in her mind. Out of all those hundreds, only a dozen or so in flesh and blood. He's in her mind; he won't go out of it. And deep down below all the doubts she knows she's got him too, at least for now. He can't help it any more than she can. She knows it when his voice flukes up and he sounds as if he's in pain. 'What you doing to me, Rose? You tell me what you call this.'

She doesn't know what she calls it. She's caught in it, like a cat dancing in a rainstorm that's forgotten its own nature so completely it doesn't even remember to hate the wet. She, Rose, who never put a paw out of place before. At all the wrong times she imagines herself naked, with him. It wouldn't surprise her to find herself lit up at night, as if someone had painted her skin with the stuff that makes clock fingers glow in the dark. In the typing pool, the clatter of keys and the jingle of the carriage return fades, and she's with Frederick, peeling off her stockings, tangling her legs in his. But the smell of women brings her back to the big room where they sit in rows, in uniform, beating out words.

At the end of basic training last year, she saw her own reflection in the eyes of the officer who was checking length of hair and absence of jewellery. Her own body, packed away in a ratings uniform for the duration. She blinked and shifted her gaze from the regulation eyes front. She was part of a row of women standing at attention, quiveringly still. But inside she was prickling with life, her skin burning, her hair springing under her cap. The uniform didn't do away with that; it made it stronger.

Basic training was a shock to some of the girls. It wasn't so much getting up at dawn and being yelled at and working all the hours God sent and then being told to do it again, but the fact that nothing was personal. It didn't bother Rose. They thought they were knocking you into shape, but what they didn't reckon on were all the things that had shaped you already, the things that had knocked you till you all but went down and stayed down. But you hadn't, and you never would.

Rose looked light but she was tireless. She wasn't afraid to heave coal, riddle the huge boilers, shovel out the clinker and wash down the boiler-room walls.

The only thing she didn't like was scrubbing corridors. It was the way they wanted you down on your hands and knees, arse in the air, skin chapped to the elbows. There were mops but they wanted scrubbing brushes used in basic training. And maybe forever after: that was the way the Navy was. But it wouldn't be Rose doing the scrubbing, not after these two weeks.

Rose's mother had scrubbed like a demon in her bad spells. Floors, walls, windows, chairs, table. On those days Rose had come home from school and smelled the carbolic and her heart had sunk. The little ones were out in the yard. They were wary, quiet as mice, sheltering by the coal bunker and waiting for Rose. As soon as they saw her they rushed to grab her round the waist. They wanted their dinner; they hadn't had their dinner. Rain clung to their clothes but they hadn't dared ask to go in. Dickie and Iris were scared of Mum when she got her bad times, when she became a stranger and looked through them.

Rose knew as soon as she smelled carbolic that there'd be no more school for days, maybe weeks, depending how Mum was. She couldn't be left when she was bad. She would clean until her hands bled and then all the life would die out of her and she'd lie on her bed eating nothing, drinking a cup of tea if Rose was lucky, speaking to no one. When Dad came back from work he would look into the bedroom, and go out again without eating the tea Rose had made. Rose couldn't blame him. She'd have done the same herself if it wasn't for Dickie and Iris.

Rose never let them see that she hated scrubbing the floors. She wouldn't give them that satisfaction. She did what she had to do, never spoke to an officer unless spoken to, rolled up her hair so it didn't touch her collar, kept her place where she belonged. But a part of her stood separate. Nothing would get the better of her. After basic training she was going to train as a typist. If she got on, she might become a telephonist one day, or even a radio operator. With the war, there were chances there'd never been before. She'd have something for life that no one could take back when the war was over. That was the reason she'd volunteered for the Wrens, or part of the reason. She wasn't going to wait to be called up. They might send her anywhere. She'd end up in a factory, making shells to the din of *Workers' Playtime*, or shovelling swill on a farm in the back end of nowhere, under a sky the colour of mud, while some pig-ignorant farmer tried to get her into his bed.

Uniform's all right, it saves coupons, she tells herself. If she'd been able to go to the grammar school she'd have worn uniform there, a black blazer with a gold crest on the left pocket. She thinks the thought quickly then sheers off from it. She's in uniform now, like everyone else. But when Frederick walks towards her, all fine and supple with life, she can't turn aside from the thought of the death he's kitted out for.

Thick rain continues to fall. It's April, a sharp night but not cold. There's a cough in the dark close to her, and Rose shivers. There'll be couples all along the row of bus shelters, locked together the way she wants to be. In the dark each pair carves out its tiny privacy and the rain on the roof drowns out the sounds they make. Rose tenses, listening, feeling her uniform skirt rasp her knee through the nylons Frederick has given her. She must be mad, wasting nylons on uniform. It'd be against regulations if anyone thought a girl would be stupid enough to do it. Probably it is against regulations.

The dark blue uniform suits Rose. She has the kind of body that makes itself felt through boxy cloth. And then there's her skin, that fine-grained olive skin that still looks good when fair-skinned girls flag from lack of sleep.

'Where're you from?' Frederick Lafayette asked her the first time she danced with him.

'Staffordshire,' she said. 'The Black Country.'

He laughed, deep in his chest and then high and sweet like a little boy. As soon as she heard it she wanted to make him laugh again. That voice of his. That grain in his liquid voice, like comb suspended in a honey-jar.

'How come you call it that?' he said. She soon found that he had two ways of speaking, as she had. His home voice, and then something flatter, for every day and officers. It took a minute for him to feel his way back inside his real voice, each time he was with her. And Rose dropped the voice she'd been learning so that one day, if the war went on long enough, she could be a telephonist, a wireless operator …

'It's a real place,' she said. 'Do you know where the Midlands are?' Probably he thought all Brits were the same, living elbow to elbow in their packed, rainy little island. The Yanks didn't seem to think life over here had any scale. One she'd met didn't know there were other cities besides London. He'd laughed disbelievingly when she told him about Manchester and Birmingham, as if they were villages she was trying to make big.

But Frederick frowned. 'They give us a map,' he said coolly. He was a reader. An electrician by trade, but he went to night school back home, to study economics. He intended to go to college one day, when the war was over. He reckoned that there'd be scholarships for GIs.

'How about you? Were you a college girl?' he asked the second time they met. She glanced sharply at him, but he was serious. He couldn't tell about British accents, any more than she could tell about American ones. He really believed she might be a college girl. College over there meant university here, she knew that. His mistake struck inside her like a bell, shaking everything.

'I got a scholarship to the grammar school,' she told him. 'But I had to get a job.'

He nodded. She saw that he understood.

'I went to look at the grammar school once,' she went on, telling him something she'd never told anyone. 'It was over the other side of town, so I went on the bus after work. It was getting dark and they'd locked the gates. I looked through the railings. There were still some lights on in the buildings. They were huge, those buildings. Like another town inside the town, separate.'

Frederick said nothing. Did not bring out any experience of his own, did not say she'd done well for herself since. He put out his hand and cupped the side of her face. It was the softest touch she had ever felt, his fingers touching her jawline as if it was beautiful. She rested her head in his cupped palm.

A couple of yards from Rose the red tip of a cigarette pricks the dark. It lights up a man lounging against the back wall of the bus shelter, eyes down. Then the soft, pitchy curtain of rain and blackout settles round her again. The man must have turned aside, because she can't see his cigarette end any more. But he hasn't moved away. She'd have heard him. She's an expert on footfalls, man or woman, boot or shoe.

She can hear trains clunking in the yard. Always trains now, night and day. Things are hotting up. Everyone knows it's coming. A vast prickling excitement is building over the tiredness they won't get rid of ever, not if they sleep for a month of Sundays. Ask any one of the girls what she wants most and she'll say, 'To have my sleep out.'

He'll go soon. That's what he's over here for, to go. All those tall easy Yanks, full of food from the PX, food Rose hadn't seen in years until she met Frederick. Tinned ham and corned beef and tinned pineapple. It's true that eating as much meat as you want gives you a different energy. The Yanks are full of it. They spill out of their lit-up cities and come over here not really believing in the darkness. Next to them, the British look like thin and tired. But the same thing's coming to all of them. The tension's like a boil, swollen to bursting-point. Fights break out and are broken up; trains clank down the rails all day and all night. It's coming. Everybody knows it and they speak about it in a different voice from the voice that's served for long grey years. Something's coming that you want and want – but when it's so close that you can nearly touch it, you're afraid too. You want to pull back, to hide in waiting again.

It's always when she stops thinking of him coming that he comes. A finger touches the top of her spine. His voice grazes her ear.

'Jeezus, I didn't have a hope in hell I'd still find you here. You wet, baby? You got rain on those pretty shoes?'

They laugh. He has small feet for a tall man and Rose's feet in their uniform boats look nearly as big as his.

'Don't start on my feet again,' says Rose.

'I have no *intention* of starting there,' he assures her gravely. 'Come on. We're gonna go find us a park.'

It's easy in the dark. No one sees them. They're a courting couple like any other, hungry for their own patch of earth that's stayed dry under the canopy of laurel. There's an etiquette to finding your space. You can be three yards from another couple, but you don't see them and they don't see you. At night everyone is free, even Rose and Frederick. The park is safe, not like the street. When they walk down the streets, Rose watches ahead, bracing herself when she sees a clump of men in uniform. The ratings are rowdy, but some of the GIs scare her. The white ones. They spit on the ground as she passes with Frederick. They look at Frederick with something she hasn't ever seen on a man's face before when he looks at another man. Not before a fight, not anywhere.

'They bring their Jim Crow law over here with them,' Frederick says. The Americans separate their army into two armies, black and white. That's Jim Crow law, Frederick says. She tells him of a story she's heard, about an old farmer way down in Devon somewhere. They asked him what he thought of the Yanks stationed nearby. 'I love the Americans but I don't like those white ones they've brought along with them,' he said.

Frederick told her how his daddy had brought the family from Atlanta, Georgia up north to Chicago, and never gone back. Never would go back, never would set a foot south of the line again. Not for a visit, not for nothing. His daddy was buried in Chicago soil. He'd never wanted that Atlanta earth to touch his body again.

Those white GIs would scare her if she let them. They see her walking with Frederick and you would think it was their country, not hers. Once, in the crush of the pavements, a GI had grabbed her breast, openly, although Frederick held her arm. As if Frederick wasn't a man. He grabbed and kneaded, tweaking her nipple, grinning at his mates to show them, as if she was anybody's. Frederick was looking ahead the way he did, his face impassive. In the crowd, he hadn't seen what was happening. Rose said nothing. She hardened herself too, shutting her nostrils to the close angry smell of the men and the beer on their breath. She shut her ears to the things they said. She stared straight ahead, as Frederick did, and would not give them the satisfaction of knowing that she felt anything.

They'd be gone soon, she told herself, and she felt easier. But then she remembered that when they went, so would Frederick.

The park is full of scents. There's the sharp smell of city earth, and a honeyish smell from a shrub she can't name. Rain rolls off the leaves and spatters their clothes and skin as they push through the branches. Rose doesn't like the park, but it's the only place. They find a space and he spreads his jacket on the earth. It's damp, but she's known worse. When they first met it was January, with slush on the ground, a raw wind fingering up her skirt and Frederick with the worst head cold he'd had in his entire life.

They lie under the dirty old laurels, on the dirty old ground.

'Welcome to the black country,' he says. It's an old joke between them now. She tells him that one day she'll take him to see the real thing. What would Iris and Dickie make of Frederick? Iris is bashful. She won't say much to anyone she doesn't know. But Dickie's gone the other way, living his own life at thirteen, hardly coming home except to sleep. She doesn't have to worry about what Mum and Dad think. Mum's been dead five years now, and Dad's married again. Iris is still living with them, but she wants to lodge above the shop where she works. She told Rose about it, secretly, last time Rose was there.

'But Auntie Vi doesn't want me to leave home.'

'She's no more your auntie than my elbow. And it's your wages she doesn't want to leave home,' Rose pointed out.

'She's all right, Rose.'

'She's soft. She'll do anything he tells her.'

'I'll wait until I'm sixteen, then I'll go.'

'You're only fourteen and a half.'

'I know.' Iris ducked her head so her hair slipped forward over her cheeks.

'Listen, Iris. Soon as I get a place of my own, after this war's over, you can come to me. And Dickie too if he wants.'

Iris looked up. Disbelief and longing fought in her face, but the idea was too big for her. 'It's a nice room, Rose. It's lovely. Mrs Lambert let me go up and look at it. It's got a window that looks over the street. You can sit and look down on the people. All their hats go bobbing underneath you and they never look up so they never know you're there. 'F you open the window a crack you can hear what they're saying. I was thinking, I could sit there after work. And Mrs Lambert's going to let me paint the walls.'

'Where're you going to get paint from?'

'I know, but when you can. After the war.'

'She'll let you hook your own rag rug as well, will she?' asked Rose sarcastically. But Iris just gave the willing smile she used to hide the times when she wasn't following what Rose said.

'It was nice the way Mum gave us both flower names,' she said at last. Iris was always busy like that, cobbling up a mum for herself out of nothing. A mum who thought about her and loved her but just happened to have gone away.

'Maybe she knew he was going to marry a woman called Violet after she was dead.'

Iris had risen silently and gone out. Rose lit a cigarette and dragged in smoke. She wanted to smash everything in the room. After a while she stood up and went into the back kitchen. Iris lifted her face from the blue-and-white towel that had hung from a wooden bar as long as Rose could remember, washed so often that the blue had all but gone. That towel's lasted longer than my mother, Rose thought suddenly, remembering her mother's hands fastening it back in place after the wash.

She must not say such things to Iris. Iris's face was mottled with crying. Those red patches always sprang up on the same place, on her temples and around her eyes. When she was a kid it took hours to calm Iris down after one of her do's.

'Here, have a drag of a fag,' said Rose, handing the cigarette to Iris.

A faint smile appeared. Iris took the cigarette with a practised gesture.

'You are a daft ha'porth,' Rose said.

'I know.'

'I brought chocolate for you too.'

'Chocolate!'

'American chocolate. It's called a Hershey Bar.'

'Where'd you get it, Rose?'

'That's for you to ask, and me to know. Here, catch.'

'Are you courting a Yank, Rose?'

'Maybe.'

'What's he like?'

'Handsome.'

'Did he give you those nylons too?'

'No, that was the man in the moon.'

'Can I try them on?'

'You're taller than me. Your suspenders'll burst them.'

Iris was tall, like Dad. She looked beggingly at Rose, her mouth full of chocolate. 'Please, Rose! Just so's as I can see how they look on me.'

Her sister's legs were long and pale. The stockings only went halfway up her thighs. American Tan stretched over white skin. That's what some girls call soldiers like Frederick. Tan GIs.

Rose and Frederick know just how many buttons to undo, how far to pull up her skirt. Rose arches her back automatically to unfasten the hooks of her brassiere. Then she looks around. The rain has stopped and the sky is clearing fast. A thick, curdy mass of cloud blows over a brighter space where the moon is hidden. They are the only ones left under the laurels now. She thinks that the other couples must have gone because of the rain, dripping and seeping everywhere. But it's not as dark as it was. Now she can see him a little. Quickly, Rose pushes his hands aside and kneels up.

'Rose, what you doing?' he complains.

'Wait.'

She sheds clothes. Skirt, jacket, blouse, petticoat, brassiere, suspenders, stockings, knickers. They peel off and fall away like cards in the hands of a dealer. Rose piles them out of the way, quick and neat as always. She kneels up, naked. Can he see her?

He can. 'Jeez, Rose, look at you.'

'You do it too.'

'What if somebody comes? You want to get me court-martialled?'

'Yes.'

He hesitates, on the brink of the cold water where she is already far out. And then he smiles. She hears the smile in his voice, though there's not enough moonlight to see it by.

'OK,' he says slowly, 'OK. If that's the way you want it.'

He takes off his clothes more slowly than her, folding each item with a care that shows her he is suddenly nervous as he's never been before. Then he's naked too. She puts out her hand and it shows pale against his arm. She has never seen him like this before. She does not really know what he looks like. They know each other by touch, through clothes, standing up on the coldest of nights, lying down where they can.

Rose lies on top of him for a long while. Neither moves. If one of them moves an inch it will all start, a ripple in one flesh spreading to the other. How long can they hold still, like this? She can't tell where he ends and she begins. He's different from the other men she's known, who have no sooner got her legs open than they are pumping into her as if there's a fire, their faces twisted and their weight crushing her breath. Afterwards they don't want to talk, don't really want to see her even. They haul themselves off her with a suck and a heave. They have no idea that there's anything left to want.

Worst of all are the ones who are doggily grateful, as if it's all been done for their sake, a gift they got away with because Rose is stupid, or easy. And maybe most of the time that's true, thinks Rose.

Suddenly she is chilled, and as lonely inside herself as she's been all those other times. She moves one leg, very slightly, against his thigh. She skims her right hand across his chest and touches his nipple, the feathery touch she's learned from him. He gasps deep in his throat, between a laugh and a groan. She leans forward. His face snaps sideways and he begins to move inside her. She tastes his mouth as if it is a fruit she's read about but never imagined she would eat.

It is cold now. The moon's brighter, too bright. Rose can hear wind tickling the leaves along the path. It sounds like the rustling of a newspaper with bad news in it. As soon as they've done it, outside comes pressing in on them, she thinks. Their heads, screened by rhododendrons, are only a few feet from the path. Twice she's heard footsteps. She moves her head so that she can see past Frederick's shoulder, and looks up at the moon through the laurel leaves. It's still pushing back the night clouds. For a second she lets her gaze follow the long curve of his shoulder, his back, hip, buttock, thigh, then the legs going away. She can't see his feet at this angle.

But if she can see him, so can anyone. Military police patrol this park with torches sometimes. Frederick eases himself up on his elbows, and looks down at her. She wonders what he can see, but for once she can't find her mirror face to look back with. She just lies there and lets him see her, naked as a baby. Then he is up and brushing loose dirt from his hands, bending over his pile of clothes. Rose sees that he is ready to turn from her, back into the world of uniforms.

'If my mama could see me now,' he says, looking down at Rose over his shoulder.

Rose does not reply. She does not want to hear about anyone's mama. She knows enough about Frederick's family. His brother who is still in junior high. His baby sister, and his father in the Chicago soil. Every time he speaks of them she hears responsibility in his voice. He has got to take care of them. His brother is a bright kid and he'll have the chances that time wasn't right for Frederick to have.

His voice is telling her that his life is elsewhere, not here in these rainy parks he soon won't see again. Better his family don't come too close, get too real. Would they like her? What would they think about Frederick going with a white girl? A Brit, that's what they'd call her. She'd be foreign to them. The brother is going to college one day. *If my brother don't study hard my mama will whup his ass and then I'll come home and whup it a second time.* Frederick smiles as he says it. Rose guesses that there won't be too much whupping required. Frederick has confidence in a brother who doesn't need to be driven, in a future that's burning its way out of the past. What would his family say to Iris, and Dad, and Auntie Vi?

Elsewhere is nowhere, Rose thinks. These days are what we've got. You have to take what you can.

Quickly they get dressed like strangers, back to back. But at the last moment, late as they are, he wraps his arms around her again. Soon he is rocking her and they are cheek to cheek.

'Cold,' he says. 'I ain't been warm since I left home.'

She tries to remember where Chicago is on the map. 'Is it warm in winter, where you come from?'

He laughs. 'Uh-uh. But it's a different style of cold back home. I never been bone-chilled like here. We better go now, Rose.'

'I want to live near the sea,' she says abruptly. 'The noise of it.' Another thing she has never told anyone.

'That's why you joined the Wrens?'

She laughs. 'No, it was because of the buttons.'

'The buttons?'

'Yeah. Wrens don't have brass buttons. If you have buttons, you have to polish them and they have to shine all the time.'

'You worked that one out before you joined up?'

She nods, feeling her head move in the hollow of his shoulder. But then her voice comes again, muffled. 'It was the sea. I'd never seen the sea.'

When you are slack with love you get careless. Rose and Frederick step out of the park, but nothing outside their two bodies touches them. By the rank overgrowth of privet at the park gates she hears rustling, snuffling, and thinks of badgers though there are no badgers here. The gates are shut but with the railings gone it's easy to climb over the stone wall studded with stumps of metal. She goes first, with Frederick holding her hand to steady her, and then he follows. Down on to the pavement under the street lamp with its muffled blackout glow. But they're all right because they know where they are going. This is their place.

'Nigger lover,' says a voice by her ear. She's so far from herself that for a second she thinks it's a joke. It's a Yank voice, like Frederick's.

'Fuckin' nigger lover,' says a second voice, and then another. They are coming at her from everywhere. Then shadows pull away from the dark. Three men, four, five. They don't wait, don't say any more, don't shape up for a fight. Just fall on Frederick, banging Rose to one side so she slams into the stone wall.

She grates against the rough stone as she falls. She is down on the ground. She touches the side of her face where it hurts and her fingers come away slimy with blood. But Frederick is gone. She wants to call to him but cunning sits on her tongue, holding it down. They mustn't know that she can move.

She looks along the wet pavement to where it's happening. There is a mess of dark, jostling shapes, on the ground. They've got him down. She knows that in a fight you mustn't fall. You have got to stay on your feet. She heard Dad teach Dickie that. If they get a boot to your head you won't get up again. She clambers painfully on to all fours, pushes herself off the wall, begins to stagger towards them. But one of them turns casually, sees her coming, and throws her off easily as if she's nothing. The back of her head hits the pavement.

She lies there looking up. There is a taste of vomit in her mouth. Maybe she has been sick without remembering it. Her ears are noisy, as if they've got water in them. The moon is still up there, looking at her more brightly than she could ever look at it. She can't remember why she is down here looking at the moon, and then she can. She raises her head but it won't hold up; she raises it again and heaves herself over and begins to crawl forward with her head down. But they are too far and she can't get to them. The fight is moving down the pavement away from her, taking Frederick with it. There are terrible noises coming out of it that don't sound like anyone she has ever known. She is crying out now, trying to reach the bodies that sway and lunge. They have got him on the ground, she knows it, and she can hear him grunting and groaning as if they are on top of him and his life is being pushed out of him like the little ones being pushed out of Mum while Rose sat in the yard and played with pebbles.

'Frederick!' she screams. He doesn't answer, but one of them leaves the pack and falls on her. He drags her up off the ground, he gets hold of her head, he is grappling for her mouth but his fingers miss and poke her right eye. She screams again. He is blinding her but she knows no one will come. She can smell the man, his sweat and something he puts on his hair and his uniform smell and his PX food smell. Some parts of his smell are the same as Frederick but most of it is strangeness. He pulls her head back and gets his whole right hand over her mouth, half over her nose too so that she struggles for breath, lashing out with feet and nails. She twists her head, trying to get a grip, trying to bite his hand. His left hand grips her throat.

'You carry on like that, I'm gonna hurt you.'

Her eyes are bursting in her head, hurting her. She can't see the moon. All she hears are her own whimpers.

They are gone. She's down on the pavement. Her cheek is against the ground and the cold stone is greasy with rain. She lifts her head and looks in terror along the length of the ground, trying to focus.

He is there. She knows it's him though the shape on the ground looks smaller than Frederick, even when he's lying down. She shuffles towards him, saying his name. The moon is weak now. She can see him but not yet name the parts of him. Slowly the shape thrust towards her becomes the sole of his boot. She raises herself on her knees to see him.

He is on his back, arms cast up around his head. He looks as if he's been thrown there. His face is sideways, his eyes almost shut but not quite. A strip of white shows. She shuffles until her face is touching his, and feels for his breath with her fingers.

It's there. She can feel it. She thinks she can feel it. But his face is split, pulped like a fruit.

'Frederick? Frederick!'

But he doesn't answer. His lips are open. His top front teeth are gone.

She looks down the long, shining pavement. At the far end, a hundred yards away, a shadowy couple walk, twined together. They are in a world of their own. They saw nothing, heard nothing. She begins to call and wave her arms as if she and Frederick are far out to sea, clinging to the hull of an upturned boat. The couple drift on, out of sight.

'What'd they do to you?' he asks her days later in the hospital. His voice is grating. That's because his windpipe was hurt where they tried to throttle him. He clears his throat as if he's got a cold.

'Nothing,' she says quickly. 'They held me down, that's all.'

Suddenly she realises what he's been afraid of. He thinks they raped her, to show her that she's anyone's. That's why he hasn't wanted to see her all these days. That's why the nurses were told to say he was too sick to see anyone. The swellings are down and the stitches due to come out. He has had an operation on his jaw, which is broken in three places. They've put a plate in.

'You reckon they'll be giving me a medal?' says Frederick. His voice is a thousand miles away from her. The gap in his teeth makes his words seem to stumble.

'They didn't touch me,' she says urgently. But he just nods, neither believing nor disbelieving. She puts her hand on his arm and he lets it lie there. His face has changed so much, as if the doctors tried to put everything back right but did not know where the right places were. She knew: she could have told them. Now she sees that the smallest change to a face makes it so that you can't read it any more. Eyes, forehead, cheeks, mouth. She looks at them. His skin colour is different, ashen with what pain's done to him. Deep bruising still discolours his face around the jaw line. They stove in three ribs; she knows that. The nurse told her. His collarbone had been dislocated. There are other troubles. A catheter line leads from the bed to a glass jar. Rose is afraid to ask Frederick about his injuries. She would have asked a nurse, but they are all in a hurry, clacking past as if the visitors are trouble they don't want.

'My mama wrote me,' Frederick says abruptly, nodding towards his locker.

This is the face that lay so close to hers that they seemed to share the same breath. The locker top is smooth and empty. He must have put the letter away. He didn't want anyone to see it.

'She don't know nothin' 'bout all this and she ain't ever gonna know nothin',' he continues.

'What's her name?' says Rose at last.

'Lucile.'

'That's a nice name.'

'Yeah. Pretty. She writes she's prayin' for me night and day, 'cause she knows I'll be goin' into danger soon. Mama's a Baptist. Not my daddy though, he was political.'

He is talking in the voice he must have had as a child. His eyes are turned away from her. He is back with them, not with her.

'He brought us out of Georgia when I was eight months old,' he goes on. 'My daddy used to tell us stories. They weren't fit for a child's ears, my mama said, but he said we should know them; that way we would understand what the law was for, and why you have to get to a place that has laws the same for everyone. He used to say that we hadn't reached that place yet and maybe we never would reach it. But we were on our way. 'Cause it ain't right for people to do what they like. I used to wonder when my daddy said that. Used to think it'd be pretty good to do just what I liked.'

She is tiring him. She takes his hand, but it lies slack in hers. She releases it gently, to rest on the boiled bedcover, palm up.

'Frederick,' she says. His gaze slides towards her, and then away. The whites of his eyes are still bloodshot and yellow.

'I never was baptised,' he says. 'I never heard that call. I followed my daddy.' There is a film of sweat on his forehead now. Soon the nurse will come and tell her that he needs to rest. Those doctors and nurses think they know everything. Dad wouldn't let a doctor near Mum, because they'd have taken her away. Better she lay there, her toes poking up under the bedclothes and her face shut. She lay like that for weeks sometimes, and the bad times came more and more often until the good times were squeezed to nothing between them.

That nurse is crackling her way down the ward towards them, twitching bedcovers and checking charts. Visiting hour is over.

'Goodbye, Rose,' he says.

What's left? There's nothing left.

'I'll come again tomorrow,' she says. She'll come and come and each time he will be there, not here. She wants to seize him back, all of him, pull him back across the ocean from where he's gone. She knows where Chicago is now. She's looked at the map. Chicago lies on a lake as big as the sea, but it's hemmed in by thousands of miles of land. The lake is so big that they even have tides there; it says so in the back of the atlas. But they are not real tides. You'd think from the size of the lake that it was the sea, and that you could sail away on it to anywhere in the world. But you never could.

PROTECTION

❧

Florence wakes. The bedclothes have slid to the floor and she's cold. She sits up quickly and listens. Something woke her but she doesn't know what. Perhaps it was her own voice. That happens sometimes, when her dreams are too strong.

Is something wrong with one of the girls? They don't come to her unless they are ill. There's no need, when they've got each other.

The house is still. It creaks and stirs but she's used to that. A house this age is a living thing. It was nothing, she tells herself, but her body knows better. Her skin prickles. *Don't pretend. You won't get out of it that way.* She leans over the side of the bed, scrabbles for the sheet and wraps it around her.

She never draws the curtains. She can lie in bed and see the stars. When there's a full moon the wash of light is almost strong enough for her to read by it. She recites these facts, telling them to herself as she tells them to

267

her London friends. Why live in the middle of nowhere and still draw your curtains?

Her heart is still thudding. She's cold, not because the night is cold but because of the start of sweat all over her body. Something frightened her, while she was still far down in her sleep.

A streak of light travels across the window. Instantly she knows what it is and she ducks down, away from it. She reaches under the bed and picks up a length of pipe, heavy in her hand.

Jack doesn't know about the pipe. It's only when he's away that it comes out from behind her shoes at the back of the wardrobe. Everyone says there are no burglars here. This is the back end of nowhere. There are cottages and farmhouses, but not a big house for miles. Besides, even if a burglar tried, he wouldn't find the way down the twisted lanes.

'But all the same, you should have a dog.' Her friend Rosamund said that, when she came to stay.

The pipe is cold and smooth. She will cave in his skull if he comes near her girls. She has prepared for this moment in her mind, and now here it is.

The light flickers across the window again. She knows exactly where he is: on the path that skirts the boundary of their property and then climbs the hill through the woods. He's looking across to the house, shining a torch to see how big it is and whether anyone is awake. She even knows the words for what is happening. He is casing the joint. But that's an American expression and she is English, in the heart of the English countryside, with her lead piping. Her thoughts jump and spurt like matches being lit one from the next.

She must keep quite still. If she goes to the window to look out he will see the movement. If she had a dog it would be barking now. Florence listens. Her window is open a little at the top. She hears nothing and everything. The night is still. Not a branch stirs. A tawny owl cries softly; a male, she thinks, a locating cry. At night the wood sounds even closer than it is, as if it laps the walls of the house like water.

The doors are locked. She runs through them in her mind. Back door: yes, she shot the bolt across. They never use the front door. She thinks its iron key is rusted into the lock. The downstairs windows are all shut, and at night she puts the catches across them. The girls always pull their upper window right down, but they are on the other side of the house. The torchlight won't discover them.

She is out of bed. She crouches on the floor, naked, the sheet fallen from her, and goes on all fours towards the window, until her head is below the sill. She creeps upward, head back, so that her eyes will see before her pale hair is exposed.

There's the bulk of the wood. He'll have to come right out and cross open ground to get to the house. He can't come any closer without her seeing. She waits but the torch beam doesn't probe again. He's gone, she thinks, and then another thought runs through her head, electric. *He's gone round the other side of the house, the girls' side.*

Then she sees it. Another flash of light, but this time from deeper inside the wood. He is on the path. She knows exactly where he is and how the path twists as it climbs the hill. Now the light will come again. Yes. One light stabs, then another, another, another. There are four torches. Four men. Her breath goes out of her.

They are following the path. Four of them. If they spoke she would hear them, they are so close. So why shine a torch at the house and give themselves away? Maybe they wanted to get their bearings. The house is a landmark because that's where the path begins.

They are going away, up the hill. They're not interested in the house.

If they'd come in daylight she wouldn't have known they were there. It was only the torches that gave them away. She could have been working in her studio while they passed within yards of her.

So why come at night?

She reaches for the sheet again, and pulls it around her with one hand. She won't switch on the light. If they looked back they would see it pour through the window frame and they would know that they had woken her. They might guess that she had looked out and seen their torches. And they might not like that.

Lights bobble and waver through the trees. As the path goes up it hides itself behind a fold of the hill. It's very steep. They will trample the leaf mould and release the mushroomy smell of undergrowth in autumn.

There are deer in the wood, and pheasant. Of course, she thinks to herself in huge relief: poachers. Even the word has something soothing and domestic about it.

The wood goes dark. Whatever they're up to on the hill, it's not her business. She can go back to bed, but first she'll make sure that the girls are all right.

She takes Jack's heavy brown woollen dressing gown off the hook on the back of the door and wraps it around her. Her fingers graze the light switch, but she doesn't press it down. She'll close her bedroom door and turn on the landing light, because that can't be seen from outside.

But I can draw the curtains, she thinks. She drags them across until there is no gap at all. She knows that never again will she sleep under a window full of stars.

As always, Florence hesitates before pushing open the door of the girls' room.

'Twins!' people used to say as they peered into their pram, as if Florence might not have noticed that she had two babies in there. 'They're lovely babies, dear, but sooner you than me. All that work!'

What nobody said and nobody seemed to know was the loneliness of having them. With two beautiful babies, you never have to worry about them having someone to play with. No, thinks Florence, you never do. The only trouble is that every time you come into their bedroom you think you're interrupting something. It's like living with a newly married couple who are perfectly polite but have no real interest in anyone but themselves. But with her girls the honeymoon has gone on for years, fierce, secretive and so intimate that it seems to suck all the air of the room into itself.

The girls are asleep on the big bed. They won't give it up. They like its iron frame and coiled iron springs. When the mattress gets too uncomfortable they beat the lumps out of it with their fists. It has a smell that Florence dislikes, but Marian butts at the striped ticking like a goat and buries her nose in it.

'It smells of sleep,' she says.

To Florence it smells of the faintly urinous second-hand shop where she and Jack bought it years ago, as their marriage bed. She scrubbed the ticking and slung the mattress over two chairs, out on the Kilburn pavement. She brought out a third chair and sat there with her book in the fierce sun until the mattress cover dried and the stains were almost bleached away.

'It's our bed. You're not getting rid of it,' Clare told her father when he offered them twin divans. It was at the start of the magazine job. He came home so pale with excitement that Florence thought he was ill. They had a backer for the magazine at last. He came from the Persian Gulf, and his name was Alistair. Jack was to be editor.

'The Persian Gulf?' murmured Florence.

'He read English at New College,' said Jack, as if that explained everything.

'At Oxford, do you mean?' she asked.

'Yes, of course, at Oxford,' he said impatiently, his pale eyes ablaze in his pale face.

The mention of Oxford made her feel tired and sad. It would be another of those schemes that came not to nothing exactly, but in the end to Jack looking as if he'd been dipped in a dirty river and left on the towpath to dry himself and wander home as best he could.

'But Alistair is a Scottish name,' she said.

'Not Alistair, for God's sake. Al-Istrahar. Everyone calls him Ali.'

'Do they?'

She was wrong, and Jack was right. She saw it in his face when he came back triumphant a month later, bringing her ham from the Lina Stores. He had an office with a desk and a pair of shabby leather armchairs. He had a local where he drank with contributors, and a girl to type for him. There was a salary, to be paid every month.

'Why does he do it?' she asked Jack. The magazine had been going for ten months; ten issues. Florence visited him in the small office where he put his feet up on the desk and talked excitedly into the telephone.

'He likes poetry.'

'He likes poetry? Is that why he does it?'

'You don't understand, Florence.' He waved his arm around the room. 'The cost doesn't mean anything to him. You'd think longer about buying a bunch of violets.'

Violets don't last five minutes once you get them home, thought Florence. 'Does he write poetry?' she asked.

'No, thank God. He has too much respect for it. I wish there were more like him.'

There was money for furniture now.

'We like this bed,' Marian said, her eyes as pale and fierce as Jack's. 'We don't want *twin* beds.'

'Thank you,' said Florence.

'*Thank you*,' said Marian and Clare together.

'Paint your room or something then,' said Jack, taking a handful of half-crowns and florins out of his pocket for the girls to pick through.

'Any colour we want?'

'Not black,' said Florence. 'The landlord would make you paint it over.'

'We'll move to the country,' said Jack. 'You can have a studio, Florence. The rent will be half what we pay for this place. I'll build you a studio in the garden.'

He might even do that, she thought. He was good with his hands, when he wanted to be.

Marian is sleeping with her arms flung behind her head and her legs tangled in the sheets. Clare is curled neatly, facing away from her sister. The landing light dramatises the ruck of the bedclothes so that it looks as if they've been fighting. The room smells of skin, hair and sweat. They smell like women now.

Clare has sprayed her sister's perfume over herself before going to sleep. Imprévu. Marian had it for their birthday. She doesn't like it any more; she's gone off perfume, in the fierce, sudden way that Marian's loves turn to hates. She won't give it to Clare, though, because it's hers. Clare can borrow it, but not have it.

Florence sighs. It's typical of the arrangements between her girls. They talk of 'lending' and 'borrowing' things which can in fact never be given back: sweets, shampoo, Easter eggs. The house rings as they drive their bargains. They shout and slap, and sometimes they wrestle each other to the floor. If Florence intervenes they stare at her, at bay, out of their identical faces.

They are not identical, Florence reminds herself for the thousandth time. Clare's hair is slightly darker. Marian has a mole on her stomach. She has always been able to tell them apart. She has always wanted to tell them apart.

But if I dyed my hair, and Marian had her mole removed, you wouldn't know which of us was which.

Of course she would, you clot. I'd have a scar.

Clare breathes quietly, while Marian mutters to herself under her breath. Neither will wake. All through their childhood they slept twelve easy hours, as long as they were within sound and touch of each other. When Marian had her tonsils out, Clare sat up all the first night, haggard and silent, with her arms wrapped around her knees as she waited for her sister to come home. But Marian was away five nights. Florence wanted to take Clare into her own bed, but Clare resisted, stiff as wood.

'She's dead,' said Clare in the middle of the fourth night. 'She's dead, and you're not allowed to tell me.'

The girls were seven then, and children under fourteen were not allowed to visit the ward. When Marian came home, Clare didn't say a word. The girls went upstairs together, and Florence, following them, saw Marian sitting in the centre of the big bed while Clare felt over her face like a blind girl, patting Marian's eyes, her lips, her cheeks and lips. For a long time after that Clare's hands shook.

They are quite safe. The house is locked, with the bolt in place. The windows are secure. Those men have gone their way, intent on their own purposes.

She will go downstairs, make tea and read for a while to settle herself.

The kitchen, like the girls' room, faces away from the hill. The windows are small and the blackout blinds from the war are still in place. Florence keeps meaning to rip them out. Now she goes to the windows, one by one in the dim light from the hall, pulls down each blind and secures the strings. After that she switches off the hall light, closes the door and turns on the kitchen light.

The whole point of this place is that we are free. We can do as we like.

The kitchen is warm and it smells of the stove, banked up with coke to last the night. The plug sparks blue as she turns off the kettle. She makes tea, soothing herself with ritual, and finds the packet of Rich Tea biscuits which she keeps hidden from the girls. It's surprising they haven't found them yet. They eat everything, with such speed and lack of conscience that keeping up with their appetites is like holding back a river with one of the twig dams of her childhood. They will eat six slices of toast each when they come home from school.

Florence bakes all their household bread. She has learned to do so, just as she's learned to clean the kitchen floor, riddle and feed the stove, chop wood for the fires, unblock drains, and also top up the oil, clean the plugs and deal with the radiator of their old Morris Traveller. By nature she's quick and efficient, and would rather do things herself than worry about finding the money to pay others. Money is time for her work. The girls have a long day at school, and then homework. They can't be expected to do much during the week, beyond washing up on alternate nights and bringing in logs from the woodshed.

Sometimes, by the end of the day, Florence is almost too tired to speak. She gets up at six thirty: late, she knows, by the standards of the women whom she sees selling eggs and cheese on market day.

'You're not in Kilburn now,' she says to herself as she stands in the doorway with the first cup of tea of the day, looking out at the pale landscape blowing away from her for miles. 'Be thankful you don't have to keep chickens.'

But it's night now. She won't be able to sleep, even if she goes back to bed. She keeps seeing those four points of light, jabbing into the dark of the wood. Again, fear floods through her. She can smell it, coming out of the seams of her body. She leaves her tea and goes back upstairs. She must be with her girls. Silently, she enters their room, crosses the floor, and lifts a corner of the curtain.

This side of the house faces away from the hill and the wood, over disused pasture which is full of tall ragged weeds and dozens of scuttering rabbits. She has the pipe in her hand, although she can't remember when she picked it up again. Suddenly it seems dangerous, as if it might spring out of her hands and smash the girls' skulls. She peers into the dark. The clouds are rubbed thin and there is faint light from the quarter-moon. She waits. Behind her, the girls breathe. Jack's dressing gown itches against her skin, but she doesn't move. Very slowly, the long field comes into focus. Rough, lumpy land, full of shadows, bounded by the ruins of a drystone wall. There are so many gaps in it that the wall is more the idea of a wall than the thing itself.

Something is approaching from behind the house, where she can't see it. She knows it, not with her mind but in her flesh, and the house knows it too. Across her back, down to her fingers, along the inside of her thighs, the skin prickles with the ancient fell of hair rising. It knows what danger is, even if she doesn't. She should have woken the girls, bundled them into the car, got them away down the track to safety. She should have turned off the landing light.

They come into her field of vision in single file. There are four of them and they move quickly through the wall and downhill across the pasture. They are carrying things, but she can't see what these are. The torches are switched off. The men are accustomed to dark and moonlight now, just as she is. They are walking faster than they walked uphill. If these *are* the same men ... but she knows that they must be. No one ever comes here.

'That's the beauty of the place,' Jack said, and then he spent three nights a week in London.

They're almost out of sight. They're heading towards the lane, she thinks. It's about half a mile away, and you can't see it from the house. She waits, quite still, listening, working out how long it will take them.

The sound of the engine carries clearly across the fields. It revs, settles, and then she hears the car – or no, a van – begin to move. Florence listens to the sound of the engine until it fades into the night. They'll be heading for the main road, five miles away. She thinks she can still hear them. She shakes her head to clear it, and then the pulse of the engine is gone. Whatever they came to do, they have finished with it.

She's been holding her breath. Slowly, deliberately, she breathes out, letting her shoulders drop. She glances behind her. The girls' arms look as if they are carved from alabaster: Marian's above her head, Clare's curled, as her body is curled. Her hands pillow her cheek. Awake or asleep, Clare drops naturally into poses.

Alabaster dissolves, though, if you leave it out in the rain. Florence prefers to work with Carrara marble. Her girls are here and helpless, because Florence has not been thinking properly about the loneliness of the place, and about what they were doing there.

The men could have brought their van up as far as the house, on the track that leads off the lane. Florence made Jack take down the wooden sign that pointed up to the house, because she's here on her own with the girls so much of the time. Perhaps the men didn't notice the track … But they must have done, as soon as they began to walk in this direction. It would have made sense to turn back for their vehicle. Instead, they left it, and came up across the fields, silently.

Why would they come up silently, unless they knew that someone might be disturbed? Why would they shine a torch at the house, unless they wanted to be sure that no one was awake?

They knew we were here, thinks Florence, and a shiver begins in her legs and goes right up through her body. They must have known their way. The path up the hill led to an Iron Age fort and it was marked on the Ordnance Survey, but these men didn't need a map.

'There'll be no one to disturb you,' Jack said when they first saw the house. 'You'll have the whole day to yourself, once the girls have gone off to school.'

They leave for school each morning at seven thirty-five. Seven forty is too late, and seven thirty gives them five cold, annoying minutes on the platform when they could have been in bed. Florence drives them the five miles to the station, and they go another ten miles by train to school in the county town. They make their own way home, catching a bus from the station. It ambles around the lanes, but brings them within a mile of the house, and from there they walk. Or rather, they dawdle. They like these hours that belong to no one but themselves. Often they are not back until six, or later. Next month they'll be coming home in the dark.

She tiptoes out of the bedroom, and closes the door. She won't be able to sleep now. If Jack were here they could talk about it. He would tell her to calm down. He would make her see how much safer the girls were here than in London.

Of course he would, she thinks suddenly. If he's going to leave us here three nights a week while he's in London, he's got to believe we are fine here. He's quite happy to talk about tramps and poachers.

She had argued with him about the car. They'd never had one before, and although Florence could drive, he could not.

'I could drive you to the station if we had a car,' she said, but he shrugged.

'There's a bus. Why do we want a car? All these *things*, Florence! They tie you down.'

'Quite the opposite,' said Florence. 'They free you. This isn't London, and I can't get materials delivered. Do you think I want to be wheedling with taxi-drivers to let me put stone in their boots?'

He had to concede that she couldn't lug stone on to the bus, and then trundle it up the track on a wheelbarrow.

'Didn't you think of that when we looked at the house?' asked Florence. 'And if we have a car, it'll make it much easier if you want to come home instead of staying up in London. I don't mind how late it is. I can pick you up from the station.'

'I can't be going back and forth all the time. I'll sleep in the office, or on someone's sofa.'

She didn't suspect him of sleeping anywhere else. He was probably right to stay. The magazine was like a baby, and needed constant attendance.

They got a fourth-hand Morris Traveller. It sat at the top of the track, saying to Florence: *You could. You could.*

I should have got the girls into the car as soon as those men were away up the path, thinks Florence. There were four of them. If four men put their shoulders to the back door it would burst open.

There is no telephone in the house, because it would cost too much to bring the line across a mile of fields. Florence had never minded. She had always felt safe here, lapped by miles and miles of darkness.

The next morning, Florence says nothing to the girls. The postman brings a letter from Jack, about a poet whom he has finally persuaded to contribute, and a sheaf of bills. She asks the postman if he would like a cup of tea, and he sits down in the kitchen, slinging his heavy bag to the floor. It's a long haul from the village and he always makes that plain.

'It's a quiet life for you up here,' he says, sipping tea. 'Wouldn't go for it myself.'

'I've got my work,' says Florence. 'It suits us.'

He nods. 'You should get a dog,' he says. 'Wonderful company, a dog.'

She opens her mouth to tell him she doesn't like dogs. Suddenly she thinks of the warm bulk of a dog at her side, like a soldier. Not only at her side, but on her side. 'Maybe I should,' she says.

'If you're interested, there's a Stafford going at the pub.'

'A puppy, you mean?' A puppy was no good.

'Two years old. Beautiful dog. Steve married again, that's where it is,' adds the postman cryptically. 'I'll tell him you're interested if you like. It's a lovely breed. Lovely temperament.'

'Are they … Do they make good guard dogs?'

'Burglars won't take on a Staffie.'

When Jack comes home at the weekend, Florence says nothing to him, either. He is pale from overwork, and lit with an exhilaration that has nothing to do with her or the girls. Three times he has to walk down to the village to make calls from the phone box. His other world calls to him like a siren, bright, compelling and far more real than the grey house, or the hill. Marian and Clare take little notice of him and spend the weekend in their bedroom reading magazines borrowed from girls at school. At night he sleeps deeply, obliviously. To him, the countryside is nothingness. If asked, he will say how peaceful it is. Empty.

The four men walk across Florence's mind. They go up the hill, finding their way by torchlight. They come down fast, looking for escape. If she went up the hill she might see where they have disturbed the earth. She is afraid to see it, and deliberately does not walk that way, even when Jack suggests that they go up to the old Iron Age fort on top of the hill.

'No,' says Florence, 'let's go to the river.'

Soon he'll be gone, back to London. She fears it but also longs for it. She has arranged to go down to the pub and see the dog on Sunday evening. Secretly, she has bought dog food, a bowl, a blanket and a basket. She doesn't know what else dogs need.

The dog is called Richard.

'You won't change his name,' says Steve, and it's not a question but a command.

'Of course not,' says Florence. She understands that Steve doesn't want to part with the dog. She sees the new wife, flitting through back rooms, watching the transaction. She wants the dog gone.

'Richard,' says Florence.

'Put out your hand for him to smell,' says Steve, and she does so. The dog snuffles the back of Florence's hand and then she turns it over and he tastes the salt of her palm. The touch of him is strange at first. He nuzzles her then, and she feels herself dissolve with tenderness for him, because he has not rejected her. Steve talks to the dog in a low, serious voice. 'You're going to live with this lady, and look after her,' he says, as if there's no question that, once having seen the dog, Florence can fail to want him.

He is right, of course. Florence pays the price for the dog, and takes the heavy lead, the collar, and the framed photograph of Richard as a six-week-old puppy.

'But don't you want to keep it?'

'Best it goes with him.' Steve holds out his hand to shake hers, to seal the bargain and maybe to end something which has become too hard. Then he says, looking straight into her eyes, 'You'll be wanting a shotgun. For the rabbits. Licence is easy enough to get.'

'Yes,' says Florence. 'I was considering it.'

Steve nods, and that is the end of it. The dog goes with Florence, easily.

As she goes to sleep that night, with Richard on the floor at her feet, it occurs to her that Jack will not like the dog. But he is not a new husband, she thinks to herself, and laughs in the darkness.

Richard is gentlemanly with the girls, as if they are precious but foolish things for which he is willing to take responsibility. They want to come first with him. They coax him into their room, and he stays there for a while, dutiful, but watching the door. The house is under his protection and Florence is lord of all.

At the weekend, Jack comes home. In his case there are copies of the latest issue of the magazine, moist with newness, smelling of ink and promise. He takes them out to show to Florence. She watches how his hand strokes the glistening cover. He opens the magazine to show her two new poems by Hugh Carteret.

'I had to go over to Paris to persuade him,' says Jack, casual, offhand to any ear but Florence's.

'You went to Paris?'

'He lives in the most extraordinary rooms. There were drafts pinned all over the walls and spread out on the floor. That's how he works. He has to see it all in front of him. It's a very physical approach.'

'Presumably he lives alone.'

'I don't think so,' says Jack, smiling. 'Not from what I saw.'

Florence imagines the woman who would be fool enough to live with Hugh Carteret, a man who papered their home with his own words. She bends down and gives her hand to Richard, who is under the table.

'Whose dog is that?' asks Jack.

'Mine.'

'But you don't like dogs.'

'It's very isolated here, when you're in London. We need a dog for protection.'

Jack looks at her, startled, his eyes wide open. '*Protection?*'

'I feel safer with Richard. The girls— Everybody thinks it's a good idea.'

He says nothing more. She sees him glance down at his double spread again, but she withholds praise. It is almost time to take Richard for a walk. Jack tires her. He sits there with his magazine, misty, irrelevant.

Florence and Richard go up the hill, following the path the four men took. It's the first time she has set foot on it since that night. There's been rain, and any marks have been washed away. The wood pushes in around her but she is not afraid, even though she knows now that it's neither empty nor peaceful.

The men will come again: four of them, or perhaps only two, and some nights a single man. There's no stopping them. Richard will stir, and tense, and growl, and she will know that they are moving up the hill like shadows, pointing their torches to the ground. They will climb to the top, where the ghost of the Iron Age fort shows through bitten grass. She thinks they won't shine their torches against her house. Word will have got around. Steve at the pub sees everybody, more or less.

She has Richard, and a shotgun is easy enough to get.

A SILVER CIGAR IN THE SKY

❧

Around her, the crowd gasps. The Zeppelin wallows above the city and the crowd breathes out, willing it higher. Breath from thousands and thousands of lungs becomes hot air to push the Zeppelin up and away, out of danger.

It's going to crash into the Wills Building.

It's going to impale itself on the Cabot Tower.

It's going to catch and crash and sag before bursting into flame and spewing a river of fiery struts, fabric, metal and men on to the streets below.

The woman next to Iris grabs her arm. 'My God,' she says. 'Look at it. Just look at it. It's going to hit the tower.'

'It's all right,' says Iris. 'It's not as low as it looks.'

'How do you know?' says the woman, offended.

'I've seen one before.'

The crowd breathes in, breathes out in a long sigh of relief and maybe, for some of them, just a sliver of disappointment. Drama has loomed. It has almost touched them. But the *Graf Zeppelin* sails on, massively chuntering to itself, towards the Docks where more crowds line the wharves. Boys hurl their caps into the air and fathers swoop children on to their shoulders for a better view as the airship turns. It is right over them now. They gaze up at its belly and giant fins. They are in the shadow of the air-whale.

It's going along the water. Heading for Avonmouth.

It's going up by Hotwells.

To the Suspension Bridge!

Go up over the Downs, you'll get a good view there.

Those who have motor cars jump into them and set off in pursuit of the Zeppelin, sounding their horns while passengers hang out of the windows to track its flight.

The motor cars roar past Canon's Marsh, along Hotwells, up Clifton Vale. The airship is hidden by the turn of the hill. They're going to miss it! They burst out on to the level and race for the Downs.

Iris Daniels has no motor car, and it's not likely she ever will. She has come on her own to see the Zeppelin, saying nothing to her sister. Iris often goes for a long, solitary walk on a Sunday. It gets the fidgets out of her, she says, after the working week. She's a dressmaker who would rather rip out a seam than send a client away with a less than perfect fit. She's been back in Bristol for twelve years now. It was hard to begin with, but now she has to turn away clients. She spends long hours in the attic room that serves as her workshop.

Iris's lips are parted. She stares at the Zeppelin as it chugs away over Bristol, touching nothing and impaling itself on nothing. The *Graf Zeppelin* is on a peacetime visit as part of its tour of Britain. She read all about it in the paper. This is a display flight, commanded by Dr Hugo Eckener, director of the Luftschiffbau Zeppelin company. Iris has read the newspaper article with attention. She knows that the *Graf Zeppelin* is a friendly guest in the skies over Bristol, but her heart and her breathing refuse to believe it. Her heart bumps with fear. Her breathing is tight. Her body expects injury or death.

The Zeppelin has gone, and around the Docks, Navy Week continues. HMS *Warwick*, HMS *Velox* and HMS *Versatile* are visiting the city. The children who waved and cheered at the *Graf Zeppelin* are the children of peace. They weren't even born, thinks Iris. It's almost fourteen years since the end of the war. Sometimes it makes her dizzy, the way time rushes on and leaves you standing.

'Iris! Iris!'

'She's off in a dream.'

'Wake up, Iris. Are you coming tomorrow night, or not?'

She blinks, and looks around at the girls. 'Coming where?'

'Coming up west with us tomorrow night.'

'Oh … I don't know—'

'Do come, Iris,' pleads Grace. 'Mother's so strict, but she won't mind me going if you're there.'

Iris is a married woman, and therefore able to throw a cloak of respectability over almost any outing. 'Strict' is one way of describing Mrs Butterfield, thinks Iris, who has been invited home to tea with Grace in Clapham. A more observant – or less cowed – person than Grace would see a harridan with an evil imagination who persecutes her daughter.

'I don't know why you let her get away with it, Grace,' says Pansy, who looks delicate but is the most fearsomely self-willed girl Iris has ever met. 'Ask her if she knows there's a war on. Tell her they've put you on the evening shift. Watch out, girls, here comes the Stoat.'

'I'll come,' says Iris quickly. 'I'd like to.'

The Stoat – Miss Stote – is their supervisor. In a flash they are back at their desks and the rhythmic pounding of typewriters fills the room. Iris has never spent so much time with other women. Her marriage and brief life with Edward have fallen away, as if into the bottom of a well. She can peer down and see them shine but she can't get at them. She's earning good money, though. The two rooms where she and Edward set up home together are bright with bits of china she's picked up from market stalls, and pretty cushions. She keeps it all ready, as if he might walk in any moment.

His last leave was awful. She meant it to be perfect, but it was such a shock, somehow, to see him thickened and brown in the face and restless as she'd never known him. They only came back to themselves when they went walking, late into the velvety summer nights, not talking, just arm in arm, stopping at a coffee-stall and then walking on again as if they could get to a place where there wasn't a war. He was all right, he said. He didn't want to talk about it much. They did talk, though, one night, about what Iris would do if he got killed. That was typical of Edward. Very serious, very responsible, old for his age. He'd always been like that. He'd made his will and it was in the top right-hand drawer of the big chest of drawers in their bedroom. He wished there was more to leave her. If there was a baby—

'Don't talk like that!'

'Don't you want a baby? I do.'

He'd never have said a thing like that before. He'd have been too shy, even with her.

'It's not that. It's you talking about leaving things. I don't want things left to me. I want—' But she stopped herself. She wasn't going to be weak and say, 'I want you to come back,' and make him think that she had any doubt of it. His neck was brown and roughened, and his face and forearms too. His hands were calloused. He undressed and there was a line where the weather-beaten colour ended. Beyond it, his skin was white and fine-grained. She pressed her face into the silky skin of his shoulder, and felt the new muscle under it.

'Of course I want a baby,' she murmured.

But it didn't happen. His leave ended; he went back. A week passed, and another, and then it was clear that there wasn't going to be a baby. She couldn't write a thing like that in a letter, though, especially with his letters being censored. They should have made up a code, like one of the girls at work had done with her best boy before he was sent out, but Iris and Edward didn't think of it.

Iris gets out her best silver dress, made last winter and only worn twice, her silk stockings and best cami and lays them on the bed. She can't help feeling there's something wrong in wearing the silver dress without Edward when Edward might— No. Don't think of that. Edward said: 'Make sure you don't stick in here, Irie, night after night.' And the girls at work are the only people she knows in London, apart from Edward's parents and his awful sister.

Pansy has got tickets for the show at the Royal Fortune, where Iris has never been before. It's near the Lyceum, apparently. They all paid into a kitty and they're going to have an early supper at the Corner House first. Her good coat will be warm on top. She strokes the fabric of her silver dress. It fits like a glove again, now that she's altered it. She lost weight when Edward went out.

The thing Iris likes best about the show is the costumes. They are wonderful. She'd like to look at them close up, to see how the designers manage to make them fit so well and yet the girls who wear them can dance as free as if they were in the altogether. In one number, all the girls have plumes of ostrich feathers attached to diamanté bands in their hair. Iris costs them in her head. She'd choose a slightly different shade of blue for the satin of their bodices, though. Even under the lights, the colour is harsh against the girls' skin.

'Come on, Iris! It's the interval. We're all going out.'

Iris smiles and shrugs on her coat, but leaves it open, so that the gleam of her dress shows.

'Aren't the costumes lovely?' she says to Joan.

'You'd need to have a figure like yours, or Pansy's,' says Joan, rather mournfully. She is heavy-set, and doesn't help herself by wearing pink. Her dress is too tight, straining across her hips. She needs to offset her colouring. A dark, misty green and some clever cutting would do wonders for her. Although, with her figure, she'd look better in something tailored ...

'I'd love to make a dress for you, Joan,' Iris says.

'Oh – Iris!' For Iris's clothes are the envy of the office. 'Would you really? But wouldn't it be awfully expensive?'

'I can get the stuff for you cheap. There's a place I know. I'd like to, Joan, really.'

Joan stumbles over the end of the row of seats, blushing with pleasure. I ought to have thought of it before, thinks Iris.

The streets are packed. The Lyceum's just out for the interval, too. Crowds swirl around the stalls that sell roast chestnuts, chocolates, coconut ice. Grace has gone to the cloakroom. Suddenly Pansy grabs at Iris's arm, almost pulling her over. 'My heel!'

Both girls examine the shoe. The heel has come away from the sole, but cleanly.

'You can get that repaired.'

'It'll mean a bloody taxi.'

'Pansy!' exclaims Joan. 'It's not your heel that's gone. I'll tell you what, girls, I'll get us all some chocolates.'

Joan plunges across the road to queue at a stall. The crowds swallow her. So many people – it must be all the shows having their interval at the same time. If Grace comes out, how's she going to find them?

Something changes. Iris can never remember quite what she noticed first. A thick thrum in the air, like a train coming down the line. A stillness. Sweep and ripple through the crowd as one head tips back and then the next. A taxi squeals to a stop and the driver jumps out and runs down an alley.

'Oh my good Christ,' says Pansy, and her face is a white disc, turned to the dark sky.

Except it's not dark. Something vast and rimmed by light swims over the gap between the buildings. It looks like a cigar. A silver cigar, filling up the black sky.

The air packs itself together and slams at Iris. She is on the ground. There's a stink of smoke and a shrieking noise by her ear like a kettle that no one has pulled off the hob.

Slowly she moves bits of herself. A hand. Her legs. The smoke panics her. She has got to get up out of this. She watches herself shake as if she were someone else.

Up you get, Iris. She stands. She can't see Pansy anywhere, or any of the girls. No, there's Pansy sitting on the pavement, her mouth square like a baby's, screaming. But that's not the kettle noise. The shrieking comes from somewhere else. She looks around. Someone must have picked her up and put her down in a different street. The buildings are all wrong. She turns. There's the Lyceum. People are running and screaming now, like Pansy. But over there, where the stalls were, no one's running. There are heaps on the pavement. Bits of building fallen down. Everything trembles as if it's going to fall, or perhaps it's her, shaking.

Iris picks her way over the rubble. A man tries to get hold of her but she pushes past him. Her coat has gone. Her dress is ripped down the front. I must look a sight, she thinks. Lights flare, and Iris picks her way.

Someone is mouthing at her. She can't hear the words, and she takes no notice. It has gone very quiet. Something's lying on the ground in front of her, half hidden by bits of building. At first Iris thinks it's a dummy out of a shop window, then she sees it's a person. It hasn't got any clothes on, but then she sees rags of pink over the jammy-wet flesh. She doesn't dare look any closer. Nothing moves. Slowly she gets down on her knees and starts to pick at the rubble.

*

The excitement of the *Graf Zeppelin* friendly visit is over, and Iris slips out of the crowd. She won't catch the tram home; she'll walk. It will do her good. She shouldn't have come down here. Why ever did she think she wanted to see a Zeppelin again? It was a stupid idea, not like her. What was in her head? Laying a ghost, or some such rubbish. Lucky that Sarah and the boys didn't come down. It wouldn't do for them to see Auntie Iris in such a state.

She's lucky. She should count her blessings. Living with Sarah and Ray ... They're as good as gold to her and, besides, they need her. She pays a third of the rent, and her keep. She has the two attic rooms, one for her dressmaking, the other as a bedroom. The boys are seven and nine, and Iris loves them more than she ever thought she'd love anyone, after Edward. She's making good money, and she saves regularly for them, into a Post Office account they'll have when they're twenty-one. Sometimes she gives herself a treat and imagines their faces when they see how much it has added up to over the years.

But who would have thought of the Germans sending over a Zeppelin in broad daylight, and that everyone would clap and cheer? Sarah was only fifteen when the war ended, thank God, and Ray a year older. They were courting then, and they stayed together. Iris doesn't think they've ever been separated for as much as a night.

She used to be so jealous of Edward, for being dead. She used to wish it had been her. But these last few years, when she looks at his photograph, he is so young. She thinks about everything he's missed. He isn't smiling in the photograph. He was like that: serious, responsible. He wanted her to have a baby. He never knew Sarah's boys.

It's over, she tells herself. The boys weren't born or thought of then. The war means nothing to them: it's something that's past, and photographs of people they've never met. But that's good, isn't it? It means they're living in a better world. Thinking, walking, Iris calms herself. By the time she reaches Whiteladies Road, her hands have quite stopped shaking.

DANCERS' FEET

❧

At last the ferry swung out into midstream, churning the grey-brown water. It couldn't go at full speed yet; he knew that. They still had the pilot on board to steer them through the shifting sand and mudbanks of the Thames estuary. He wondered if he could ask one of the crew about where the pilot would be dropped, but perhaps they would think it was a stupid question. He would just wait up on deck, and watch.

Tilbury was well behind them now. Across the river, in the dirty haze of a late-summer afternoon, that must be Gravesend. He knew they had to pass Canvey Island, and the Isle of Grain, where the Medway joins the surge of the Thames. But by then they would be more or less at sea, and already turning north. He might not even see Foulness Island and its point.

He ran over the names in his mind. He never went on a journey without studying the map first, noting every name. These were the kind of facts he liked, hard-headed but somehow adventurous too. They would pass Shoeburyness. 'Ness' meant 'nose'; he knew that from school geography, when they'd studied the Vikings. He'd always liked the Vikings, with their long, plaited hair, beaked ships and fearsome legends. Now he was heading north, to the land that the Vikings had left behind.

But it had to be said that, to judge from her photograph, his Aunt Karolina looked nothing like a Viking. Prim and plump, she stared out at Robert as if she were already having second thoughts about him as a tutor for her sons. Only a certain broadness of shoulder suggested that Aunt Karolina might be able to row a longship.

She wasn't really his aunt, anyway, but his mother's cousin. Which made Lars and Erik ... but no, he couldn't be bothered to work out what that made them. The important thing about Lars and Erik was that they needed to learn English, and he wanted – well, not exactly to teach it to them, of course, but to go to Sweden. To travel. To get away. He was fed up to the back teeth with people droning on about how they used to travel 'before the war', and how wonderful Paris had been, or Rome or Berlin – all these places which he knew only from reports of battles on the six o'clock news. He had done nothing and gone nowhere.

His grip tightened on the railing. He'd expected a breeze, now that they were away from land, but the air was as hot and heavy as ever. The journey across London had been the worst part: Paddington to Liverpool Street on the Circle Line, with his palms sweating so much that the handle of his case slipped. He kept checking the names of the stations on the Tube map. He wished he knew London properly. If it hadn't been for the war, he would have been a Londoner. Instead, from the age of eight, he had been stuck in Devizes.

He could still smell the Tube train. It had stopped for so long between Baker Street and Great Portland Street that he'd been sure he would miss the Tilbury train. Someone broke the thick silence of the carriage to say that the heat had probably made the rails expand. Grumbling, disgusted agreement rippled through the passengers. But it had been all right in the end. He was safe on board, with his tickets, his passport, his English money and his Swedish money. He'd already stowed his case full of winter clothes in the cabin which he was to share with three other people.

'It'll be autumn up there already,' everyone had told him when he was packing. His Aunt Karolina lived two hundred miles north of Stockholm. He had to remember, his mother said, that her house would be quite different from English homes. No open fires; they had stoves in Sweden. His mother looked as if she wasn't sure that he would be able to cope with stoves. Mothers never really believe that you can do anything, he thought.

The boat pushed on slowly, feeling its way into the deep channel. They weren't out of the estuary yet, but even so, land was getting farther away. England was going away from him. He would stay up on deck until the last trace of it vanished, and then he'd go below and get something to eat. If there was anything left by then.

Something blurred in the corner of his vision, like a fist coming at him. He flinched, then quickly turned towards his attacker. A bare, pointed foot shot at him, and then away. A fraction of a second later he made sense of it. A girl was standing, holding the rail with both hands, balancing very upright as she thrust her legs out in turn, at right angles to her body. Her head was poised in a way which struck him as unnatural. She was looking straight ahead, as if she didn't know that she had almost kicked him in the eye.

'I say, steady on,' he muttered to himself derisively. Aloud, he said, 'Your legs are quite long, you know.'

'Then move out of the way,' she answered smartly, without looking at him. 'I've got to practise.'

'Practise?'

'I'm a dancer,' she explained, flashing a glance at him which immediately convinced him that it was not true. She was younger than him, he thought. About sixteen.

'You must get very hot, doing that in this weather,' he observed.

'Dancers have to suffer for their art,' she replied grandly, shooting out her right leg. Suddenly she stopped, bent down and rubbed her calf vigorously through the folds of her skirt. He had never seen a girl wearing a skirt as long and full as hers. It was nipped in at the waist and it sprang out as if she had a dozen petticoats under it.

'Cramp,' the girl explained, making a face.

'You ought to drink a glass of water with half a teaspoon of salt in it,' said Robert. 'That's what we do if we get cramp after a match. Replacing the salt, you know, because of all the sweat.'

She looked indignant. She probably didn't like him talking about sweat like that. 'It'll be all right in a minute,' she said in a distant voice. 'I'm used to it. Sometimes, after a long rehearsal—'

In one corner of his mind he was aware that the boat had lost speed again. It was barely moving. At this rate it would never get out of the estuary. The sun looked brassier than ever, and there was a heavy heap of livid cloud at the eastern horizon.

'There's going to be a storm,' he said.

A flicker of alarm crossed her face. 'I love storms,' she said immediately.

'Do you? I don't. I was nearly struck in one once, after a cricket match. You could smell the sulphur.'

'Sulphur!'

'Yes. Like the devil. We all smelled it. We ran like hell.'

'For the pavilion?' she asked, as if proud that she knew the right word.

He nodded, even though they'd run all the way into the school building, not trusting anywhere less solid.

'What's your name?'

'Robert Oldland. What's yours?'

'Sophie. Sophie … Delacour.'

She was lying again, he could tell. 'Are you French then?' he asked.

'No. Not exactly. It's a stage name. Most dancers have them, you know.'

The ferry swung slowly to the left: port, he remembered. The engines made a juddering sound, as if someone were trying to put on the brakes. He saw a cluster of people on the other side of the deck, looking down over the railings. He wanted to see, too, but he didn't want to leave Sophie, who showed no sign of moving.

'I wonder what's happened?'

'It won't be anything,' she said indifferently.

The engines grated, changing gear. The ferry shuddered, rattled, then began to move forward. The shoreline looked a long way off now, he thought. He wouldn't be able to swim that far, even if the oily, swirling water would let him.

'Have you done this journey before?' he asked her.

'Yes, but I don't remember. I was only little. I was as sick as a dog,' she said, with a sudden wide, gleaming smile.

'I'm travelling on my own,' he said. It felt like the greatest of intimacies, as if this were the most important thing about him.

'So am I,' she said instantly. She put out a slim brown foot, examined it, flexed it. He hoped she was not going to start kicking again.

'Where are you going?' he asked.

'I've got an engagement in Stockholm.'

'A dancing engagement?'

She nodded. He looked at her smooth, polished hair, her fine-grained golden skin. She might be a dancer.

'It'll be so cold there,' she went on. 'Ugh. I wish it could be summer forever.'

'I like the autumn,' he said.

'I can't see how anyone could like autumn. All you've got to look forward to is winter.'

He thought of the street he walked home along, and the smell of burning leaves from gardens. Some houses would have their lights on already, but the curtains wouldn't be closed yet. In every house it seemed there was a girl practising piano, with her back to the window.

The shore was vanishing in a pelt of cloud. The sky was growing dark with the coming storm. A woman behind him said, 'Did you see them drop the pilot?'

He had missed it. Other people had seen it and he had not.

'Ugh, it's starting to roll,' said Sophie.

She was right. The ferry tilted, long and slow and inevitable.

'I shall be sick,' said Sophie, clinging to the rail as it rushed back towards her.

'It's only because we're coming out to sea.'

'So *you* say.' Her mouth curved scornfully at him.

'Look,' he said, to punish her, 'lightning. Over there.' He pointed, and just then another thin seam of lightning split clouds which were suddenly much closer. 'We'd hear the thunder if the engines weren't making so much noise.'

'I hate thunder,' she said under her breath. 'It sounds like the ack-ack.' He glanced at her, surprised.

'Weren't you evacuated?'

'No.'

He was as sure that this was true as he'd been sure she was lying before. Another fork of lightning ran through the clouds, like a finger exploring them for weaknesses. This time he heard the thunder in spite of the engines.

'How far away is it?' asked Sophie.

'About six miles.'

The wind had got up. Some of the hair had blown out of the polished knot at the nape of her neck. People were leaving the deck now, walking carefully as the ferry rolled. A few big spots of rain hit the planks, and then no more. Lightning danced in one corner of the sky, and then another. Thunder growled. Suddenly the surface of the water was pulled up into points of foam. Sophie lurched, and Robert grabbed her arm. A nice mess they would be in if she broke a leg. Or even slid under the railings—

'For heaven's sake, hold on to the rail.'

'You're not supposed to touch metal things in a storm.' Her voice was cross but her panicky eyes made him soften.

'It doesn't count on a boat.' He was pretty sure of that. 'There's nowhere for it to earth, is there?'

Suddenly the warm, suffocating air fell away from them. The wind whipped Sophie's skirt around her legs. The thunder banged – really banged, this time – and then the sky emptied on them. The rain stung as if there were pieces of hail in it, and it was cold. Winter had come in a minute. Sophie's face was running with water. Robert's clothes clung to him. He gripped the rail with one hand as it slipped under his fingers, braced his legs apart to steady himself and grabbed Sophie as she waltzed past him down the streaming deck. Her body slammed into his and then away, but he had hold of her and he yanked her round so that she almost fell against him. He gripped her firmly.

'Hold the rail, Sophie! You're going to get hurt.'

Rain sluiced around them, hissing. They were the only ones left up on deck. He thought that the next time the ferry rolled to its left they could make a dash for the door. Then there'd be the business of getting the door open – it had been heavy, he remembered …

He had his arm tight around Sophie. He could feel her narrow waist inside the skirt. Now the boat was pitching up and down as it hit lumps of water head-on. At the same time it kept on rolling from side to side, tilting farther every time.

'We've got to go below,' he shouted in her ear. 'It's not safe up here.' She didn't seem so frightened now. Even her eyelashes were wet with rain, stuck together in clumps. His shirt was so wet it felt like having nothing on, and he was freezing cold and hot with excitement at the same time. He wondered if it was the same for her.

'I want to stay here. I hate being shut up inside when things are banging outside,' she cried.

All right, if that was how she felt then he would stay too. He braced himself more firmly, holding the deck, holding the rail, holding Sophie. No storm was going to peel them away.

There was a shrieking noise behind them, like a gull. He looked over Sophie's shoulder and saw that the deck door was open. Someone was holding it, battling with the wind and shouting a name. A woman in a long, horrible raincoat, with a man bulking behind her. 'Joan! Joe-wown! *Joan! Joe-wown!*'

Sophie's face become expressionless, smooth as wood. Drops continued to pour over her cheeks. If he'd had a cloak he would have pulled it over her head to hide her.

'It's them. I've got to go,' she said in a small voice. He felt her take a deep breath.

'Be careful. You haven't got any shoes on,' he said, feeling stupid as soon as the words were out of his mouth. But then he saw that it was the right thing to say. She was suddenly restored, adventuring again in the quick gleam of her smile.

'Dancers' feet are tough,' she said. 'Just feel this.' She grabbed the rail tightly, and raised her right foot. Her clinging skirt fell back and he saw the pale skin inside her knee and her thigh. Her feet were brown, with small, polished pink nails. The skin of the arch was wrinkled with cold.

'Go on,' she said, 'touch.'

Behind him the voices brayed again. 'Joe-wown! *Joan! Joe-wown!*'

They sounded as if they were calling a dog. But they couldn't see him or Sophie. Not properly. She was balancing and balancing, holding out her foot to him. For all the ferry's lurching, she didn't quiver. He touched her instep. He could feel how warm she was, inside.

'I can go on pointe in bare feet,' she said. Her eyes were wide and the pupils big in them. He touched her wet, cold toes lightly. He had no idea how hard girls' feet were supposed to feel. He took a breath.

'*JOE-WOWN!*' yodelled one of the raincoats again, loud but thin, as if they knew they had already lost her.

'Good luck in Stockholm, Sophie,' he said to her. 'With your engagement, I mean.' She swung her foot down, stood upright – very upright, like a dancer, and smiled, as if a curtain had swung down on a sound of vast applause. The next instant she had slipped out of his grasp and he turned just in time to see her fly down the tilt of the deck towards the open door.

WITH SHACKLETON

❧

Athud, a squeal, a pair of hot, tight arms around her neck.

'It snowed! There's millions of snow in the garden!' Clara pulls away, rushes to the window and begins to drag at the heavy curtains.

'No, Clara, be careful! Wait a minute—' Isabel slides out of bed. And there it is, the snow lighting the dark garden, heaped on the window ledges. A blackbird flies out of the laurels, breaking loose a shower of snow. There's not a footprint on the white lawn.

Clara is silent too. How far away last winter must seem to her. It snowed then, and Stephen took her up to the Heath on the sledge. Clara was only five, muffled in scarf and woollen helmet. Isabel had even wound a shawl around Clara's legs, so the child couldn't stir.

The sledge's runners stuck in the fresh snow. Stephen tugged on the rope, the sledge broke free with a jerk, and away they went, Stephen loping ahead, the sledge bounding behind.

Isabel was wearing her new red kimono, with her coat thrown on top. There'd been no question of her going with them that day. She'd watched them out of sight, and then gone back indoors, sleepy again, yawning as she climbed the stairs. She held on to the banisters. Stephen was always telling her to take more care. He liked to think of her as impulsive, skimming over the surface of life. Perhaps it's the things we believe about people that make up their charm for us, thinks Isabel. What if Stephen knew the heavy knot of fears that lay coiled inside her?

She'd dormoused by her bedroom fire all morning. Such delicious, luxurious, justified sleepiness. Mrs Elton had brought up her cocoa at eleven. Isabel loathed cocoa as a rule, but all through that winter she craved it. Thick, delicious cocoa, made with the top of the milk. Usually Isabel was embarrassed to be found on her little bedroom sofa, doing nothing. But it was all right on that particular day, and on all those days last winter. Mrs Elton put the cocoa down and announced, 'There's a good half-pint of best morning milk in there. And a boy's just this minute come to clear the steps. I'll put some ashes down once he's done, and then you'll be safe to go out. It looks as if this freeze is going to hold.'

'Wonderful cocoa,' Isabel breathed, not because she felt she had to, but because it was true.

'There's nothing like milk to build good bones,' said Mrs Elton, folding her arms and looking down at Isabel as if Isabel belonged to her. And they were off. They couldn't help it. The irresistible topic swam into view – as if it were ever out of view! – and in they plunged after it.

Isabel had bathed in approval, day after day. She could lie on that sofa for the entire nine months if she felt like it, and there wouldn't be a murmur. Not even from that she-elephant, Stephen's mother. Isabel had done what was wanted of her. Her mother-in-law had 'spoken her mind quite openly', once Clara turned four. Stephen had always wanted a large family. The Kendalls ran to large families. And naturally Stephen wanted a son to bear his name. Any man would. The fact that he didn't talk about it meant absolutely nothing. Stephen was far too considerate, but Josephine believed in frankness.

'In fact,' said Josephine Kendall, 'I don't really regard it as a family, if there is only one child.'

A stain of red touched Isabel's cheeks. Not a family! Perhaps one day a manhole would be left uncovered, and Josephine Kendall would step on to nothing with her usual splendid self-assurance and plunge fathoms deep into the sewers of London.

But at the same time Isabel could not help longing for her mother-in-law's approval. She knew it was weak, the kind of self-betrayal that made her twist angrily in her bed at night. If she'd had someone of her own, it might have been different. Isabel's mother was dead.

And do you know, my dear, she hasn't even managed to keep her own mother alive ... Isabel could just imagine those words, uttered in the trumpeting half-whisper that her mother-in-law employed with the little crowd of evil-minded old monuments who were her intimate friends. Old monuments all of them, old she-elephants trampling and trumpeting and blundering their way through the jungle of north London. And Josephine Kendall, with her hanging flaps of jowl and her massive ankles, was the oldest, most obstinate and deadly elephant of them all.

Isabel had no one of her own, except for Stephen, and now Clara. Her father lived in Brussels – 'A most peculiar place to choose, and nobody knows quite what he lives on,' trumpeted the elephants – and as for her brother, none of the Kendalls counted him.

But Stephen counts Rod, thinks Isabel quickly. Stephen likes Rod.

Clara breaks away from the snowy window, and begins to stamp up and down the bedroom carpet, her face pale with excitement. 'Can we go out now? Can we go out now this minute?'

Isabel takes a deep breath. 'Yes,' she says.

Clara swings round and stares at her mother sternly, searching her face. Isabel knows what she's waiting for: the usual adult excuses, qualifications: *After you've had your breakfast, when we've tidied up all the toys, when your cold's better* ...

'Yes,' she repeats, 'now, this minute. We'll just throw on our clothes, and go.'

Clara's face creases with delight. 'Throw on our clothes!' she cackles.

Isabel catches the excitement. She'll do just exactly that. No bath, no brushing and twisting and pinning of her hair, no patting cream into her skin. Why she keeps on with it all anyway, God knows, since Stephen's not here. And won't be for—

Don't think of that. She crams on an old tweed skirt, a woollen jumper, her thickest stockings.

'Now let's get you ready. But hush, we don't want to wake Louie.'

They creep into the nursery. Louie, the nurse, is still asleep in the adjoining room. She should be up by now. But what is Louie, after all? Just about seventeen, and still growing, judging from the way her wrists poke out her sleeves. How Isabel used to sleep when she was seventeen, as if sleep were food.

Clara is utterly silent as Isabel fishes in the chest of drawers, finding knitted leggings, woollen skirt and jersey. Clara's outdoor things are downstairs: good.

'Aren't you going to wash me?' whispers Clara hoarsely.

'Not this morning. Ssh.'

'You go to hell if you don't wash.' Clara doesn't sound troubled by the prospect, but all the same Isabel whispers back:

'That's nonsense. All that happens if you don't wash is that you smell like an old cheese.'

Clara convulses with silent laughter. Isabel grabs the clothes, lifts Clara and hurries downstairs.

'You don't have to carry me, I'm not a baby,' Clara hisses in her ear, drumming hard little heels on Isabel's hips.

The sledge, Isabel knows, is hanging on a nail in the garden shed. She tells Clara to wait at the door, and sets off across the snowy waste of the lawn. The light is so strong that she blinks.

'Here we are, Clara, you sit down here, and I'll pull you with the rope.'

'And then I'll pull you, Mummy.'

'I'm too heavy for you.'

But the truth is that she has lost weight, pounds and pounds of it. She is thin now. Her old tweed skirt sags at the waist, and her face is pinched.

'Poor Isabel, she's lost her bloom,' she heard the elephants say one day as they popped little egg-and-cress triangles into their mouths with their trunks. All the great grey ears flapped in agreement.

Isabel begins to drag the sledge uphill. It is surprisingly heavy. She turns around, but of course there is only Clara on the sledge. How could there be anyone else?

Josephine Kendall believes that it is high time Isabel pulled herself together. After all, everyone has had a miscarriage. Why, she herself …! Even a late miscarriage, although of course not very nice, is something that you must not allow yourself to dwell on. You simply have to pick yourself up and try again.

The other elephants nodded, although perhaps a shade less certainly than before.

The pavement has already been trodden. Milkmen and postmen and bakers' boys have been out already, she supposes. Her breath steams. A woman in a grey wrapper is scattering ash on the steps of a raw brick house that seems too tall for itself.

'Clara, can you get off and walk this bit?'

Clara looks sternly at her mother. 'Daddy pulled me all the way up this hill.'

So she does remember.

'Is Daddy pulling a sledge now?'

'No. You remember, I told you. Their sledges are much bigger than this, and they are pulled by dogs.'

'Dogs like Bella?'

'Bella's far too small. Remember what Daddy told you about the dogs?'

A frown almost settles on Clara's face. 'I don't remember what he said. I don't even remember what his face looks like.'

'You do, Clara. Just close your eyes and you'll see it.'

'No,' says Clara, shaking her head like a judge, 'I don't not even remember what his tongue looks like. I'm afraid it's gone,' she adds. The sound of one of Josephine's favourite phrases on her daughter's lips makes Isabel want to slap Clara. False self-deprecation followed by deadly insult: how typical of Josephine it was. *I know I ought to remember your name, but I'm afraid it's gone.*

'They are called husky dogs,' she says levelly. 'And stop kicking snow into your boots, Clara.'

She takes Clara's hand and they walk on, the sledge dragging behind them. *Close your eyes and you'll see it*. But no, she realises, it's not as easy as that. She can capture the back of Stephen's head perfectly, but his face is turned away. She gives Clara's hand a little squeeze. 'Sorry I was cross, Clarrie.'

But Clara answers out of quite a different train of thought. 'Are they biting dogs, where Daddy is?'

'No. They don't bite people. Only their food.'

'What is their food?'

'Oh – meat.'

'Is that Daddy's food too?'

'Yes, but he has other things as well.'

'What other things?'

'Things out of tins, and biscuits.'

'And things from the Stores.'

'There isn't any Stores there. You remember the pictures we showed you.'

'Actually they are building a Stores where Daddy is,' says Clara casually. 'I saw it in the newspaper. Anyway, my feet are cold.'

'Come here, let me rub them.'

She pulls Clara's right foot out of its boot and brushes off the snow. Her leggings are not too damp. Isabel takes off her own gloves and chafes the foot with her bare hands.

'Are you really cold, Clara? Do you want to go home?'

'We haven't even gone down a hill yet!' Tears of exasperation jump to Clara's eyes.

'All right, sit on the sledge again, and I'm going to wrap my big scarf round your feet, like this.'

As for where Stephen is, she's not even going to think about it. Josephine had been bursting with it when the invitation came, her trunk pointing to heaven as she trumpeted the news around her circle. Stephen, Isabel's gentle, funny, thoughtful Stephen, was going off to some unimaginable wasteland of howling winds and blistering cold, to spend weeks and weeks struggling to reach a place that wasn't even a place at all. Just a point on the compass. Josephine could scarcely have been more thrilled if she'd managed to send Stephen into battle.

'A most remarkable opportunity. He simply leaped at it. The Society …'

How many Stephens were there? There was her Stephen, so close that she couldn't describe him. Gentle, funny, thoughtful: yes, he was all those things, sometimes more, sometimes less, but they weren't really what he was. She could not add up Stephen in words. The closer people came, perhaps the less they saw each other. Like bringing something so close to your eyes that it went out of focus.

But Josephine's Stephen was quite another matter.

'I feel I must give you a word of warning, Isabel dear, at such a very exciting time for us all. You do realise that it can cause great trouble in a marriage if a man is not allowed to pursue his career because of all sorts of fearfulness and tearfulness – and of course to be invited to take part was the most extraordinary honour, although naturally no more than we know Stephen deserves. I happen to know that Archie Cannington himself recommended Stephen most highly. You know who I'm talking about, Isabel dear? I only speak to you like this because your own mother—'

'Not allowed?'

'Come, Isabel, you know what I mean. A man must feel that his wife is behind him.'

Maybe that's why I can only see the back of his head, thinks Isabel now, because I am behind him.

At last, at last she has dragged Clara up to the top of the hill. Her heart thumps, and she is sweating. She must get strong again, she must. She will drink a glass of milk every morning if it chokes her, and eat second helps of everything, as Rod used to say. When summer comes, she'll go down to Eastbourne for sea-bathing. She glances behind her. Clara is sitting tight on the sledge, her mittened hands gripping its sides. She beams at her mother. There is not the smallest cloud of doubt in the sky of Clara's face.

And now they are up there, on top. The white vista spreads. There's the city, smoking in the cold, remote and intricate as a jewel. Ants of people toil up the slopes with sledges and tin trays.

But would he still have gone if the baby had been born? His little boy, seven months old by now, bundled in shawls and peeping at a white world for the first time. Isabel would not have failed, and Stephen would have shut the door on his adventure. He'd have done it reluctantly – she had to admit that – but he would have done so. Even the most fearsome rampages and trumpeting of all the she-elephants in north London could not have influenced him.

'Mummy! Mummy! I want to slide down the hill.'

Suddenly the hill looks very steep. Has she come to the right part of the Heath? Is this the place where Stephen brought Clara? Perhaps it isn't safe. If they run over a bump and Clara is thrown off and she strikes her head against a stone concealed by the snow—

'Mummy! I'm getting cold again.'

'All right. Hold tight to the rope now, Clara, while I get on.'

Isabel places the child between her legs, tucking up the folds of her skirt. The runners of the sledge fidget on the snow. The sledge wants to trick her by sliding forward slowly, inch by inch until it's got the momentum it wants and it can swoosh forward, catching her off-balance so she loses hold of the rope and then—

But it's not going to happen, not until she's ready. She digs her heels in, takes the rope from Clara and then eases the sledge forward, under control. They are at the lip of the hill.

'Hold tight, Clara.'

Clara grips her mother's knees. Isabel shoves off. The sledge sticks. She pushes harder and suddenly the sledge shoots forward, over the edge. She gasps as the cold air flies past her. A bump in the ground jolts the sledge and then they are gathering speed, hissing down the fresh, clean icy snow with the rope taut in Isabel's hands. And for a moment Isabel is superb, steering them masterfully to the left of a bush while Clara screams with pleasure.

The slope slackens. The sledge runs out, losing speed, and comes to rest in a deep, unsullied patch of snow. Isabel clambers off.

'I didn't remember it was like that,' says Clara. Her cheeks flare like poppies. 'Is that what Daddy's doing?'

'You mean now this minute?'

'Yes.'

Those cliffs and lakes of ice, those deep crevasses shining blue, those winds so cold they burn like fire. Is that where Stephen is? She can't get close to him. She can't hear what he is saying, or listen to his breathing. He is much too far away. Just a dot, like a baby before it's grown or born. Come back, she begs him. Come closer. But even when she manages to bring him back into focus, all he does is hammer pegs into the ground and fix twine between them, before taking careful measurements.

'I want to do it again,' says Clara. Isabel looks at her. Clara sounds so exactly like Josephine that Isabel almost expects to see her daughter swing a tender, baby trunk. But she also sounds so like Stephen that Isabel's eyes prickle.

You're sure you'll be all right, Isabel? Because if you minded dreadfully, you know, I wouldn't—

'I want to do it again. Are you listening, Mummy? I want to do it again.'

'All right, but help me pull the sledge back up the hill.'

The child takes the rope in her fist. Isabel holds it too, and they begin to haul the sledge up the steep slope. Isabel is soon out of breath.

'Let's stop a minute, Clara.'

'Are you tired?' demands Clara, her face suddenly tense. She shouldn't look like that, thinks Isabel.

'No,' she replies, 'not tired a bit. We'll get our breath, and then we'll go on up.'

Clara searches her mother's face with bright, suspicious eyes. She doesn't trust me, thinks Isabel. She doesn't think I'm strong enough. I've cried in front of her. Weak, oozing tears that slipped out, hour after hour. Clara had stared, then put on a bright blank face and run off to find Louie.

What does Clara think about Stephen being gone? What does she really think? The elephants have told her how proud she must be. Isabel has told her that Stephen thinks of Clara every night, before he goes to sleep. But they are all lying, thinks Isabel. And she herself, why, she's the greatest liar of them all. Her 'gentle, funny, thoughtful Stephen'. Why does she tell herself such stuff? Why does she want to edit Stephen so ruthlessly?

He had explained it all to her. The clothing he would wear, the instruments they were taking, the pack ice, the way the ship was designed to yield to the pressure of the ice rather than be crushed. He told her about sea leopards, whose existence she had never suspected. So many things, a jumble of them spilling out on to the carpet as he stood with one foot on the fender, his eyes alight with unshared joy.

He was pregnant with his journey. She didn't understand that then, but now she does. The journey was all folded away inside him, a life that was as real and immediate as his own heartbeat, but to everyone else just a possibility that might happen or might not happen. And if it didn't happen, well, it was not a tragedy. Pick yourself up and start all over again.

For him, it has happened. He is there. He isn't thinking of her or of Clara, she knows it in her bones. She doesn't expect him to do so. He's taking measurements, skilfully and meticulously, to make a map where previously there has not been a map. It is summer there, or what they call summer. At the end of his long day he'll lie in his sleeping bag, writing up notes.

She was happy to let them go off together that day last winter, Stephen and Clara, without her. She wasn't fearful, because she had her own baby safe inside her. Such calm is a kind of folly, she thinks now. It's self-deception.

'Don't take your mittens off, Clara.'

'My hands are sweating so much they are wet,' says Clara, with her usual severe accuracy. She has pulled off both mittens. She wriggles the fingers of her left hand, and spreads them out into the shape of a star. Impossible to believe that hand was ever part of Isabel's own body. Clara is so separate, so forceful. She seizes the rope again. 'I want to pull it.'

'All right, see if you can.'

'Don't help me, Mummy, I want to do it all on my own.' Clara starts to clamber up the steep side of the hill, hauling the sledge. She'll defy me all her life, thinks Isabel. It makes her want to laugh. And if the baby – yes, you're going to say it this time, she tells herself – if the baby had been born, he would have defied you too.

Stephen was sorry not to have his son. He'd looked at her with his eyes wide, bright, blank. 'I'm awfully sorry, Is.' Sorry for her, he meant. And she'd taken it as no more than her due.

There's that small dot again, far away in the wasteland of snow. He's bending over something, concentrated. She can't see his face, but she knows it will be taxed with thought. He has got to get this right. In the glassy, untrodden waste there is not so much as a single elephant's footprint to distract him.

'Look at me! Look at me, Mummy! I'm right up at the top of the world.'

And so she is. 'That's wonderful, Clara!'

But Clara scorns her mother's hyperbole. 'Watch out!' she trumpets. 'I'm coming down!'

'Wait, Clara, not on your own—'

The next minute Isabel has to leap aside as the sledge, propelled by a flushed and shrieking Clara, hurtles towards her. It careers on and overturns, depositing Clara in the snow. Clara gets to her feet in silence.

'Are you all right?'

'I meant that to happen,' says Clara. 'I want to go again.'

Back up the hill. Suddenly Stephen is close. He's stopped for a breather; he's wiping his face and peering in her direction. But perhaps he doesn't even know that she is there. She won't distract him. With that sort of close, meticulous work, one slip can lose you hours.

When I was having Clara, she remembers, I didn't want Stephen in the room.

But all the same, almost in spite of herself, her hand creeps up. She gives a small, tentative wave. Does he see her, or not see her? It doesn't matter.

I can't tell you, Is, what a feeling there is among the men.

No, she thought. You can't tell me. She shrank from his euphoria as if it were a flame that might burn her. He was so considerate, too. He left behind a thick packet of directions, to be opened 'in the eventuality of my death'. And he told the she-elephant of the packet's existence, but not Isabel. Josephine could not resist one fatal hint, and Isabel was on to it like a tiger.

They saw Isabel at last, those elephants of north London.

Here they are again, at the top of the hill. Here is Clara, taking the rope. Isabel holds the sledge, steadying it.

'Ready, Clara?'

She pushes the sledge and it reaches the lip of the hill. It hesitates, then glides forward, gathering speed.

There is her daughter, flying away from her. Stephen, from the bottom of the world, shades his eyes to see Clara fly.

AT THE INSTITUTE WITH KM

◈

I lie and bathe in the warmth of the cows. That's what I'm here for, or rather it's what the cows are here for. It's beneficial to inhale the mild steam of cows. Everything happens for a reason at the Institute. Even lying down has its purpose. I want to resist it, but I haven't the energy any more.

I lie on my couch in the hayloft. Down below, the cows shift and stir and tear the hay from the manger, and send up billows of breath. They shit as they eat, and the shit smells both sweet and acrid as it spatters down their legs and clots the hair of their tails.

The cows are beautiful. I could think about them all day long. Their movements, their long shuddery sighs, the noise of their teeth, the sensitivity of their lips, the strings of slobber that drop from their jaws. They are benign. We lie in a row and think about the benignity of cows.

I wish I'd been chosen to learn to milk, but I wasn't. I used to work in the vegetable garden. Last summer we produced more than two thousand pounds of tomatoes. Sometimes I think of those tomatoes, too, as a change from thinking about the cows. They are not quite like the tomatoes on market stalls. They are thick-skinned and warm. As the vines shrivel, the pungency of tomatoes grows until you start to imagine that they are the fruit Adam ate in Eden.

But we don't eat tomatoes very often at the Institute. No doubt there's some reason for that.

I worked hard in that vegetable garden. Even when the sun was full in the sky I didn't rest. My hoe scritch-scratched up and down the rows of onions and I watered the tomatoes evenly so that their skin wouldn't split. If my mother could have seen me, she would have rubbed her eyes.

I used to be a strong child, I know that. I wasn't always like this. I was a stout, foursquare little boy in my white embroidered smock and loose trousers. Doesn't my mother remember that? It was only later on that this filthy disease took hold of me and made me what I am now.

I'm twenty-seven, that's all. I look at myself in the mirror and I know far too much about myself. The bony skull and the big teeth that make me look as if I'm heehawing like a donkey. Why didn't my skull have the grace to stay hidden? I'm still alive. I don't want to see it.

Some days there are as many as ten of us, lying in a row in the hayloft, absorbing the shit-sweet breath of the cows. I stare up at the pictures on the ceiling. Mr de Saltzmann painted them. They are beautiful and funny and they do exactly what they are meant to do: they divert us.

It wasn't my choice to come to the Institute. It wasn't my vision. G has been very patient about this. He could tell instantly that I wasn't a disciple. It was my mother who wanted me to come, and in the end it was too much trouble to resist her. I thought G might throw me out, and even after a few days I was afraid of being thrown out. But he didn't. He said I could work, and join in the fast.

Fasting is strange. If you've never done it, you've no idea how it will make you feel. Ever since I've been ill, people have been urging me to eat. My mother most of all. She can't bear my thinness: literally can't bear it. I don't blame her. It's disgusting to be so thin. I disgust myself. I took off all my clothes and stood in front of the mirror and there I was. Collarbones like coat-hangers. Rounded shoulders and sucked-in ribs. My feet were bony and enormous. My elbows – why should anybody have such elbows? And for God's sake, my knees. I looked at it all for a long time and then I covered it up again. These days I prefer to contemplate the cows in all their fullness.

My poor mother with her little pancakes filled with cream and chocolate sauce, her nourishing soups and her sudden frenzies for the blackest, most expensive caviar or for dried reindeer tongue which has to be bought in slivers which are more expensive than gold leaf.

'In Lapland, they just heal themselves, quite simply, with berries and moss and reindeer tongue.'

I'm sure they do, my dear mother. But what I couldn't bear was the frightened, pleading look on your face as you ordered yet another dish of sweetbreads or quails' eggs or whatever it was that offered a day's hope. I turned away. I always turned away. I literally could not swallow it.

'Please, my darling, just one spoonful for me.'

She has been frightened like that, and pleading, since I came back from the war. Pleading with me not to know the things I know. Frightened that they will burst out of me in a rage that nothing will be able to extinguish. Maybe that's what everyone over the age of forty really feels. They want to silence us. To stop our mouths with food.

So I fasted. I can't tell you what a relief it was. Everything else dropped away. We began the season of fasting with enemas. It doesn't sound too pleasant, does it? But soon we were empty. Transparent. It didn't disgust me at all. Would you ever imagine that an enema could have the eloquence of a ritual?

We did eat during the fast. I can't remember the exact progression. One day there was vegetable juice, I know that. I was so purified, and I was strong. I could have

walked out into the fields and worked. You might ask
what on earth was going on? I did at first. It made me
laugh to think of us fasting. There we were, already
skeletons, gargoyles. Why add to it? But after a while –
a few days, maybe more – I began to see the point of
it. I felt stronger. I was doing to myself what even my
sickness could not do, and by my own choice. Not only
was I still alive, I was more alive than I had been for
months. Years.

G didn't say anything. Didn't even smile or look a
little satisfied. In fact the next day someone said to
me in passing, 'You're to come off the fast today.'
And I was sick with disappointment, if you can believe
it. Because I'd been so close to where I wanted to be,
so empty, so pure, having so little and needing so
little. And it wouldn't have taken much longer
for me to understand so many things. Maybe only
another two days of fasting would have brought me
to it.

I kept awake all night long during the fast. I didn't
need sleep any more, you see. I'd realised how unneces-
sary they were, all these things of the body that we
cling to and can't imagine living without. I listened to
the cows pulling the hay from the manger and then
tearing it, and chewing it slowly, for hour after hour,
sometimes shifting from one foot to another. I could
hear every hesitation in the rhythm of their feeding. I
understood that the hesitations don't break the rhythm:
no, it is the hesitations that make the rhythm.

I was so close then. If I'd reached out just a little further I would have touched what I wanted to touch.

The Englishwoman is asleep. She's not really an Englishwoman, in fact. No, it turns out that she comes from the other side of the world. Her nose has the sharp, nipped-in look that means she's going to die soon. I understand that look very well. I'm not sure yet whether she knows its significance. But very likely she does. She works hard. She likes to be outdoors. All the English here prefer to work outdoors. She speaks French, but we don't talk much, even when we're lying side by side. Sometimes I know that she's lying awake. You can always tell. But I don't say anything. I expect she prefers listening to the cows, as I do.

I've talked about fasting, but I haven't really explained about working. Sometimes I shook and sweat sprang out all over my skin and I couldn't see anything but blackness. But that's not important. When I did my work I was strong.

'Be careful. Rest. Don't try to do too much.'

Ever since I've had this filthy disease, that is what they've been telling me. Go south in the winter, go up into the mountains, take your temperature night and morning and maybe four times in between, swallow this medicine and that medicine, pay over fat coins to fat doctors (my mother paid so many coins, I can't begin to count what she paid), take a raw egg beaten up in milk night and morning, weigh yourself before eating or weigh yourself after eating. Your life is so precious suddenly. Isn't it comical? After those years of trying to kill us, now they want us alive.

Avoid stimulation and over-excitement. An absolutely regular life, fresh air, plenty of sleep. And of course give up any thought, my dear boy, of ever marrying.

Here at the Institute, I do too much. I work until I drop. Sometimes I really have dropped, out there in the fields, in the hot August sun. And I can tell you that when you drop it isn't the end of everything. There you are, flat on your face among the stalks and roots. Slowly the blackness parts and the ringing in your head stops. You notice some little insects scrabbling at the base of the stalks. There's a noise of crickets. You've dropped, but everything's still going on and your body fits against the earth as if it's been made to lie there.

After a long time I got up and found my hoe where it had fallen. I picked it up and drove it into the earth again. The sun was hot on my back. I'd worked until I'd fallen, and then I'd got up and now I would work again. I imagined G watching me. Of course he knew nothing about it, but that was what I liked to imagine. That he was watching, and perhaps approving. That he might find something harmonious in my fall.

One of the cows isn't happy. Her udder is too full. If I knew how to milk, I'd clamber down the ladder from this hayloft, and sit on a stool at her side, and ease her pain. It looks so easy when you see somebody else milking a cow. You almost imagine that you know how to do it yourself.

The Englishwoman stirs, and turns towards me. Her face is still asleep. I shouldn't call her the Englishwoman. I know her name perfectly well.

'You're jealous, that's what it is.' How well I can hear my mother saying that. 'You're just jealous. Jealousy is an ugly emotion. It even makes you look ugly. Go on, go and look in the mirror and see if I'm right or not.'

It's true that I was a jealous child. Always wanting too much of something and spitting with rage when I didn't get it. I would lie on the ground and beat the floor with my strong boots because my sister was praised more than I was.

I'm jealous because the Englishwoman is going to die before me. She's farther on the road, she has fasted more resolutely and worked herself into the ground more obediently. She's got rid of everything, you can tell that. Even her husband. She has a husband, but she's rubbed him off like the husk on an ear of corn. G likes her. She's one of his favourites, anyone can see it, even if she seems quite unimpressed by it.

She hasn't really noticed me. Why should she? We're just lying side by side, listening to the cows, and she's asleep. So worn out and so weary and so close to death that anyone but me would feel pity for her. I don't feel any pity. She is closer to it than I am, almost within touching distance. She has stopped clinging to life, although perhaps she doesn't yet know it. How I envy her, because in spite of everything I've said, I am still clinging like a sick monkey who doesn't know how to let go. When my temperature goes up I can scarcely breathe for panic. I calm myself with the thought that it's natural to run a little fever after dark. I keep imagining that I'm putting on weight. Sometimes I'm even weak enough to say to someone else, 'Don't you think these trousers are getting a little tight for me?' and then they have to hide their look of pity and astonishment as they murmur, 'No, no, the trousers are fine, they're a perfect fit.' The trousers are hanging off me, of course.

G told me once that it was purely a fault of the organism, that it couldn't recognise its own death. He looked at me, not with pity, but as if waiting for me to learn a difficult lesson that I kept failing over and over again.

Her lips are slightly open. She's been asleep for a long time now. The cow moans again. Soon someone will come in and milk her. I hope to God they will. I would rather shoot the cow than listen to her moaning all night long.

I had another haemorrhage two weeks ago. It wasn't very big. The thing is that you mustn't be frightened and start to think that you won't be able to breathe. You can breathe right through it. I stared at the patch of blood on my pillow for a long time, as if I was looking at a cow. Please don't believe that I'm feeling sorry for myself. That's the last impression I would want to give. Very often I stop feeling jealous entirely. It empties out of me, quite late in the evening, when it's dark and a chill rises from the earth and I realise that the tomatoes have all been picked a long time ago and it's not summer any more, or even autumn. You know that feeling when you're playing a game of hide-and-seek out of doors, and it's growing dark, thick grainy dark gathering all around you, and one minute the yard is full of children and the next they've melted away. But you are still in hiding, waiting to be found. It sounds forlorn, but it's exciting too. Only you, out of everybody that was playing, still out in the dark. The dark thickens, thickens. You don't know if you want to hear a voice raised up, calling your name, or if you want to stay out in the dark forever.

The Englishwoman's eyes are open. She's breathing very gently, in through her mouth, out through her nose. The line of her nose is sharp. Yes, she has a line all around her now, defined and dazzling.

I want to say to her that it will soon be over. All the horror of it. The rotting stink of your own breath. The labour of walking. Creeping from the chair to the door, resting, gathering strength to turn the door handle. The ugliness of it all. Perhaps I don't need to tell her. Perhaps she knows. She looks quizzical, but she says nothing. Is the husband coming soon? He'd better. But however soon he comes he will never get this moment we've got. The cows below us, big and square and warm-breathing. The scent of the packed hay. If I were not myself, I would be jealous of myself. The thought is so ridiculous that I smile, and immediately the same smile lights her face, as if we're two children sharing a pillow.

'It's raining,' she says.

'I know.'

I've been hearing the rain for hours. Not listening to it exactly. The rain isn't music and it doesn't require any attention from me.

'It's pouring,' she says, as if the thought pleases her.

'Yes. Good for the soil.'

'Yes.'

If it were not for the rain, and the mud, and what it did to us, I would not have this disease. I am convinced of it. I was so glad to be alive, to have outwitted everything that tried to kill me. We drank, and drank, and drank. I can't tell you how we drank. Until we were barking at each other like dogs. The war was over, and we were not.

'C'est foutue, la guerre!'

'Et moi je m'en fous de la guerre!'

Yes, the rain and the mud. You never forget the smell of it. Rank, raw, clayey, clinging. It sucks on your boots like a lover. Fall in it and you're finished. That's what I used to tell myself when I was slithering along the duckboards. Fall in it and you're finished. But I've forgotten all that. I never think of it. It's not good to think of it, if you want to get the better of this filthy disease that seizes on every weak point. You know the way a butcher cleaves a rib of beef into chops? He finds the weak point first. A gentle chip of a cut, and then up with the chopper and whack!

So I never think of any of it. Only the noise of the rain reminds me sometimes.

'I wish I could feel it falling on me,' she says.

I don't say anything. A black bubble of bitterness has lodged in my throat. I want to cry out. I want to say to her, 'You'll feel it soon enough, don't worry. You'll be out in the rain forever.'

But I don't. I look sideways down the row of beds, all empty now but for hers and mine. They've left us here together, in the hayloft. No doubt there are exercises in progress in the room with the parquet floor. The Dervish Dance, the Big Prayer, the Enneagram. Everybody will be gathered. G will sit there with his expression of wise calm. I can picture it so clearly that my absence doesn't matter at all.

Yes, it's raining heavily. The shadows are big. We have only one small lantern to light us up here. You have to be very careful in a hayloft, in case of fire.

'I wish I could feel the rain,' she says again.

I can't think of any answer now. The black bubble shrinks, shrinks and finally dissolves. I can breathe a little more easily. She's lying on her side. Her nose is sharper than ever in her sunken face. Her eyes are fixed on me. I can't even distinguish her pupils in the darkness, but I know that look.

I have become someone else. I've seen it happen many times when a man is dying, and now it's happening with this woman. I don't speak. I don't want to break the spell of being the person she thinks I am.

I reach out. Her hand is as cold as I thought it would be. But it's not time yet, not quite, not for either of us.

In a minute her vision will clear and she'll see me for what I am. Someone she doesn't know, who has about as much meaning as a signpost in a language you can't read, on a journey that seems as if it will never come to an end. And your feet have got to labour on, until the mud reaches your lips.

Nothing can change what's got to happen. But all the same, I fold her hand in mine.

GRACE POOLE HER TESTIMONY

❧

Reader, I married him. Those are her words for sure. She would have him at the time and place she chose, with every dish on the table to her appetite.

She came in meek and mild but I knew her at first glance. There she sat in her low chair at a decent distance from the fire, buttering up Mrs Fairfax as if the old lady were a plate of parsnips. She didn't see me but I saw her. You don't live the life I've lived without learning to move so quiet that there is never a stir to frighten anyone.

Jane Eyre. You couldn't touch her. Nothing could bring a flush of colour to that pale cheek. What kind of pallor was it, you ask? A snowdrop pushing its way out of the bare earth, as green as it was white: that would be a comparison she'd like. But I would say: sheets. Blank sheets. Paper, or else a bed that no one had ever lain in or ever would.

I am a coarse creature. No one has ever married me and I have not much taste for marrying. I like my porter, and there's no harm in that. I am quick with the laudanum too. My lady takes it flavoured with cinnamon, and I keep the bottle under lock and key because sometimes she likes it too much. This little pale one won't touch a drop of anything. Won't let it sully her lips. Doesn't want to be babbling out her secrets in that French she's so proud of, as if anyone cared to listen. The little girl speaks French as pure as a bird.

I sweat and my stays creak when I move. I have good employment and I am respected by everyone in the household, not least Mr R. He's a sly one, a fox if ever there was, and my poor lady was no vixen. All she ever had, and I will swear my Bible oath to it, was a weakness.

Violent? Not she. Not my lady. Mr R brought Dr Gallion here to measure her skull. She was tied firm to a ladder-back chair and she did not resist although her eyes rolled. The doctor undertook the palpation of my lady's skull prominences. Here, he said, this is the bump of Amativeness. A propensity to Combativeness, do you see here, sir? His hands roved over her head and everything he discovered was to her detriment. He went beyond prodding at her bones to observe the way her hair grew low on her forehead, which he said showed an animal disposition. It vexed me. It was because she would not speak that he called her animal, but she could talk when she liked. She spoke in her dreams, when only I was there to hear her. If she preferred to be called mute I did not blame her. Downstairs, the pale one, chatter chatter in French with the little girl, scribble scribble on whatever piece of paper she could get, as if words were all anybody needed.

What I hated most was the way she made herself milk and water, a dish of whey for anyone to drink at, sip sop sip sop, when what she truly wanted was to be a blade through the heart of us. I knew it but the rest were dumb and blind. The old lady loved the sip sop. As for the little girl, she was taken by her, like a baby taken for a changeling.

My poor lady's skull showed an enlarged Organ of Destructiveness. Dr Gallion passed his fingers over the place and repeated the words. He nodded and Mr R nodded with him, the two gentlemen solemn together now while my lady bent her head and her hair slid over her shoulders. The doctor had loosened it from the knots and coils she wore, the better to get at her.

In such a case as this, the doctor said, it would be wise to shave the head entire, the more clearly to see how the organs display themselves.

I rubbed oil into the bristle that sprouted from my lady's scalp, so that it would grow more quickly. She was bewildered at the loss of her hair. She would raise her hand as if to touch the knot that sat at her nape, and find it gone, and then her hand would waver. I would give her a little laudanum and she would rock herself and seem to find comfort in it.

The pale one thinks she has the measure of us all. Up and down the garden she goes in the shadows of evening. She ticks us off in her steps. The old lady. Mr R. The little girl. The guests who come and go. She would tick me off too but she only knows my name. She asked it and they told her: Grace Poole.

I am a strong creature with a pot of porter. I receive excellent wages. I am so turned and turned about that if I saw a snowdrop push its way out of the earth I would stamp on it.

She was brought here to dig the frippery out of the little girl, so that the child might take her proper station in life.

Less noise there, Grace.

I can make a noise if I want. They know that. I have not yet lost my voice. If I spoke out I'd tell the pale one a story she wouldn't soon forget.

Long ago he married my lady and they were Mr and Mrs R. Amativeness is what the doctor called it. This was long before the snowdrop raised its head, but the creature with the porter was already here. Me. Fifteen, was I? As old as my tongue and a little older than my teeth. I was a lovely flashing bit of a girl then. I could stop men of thirty dead in their tracks as they ploughed. I made the air so thick around me they seemed to wade or drown in it. I was Grace Poole.

I stopped him dead in his tracks. I did not care for my lady then or know her. She did not come downstairs. They said she was nervous. To me she was a foreign land where I never wished to go.

Grace Poole, he said to me, and I saw him tremble. Is that your name?

I tilted the water I was carrying so that the jug rested on my hip. I said nothing. Let him look, I thought, and I shall look back at him.

I had an attic then. A slip of a room all white with sunlight and almost bare, but there was a bed in it. He was older than me but not by so much. He had married young and they said he was unhappy. I thought of nothing then except having him.

I dare say he had never lain down on such a bed in his life. We had to put our hands over each other's mouths so as not to cry out.

Grace Poole, he said when I released him. Grace Poole. It was the most beautiful thing I had ever heard: my own name. No one heard and no one came.

No man likes a big belly. I carried mine to a place he procured for me. He told me that he would provide for the child and give it a station in life, and I would come back to Thornfield. It was more than I expected. He was a fox because it was his nature, but he kept his word about the child. I did not resist when it was born and taken by a wet nurse, to go far away to a better place.

I took a fever when it was gone and the room stank so that even the nurse who tended me held up a handkerchief over her face, but I did not die. I pitted and spotted and what got up from the bed was no longer the old Grace Poole but the beginning of the creature you see presently. I grew as strong as you like. I came back to Thornfield and took a taste for nursing, as perhaps he had foreseen.

I did not want anyone to look at me. And there she is, the pale one, bursting with it, every inch of her chill little flesh shouting: *Look at me.*

She will never stand before him as I did and look back at him, and make him come to her. She hunts in another fashion.

So I came to nurse my lady here. She would not eat so I fed her from a spoon. She would not speak so I learned her gestures and what they meant. I brushed her hair, which was thick and soft and long enough to touch the ground when she sat. It took an hour sometimes to brush her hair, to plait it and coil it into the knot she liked. When it was finished she would put up her hands to touch it and she would be satisfied. She liked her laudanum flavoured with cinnamon and not with saffron, which was what they gave her at first. Another thing she liked was a bit of red satin ribbon which she would wrap around her fingers and rub against her cheek as she rocked herself, and at those times although she never spoke she would hum and I would think: Perhaps she is content.

Each morning: porridge with cream and syrup, so that even a little of it will fatten her. Sometimes she will take a dish of tea; other times she will dash it from my hand. But no matter how fiercely she smashes china, she never touches me. There has been long discussion over whether or not she should take meat. It is heating. It inflames the passions. She is allowed only a very little beef. I make broth for her myself, out of bones she likes to crack with her teeth when they are cooked so that the marrow is ready to drip out of them. She will eat toast sometimes, as long as it is cut so fine it splinters to pieces if the butter is hard. On the days when she puts her lips together and will not swallow, I know better now than to persuade her. I take out my two packs of cards and make them flicker down into heaps over and over. It soothes her.

But now here we are: the old lady, the snowdrop, the little girl, Mr R, my lady and the creature with the porter. Me. The little girl has come back from France and she does not know me. She peeps and cheeps about the house with her high French voice and her dancing slippers. In the kitchen they say that she is the child of a French opera dancer that Mr R has kept in France. Some say that the opera dancer is dead, others that he has tired of her. They are used to me going in and out without partaking of the conversation, as I fetch and carry my lady's food and drink. They call me Mrs Poole and none of them will cross me. Richard the footman visited London when he was a boy and he says he would rather have charge of the entire menagerie at Exeter 'Change than be left alone with Mrs R as I am. All I will ever own is that my lady has her ways.

If the pale one had not come to this house we should all have kept on safe. The little girl did not know me.

I was content with that. I liked to see her flutter about the house in her lace and silk, and dance in front of the mirror. I was no more the Grace Poole who laid herself down on the narrow bed in the sunlit attic than I was Mr R himself. I rose up from childbed another woman and I am that woman now. I have no child but I have Mrs R. Let the little girl skip where she wants and peep out her French phrases and grow up to a suitable station. But this pale one has come here, loitering in our lanes and uncannily stealing what does not belong to her. And now here is my lady disturbed night after night, murmuring and rocking. No one knows what senses she has. Sometimes I see thoughts whisk in her eyes that I would never dare to see the bottom of, and I know that Mr R will not come here again and face her.

Mr R knows that I will never leave her. We should have been safe, if that one had never come here. Of course she wants my lady gone. She spins out words in her head like a spider. She will have us all wrapped tight. I see him walking in the garden, and her walking after him, so sly and small and neat that you would never think twice of it. She calls my lady a madwoman and a danger, and he listens. She says these words and he listens, in spite of all the years I have kept my lady safe and she has never troubled him. She wants my lady gone.

She may marry Mr R. She may take him for all that there is left in him. She will never stop him dead and make him tremble all over, as I did, before he ever touched me. She can do no harm to the little girl. With her bright black eyes and her dancing feet the child will go where she chooses, and by the time she is fifteen she will turn the air around her thick with longing. We will all be what we are again.

But you could put your hand through Miss Eyre and never grasp her. I know what she is. There she sits in the window seat, folded into the shadows, watching us. She has come here hunting. I have seen how she devours red meat when she thinks herself alone. She wants my lady gone. She will have my lady put away like a madwoman. Her hair cut again, her ribbon taken and nothing to comfort her. The doctors will measure her skull with callipers.

The pale one may hunt but she must not touch my lady. I read in my Bible with my good candles burning late. St Paul says that it is better to marry than to burn, but there is marriage and there is marriage. Sometimes it may be better to burn.

I will make my lady a custard, which I can do better than any cook in England. I will sit on my stool beside her and hold the spoon to her lips. Sometimes I chirrup as if she were a bird, to make her open her lips. She holds her red ribbon in her lap and her eyes meet mine and then she does open, she does take the spoon of custard into her mouth and she does swallow.

THE LANDLUBBERS LYING
DOWN BELOW

❧

I always take my lady her morning chocolate on a round silver tray. When I was little my lady used to let me sip it from her silver spoon. I remember the rich dark taste. I remember curling in the warm cloud of her bedclothes, and the way she would caress me.

She doesn't look up from her letters when I place the tray on the bedside table.

'Your chocolate, my lady.'

'Can't you see I am busy, Scipio?'

I bow, and step backwards, but my foot catches the table leg and the tray begins to slide. I lunge for it, but the table topples, the tray turns over and dark chocolate spews over my lady's rose-coloured rug. I crouch down, fumbling for the pot and broken cup. I scrub at the stain with the tray-cloth, but it only spreads farther.

'Leave it,' says my lady. Her words fall like splinters of glass. She rings the bell for Eliza.

'I am sorry,' I stammer, 'my foot—'

'Stand up.'

I stand up.

'You have soiled your uniform,' she says, pointing at the splashes on my silk livery. 'No matter. It is too tight for you. You are growing into a hobbledehoy, Scipio.'

Her eyes look me up and down critically. 'Go and put on the midnight-blue satin, and your crimson turban,' she orders me. 'Wear your crimson sash.'

My lady knows all my uniforms. When I was little, we used to lie in her bed choosing embroidered satins and silks. I played with purple, midnight blue, crimson and gold. She bought perfumed lotions for my skin and oils for my hair. I was five years old, she said. The ship's captain who brought me here to London from across the sea told her my age, and that I was the son of a chief in my own country. My lady paid a fine price for me, and I have been her page for six years now.

I remember the captain. I remember sleeping in a little wooden room that went up and down, and how sharp the sea smelled. Sometimes the water would slop over the portholes and I would hold tight to the edges of my bunk in case I was swept away. When a grey tongue of land crept close, they said, 'That's England.'

'Remember, Scipio,' my lady says sternly, 'I cannot be attended by a hobbledehoy tonight.'

Tonight it is the concert. Two Prodigies of Nature are coming to play in my lady's ballroom. James the footman told me what this means. They are children, younger than me, and such fine musicians that the whole world comes to stare and listen.

I play the harpsichord, and I sing. I speak French and German, and I also sing in Italian. My lady engaged a French dancing-master, and I learned to dance the gavotte, the sarabande, the minuet and many other dances. My lady's friends used to give me coins when I played and sang to them. It happens rarely now, because what is remarkable in a child of six is nothing special in a great boy of eleven. I have saved all the coins. They are hidden in a purse inside my mattress.

The footmen have carried the harpsichord into the centre of the ballroom. There are rows of gilt chairs, in two half-circles. My lady has not rung for me to come to her chamber, and so James says that before I get changed into my evening uniform I should make myself useful in the ballroom. I lift the gilt chairs easily.

'You're getting a fine lad, Scipio,' says James. 'You'll make a footman one of these days, if you play your cards right.'

'When are the performing monkeys arriving?' Albert asks James.

'Watch your lip,' says James. 'Don't you know what a fine price my lady has paid for this concert?'

I have trouble fixing my turban. I look for Eliza to help me but she and Sarah are busy handing combs and pins to my lady's hairdresser.

'You should know how to do it by now,' Eliza mutters. I see my lady's face in the mirror but she does not look at me.

When I am ready I go back to the ballroom. The candles are lit and there is a man in dark clothes leaning over the harpsichord. A boy sits at the keyboard. He is very small, wigged and powdered like a full-grown man, and he is laughing.

'Let me play, Wolfi,' says the girl. He jumps off the stool and a girl with her hair dressed high in foreign fashion takes his place. She is very solemn, and the boy pulls a face at her, trying to make her laugh. She plays for a few bars; then he darts round to the keyboard and starts decorating the music with cascades of notes.

Their father says, 'That's enough practice. Come with me,' and he leads them out of the ballroom, towards the antechamber. He puts an arm round each of their shoulders. They are a family, the three of them together.

My lady receives her guests at the head of the stairs. I thought she would want me to stand beside her as usual, but she says, 'Go and serve the musicians, Scipio.'

I take them a plate of macaroons, some cordial and some sweet wine. The boy, Wolfi, takes a handful of macaroons and crams them in as fast as he can.

'Wolfi, you'll be sick like you were at Spring Gardens,' says the girl.

'Nannerl, why are you always so good?'

'She was born good,' says their father, 'unlike you, my boy.' But he says it like a joke.

'Do you have everything you need?' I ask them in German, and they all stare at me in surprise.

'More macaroons, maybe?' asks the boy, and I look down and see the plate is nearly empty.

'Wolfi, we are here to play, not to eat all night,' says his sister.

'I will get some more from the kitchen later,' I say, and I smile at Wolfi. I like him. He will have to work hard to please my lady. He deserves macaroons. 'You have ten minutes,' I tell them. 'The guests are seating themselves.'

'Good,' says the father.

Wolfi snatches a sip from his father's wine glass when he's not looking. Nannerl sees, but she doesn't give him away.

As soon as the concert begins I understand why the whole world comes to stare and listen. Wolfi can do anything. His fingers leap on the keys and he laughs sometimes, silently, to himself. He plays whatever they give him and he improvises until the music is like a fountain rising higher and higher and showering drops of notes over us all. He plays as if music lives inside him. Nannerl plays too but although her playing is very good, it is not a miracle like Wolfi's. I wonder if she minds.

They finish. There is applause, then silence. Suddenly my lady claps her hands and says, 'Scipio! Come here.

Young Master Mozart shall play for you, and you shall sing.'

She has often heard me sing. She has listened to him play, and must know there can be no match between us. But I have to obey her. Wolfi turns to me as I walk forward. Nannerl starts playing again, and under cover of her music Wolfi asks, 'Have you a song?'

My mind empties, and only one song is left. It comes from the ship which brought me to England. The captain stood me on a stool and taught me to sing it, line by line. Afterwards he clapped with his big hands and picked me up and swung me round and round. I did not understand then that he was going to sell me when we got to London.

'Yes, I have a song,' I say. Wolfi's eyes sparkle. He nods towards the antechamber, and we slip out while Nannerl plays steadily. Wolfi sips his father's wine, then says, 'Sing it to me.'

I sing it through, very softly so they won't hear from the ballroom. Wolfi nods, and says, 'I have it.' He picks up his violin, and plays a few bars perfectly. 'I like it,' he says.

When we stand in front of the audience I'm so nervous that my lady's guests are a blur of silk and satin and sparkling jewels. I cannot fix on their faces, although I know they are chattering and laughing to each other. My tight uniform squeezes my breathing as Wolfi skips through the opening bars. I close my eyes so I won't see the room, and start to sing:

''Twas Friday morn when we set sail,
And we were not far from land,
When the captain, he spied a fair mermaid,
With a comb and a glass in her hand.

Oh the ocean waves may roll,
And the stormy winds may blow,
While we poor sailor boys go skipping up aloft
And the landlubbers lying down below, below,
  below,
And the landlubbers lying down below ...'

There is dead silence, but I keep going. I daren't open
my eyes.

'Then up spoke the cook of our gallant ship,
And a greasy old cook was he,
"I care more for my kettles and my pots,
Than I do for the roaring of the sea ..."'

My voice is wobbling. They don't like it. I open my
eyes. Some ladies are making faces as they fan themselves.
My lady stares straight ahead, hard and angry. My throat
is dry and the notes stick while my song falls away in
pieces.

Only Wolfi doesn't care. He plays on, wave after wave
of music, right to the end of the song and then he rattles
out a final drumbeat of notes. My lady rises from her
seat and beckons me with one gloved finger.

'A song more fit for the gutter than for my guests, Scipio. You had better go and assist in the supper room. Ask James for your duties.'

Since that concert I have never entered my lady's bedchamber. Once I said to Eliza, 'Does she ever ask for me?' but Eliza shook her head. I clean knives and polish silver. I sleep in a cubbyhole below stairs, with my purse deep in the straw of my pillow. James still says I could make a fine footman one day, but I don't listen. He wants to make a pet of me, and he says what he thinks will please me.

'You've a footman's calves,' he says, and I feel his hand on my leg, prodding my muscle. He wants me between his thighs, but I've learned my lesson. I keep my head down and polish knives until the skin on my fingers is raw.

One hot day in July, Albert brings in a bill advertising a concert at the Swan and Harp in Cornhill.

'It's those blessed Prodigies of Nature again,' he says, sarcastic. 'Half a crown entry, they want.'

An itch to go there seizes me. There won't be any fine ladies in a tavern in Cornhill. I can go as well as anybody. But half a crown is a huge sum.

I wonder why Wolfi and his sister are playing in a tavern now, instead of great ladies' ballrooms. Perhaps they have grown too tall. Perhaps the ladies are tired of them.

When the day comes, I go to my hiding place and weigh my purse in my hands. I run and beg Sarah for a little sweet almond oil. I rub it into my skin until the ashy grey has gone and then I rub it into my hair. I ask James if I can have a clean shirt. Does he really believe that I can become a footman one day?

'Yes,' says James, pleased, and he finds me a cambric shirt, and a pair of clean breeches. I dress myself and hang my purse around my neck. It is the easiest thing in the world to slip out of the area door, up the steps and away down the street. I walk fast, but not too fast. If anyone sees me they'll think I've been sent on an errand.

There is a thick crowd milling outside the Swan and Harp. I wriggle my way through, towards the front. These people would never be allowed near my lady's doors, laughing and shouting and all with ready money in their hands. They push me in on their tide. The man on the door doesn't even look at me; he just counts the coins I give him.

Inside the tavern the air is thick with smoke and laughter, and pot-boys weave in and out, carrying jugs. In the centre a space has been cleared and a harpsichord stands ready. I find a seat at the side, in the shadows, and pay twopence for a glass of ginger shrub. My heart beats fast with excitement. Nobody here knows that I used to be my lady's page. No one is going to shout at me, 'What are you doing here, you lazy good-for-nothing? Get back to the scullery, there's a box of knives to clean.'

It is Wolfi who plays first. He has changed so much. He is much taller, and he's so thin that I think he must have been ill. He isn't wearing a fancy miniature man's suit, but a handsome shirt and breeches. His hair is tied behind. He is still a boy but he doesn't look like a Prodigy of Nature any more. Nannerl is there too, and it is announced that Wolfi will play first.

Wolfi bows to the audience and they fall silent. My lady's guests were never silent. Their chatter went on all the while, sharp as bits of glass. Wolfi plays better than ever. His father says he will play works of his own composition, and he plays a minuet and then a contredanse and some jigs that remind me of Biddy singing in the kitchen. People call out the names of their favourite songs and if he knows it he plays it straight off, but if he doesn't he'll ask them to sing a verse through, and then he has it. His father announces that he will play blindfold. The audience cheers as one of them is asked to come up and check that it is a true blindfold and now Wolfi is playing again, faster and faster, as if he has been wound up so tight that he will never be able to stop. They take the blindfold off and he stands and bows and the crowd stands up and shouts and whistles. Wolfi looks very tired.

I forget about sitting back in the shadow. I am on my feet clapping, and that's when Wolfi sees me. His face lights up and he gives me a little wave. When the cheering has died down he calls out: 'Scipio!'

I think of running away, but he looks so tired. He's beckoning me eagerly. Nannerl gives me a small, shy smile. Their father is peering in my direction, but he doesn't know me.

'Scipio!' calls Wolfi again, and I go forward.

Wolfi beams and seizes my hand. 'My friend will sing, and I will play,' he announces. The crowd clap and cheer and wave their mugs. Wolfi picks up his violin and plays the first bars of my song. He remembers them perfectly. I clench my fists. The memory of my lady's concert sweeps through me. I can't do it. I can't fail again. Wolfi stops, glances at me. He smiles but I can see he's worried.

Suddenly I make up my mind. This is not my lady's concert. Wolfi likes my song, and he knows more than my lady. I stand as tall as I can, and look straight at the audience. Their faces are warm with the music they have heard and the drinks they have drunk. Wolfi draws his bow across the strings. We are off.

By the third verse the tavern crowd is singing along with the chorus and clapping out the rhythm. An old man bawls 'Way-O, Way-O', as sailors do when they pull the ropes. The noise roars in my ears like the sea as we hit the last verse:

'Then three times 'round went our gallant ship,
And three times 'round went she,
And the third time that she went around
She sank to the bottom of the sea.'

They shout and drum their mugs on the tables for more as we bow, and I see that Wolfi is laughing as he laughed the first time I saw him, not silently this time but aloud as if this is what all the miracle of his music is meant for. But at the same time I am afraid of the faces. They are so hungry. If they don't get what they want, they will turn. I think of the captain. He taught me each line patiently. He set me on a stool as he hunkered by me, and his face was inches from mine. I don't think he hurt me. I don't remember. He would not have wanted to spoil me. He sold me to my lady for a handsome sum.

I don't wait for the end of the concert. You can stay too long, and then people don't want you any more. Once Nannerl starts playing, I smile at Wolfi, and give him a wave as I slip away. I check that my purse is still safe round my neck. There's enough money in it for food and a bed until I get work. I'm not going to be a footman. I'm heading for the docks.

The sea was grey in the portholes; I remember that. It churned around the ship and slopped all over the glass. I held tight to the sides of my bunk, for fear I'd be thrown out. I thought the sea would come in and fill the cabin. But I think there was a time when the sea was lazy, and a different colour. Blue, maybe.

WRIT IN WATER

❧

They made him a plaster saint of poetry with his eyes turned up to heaven. But it wasn't like that.

Winter. Rome at last. The terrible voyage from England was done. We'd found lodgings and a doctor. All he had to do was to get well.

By day the noise of the fountain was almost hidden. There were women selling chickens and fresh milk, children playing, pails clattering, the creak of wheels and the clop of horses' hooves. We used to count the different sounds, and he always won. But at night the fountain played clearly. Bernini's fountain, with its fantastic coils of marble and gushing water.

'Our Roman water is pure, not like the filthy water in Napoli,' said our landlady, with a toss of her head. Signora Angeletti was slippery with the truth, but she was right about the water. I made sure there was always a full pitcher by his bed. Fever made him thirsty.

They've burned everything in our lodgings. The table we ate off, the bed he lay in. Even the shutters that I swung open at dawn so that he could gaze down the steps to the piazza and the life of a new day. They stripped our rooms. It's the law here. The Roman authorities are terrified of consumption.

'Please move aside, Signor Severn. We have our duty to perform.'

But the ceiling remains, the one he lay under. They couldn't take away those flowers he gazed at every day until he died. Sometimes he thought he was already in his grave, with flowers growing over him. He dreamed of water bubbling out of the earth, and violets in damp, sweet grass.

'You should be painting, Severn! Here you are in Rome and you do not paint at all.'

When we first came, when he was strong enough, he would sit in the winter sun and watch the artists in the piazza.

'You have more talent than any of them, Severn.'

I still have this little sketch of him: see. There were others but they've been lost. Maybe someone has taken them; I don't know.

When you draw something, you never forget it. It was night, and there was one candle burning. That was enough light to draw by. It was a still, mild night, even though it was only February. But spring comes early in Rome. It was the last night of his life.

The flame of the candle barely moved. The fountain was loud. He was asleep, cast up on the pillow like a shipwrecked man. His hair was stuck to his forehead with sweat.

I shall never forget that night. He'd tried to prepare me. Warn me.

'Have you ever seen anyone die, Severn? I have. I nursed my brother Tom.'

Sometimes, after a fit of coughing, he would lie so still that I thought he was already dead.

'I must warn you, Severn, if you persist in nursing me you'll see nothing of Rome but a sickbed and a sick man. Believe me, it's better to give me the laudanum.'

There was a full bottle of laudanum. I gave it to him drop by drop, as Dr Clarke ordered.

'Give me all of it, Severn. You don't understand what it is to die as I am going to die.'

But how could I allow him to destroy his immortal soul? I did not trust myself. I gave the laudanum to Dr Clarke, for fear I'd weaken.

He asked me to go to the cemetery. He wanted me to describe the place where he was to lie. I told him about the goats cropping the grass, the young shepherd guarding his flock, the daisies and violets that grew so thickly over the graves.

'It's very quiet,' I told him. 'You can hear the breeze blowing through the grass. There's a pyramid which marks an ancient tomb.'

He lay back and closed his eyes. After a while he asked me whose tomb it was.

'I enquired,' I told him. 'His name was Caius Cestius, and he was a great man of the first century.'

'A great man ... A very rich man at least, my dear Severn, if he had a pyramid built for his tomb. Is it large?'

'Large enough.'

'Does it cast a shadow?'

'I suppose so.'

His cough caught at him. I propped him with pillows. 'You should not talk,' I told him.

He moved his head from side to side, restlessly. Then he said, 'You must understand that I will not regain my health now, Severn. I have studied enough anatomy to know that.'

We lived in our own world all those weeks. The next cup of broth, the next visit from Dr Clarke, the beating-up of pillows, the lighting of fires and measuring of medicines. Some days I hadn't a moment to call my own. Some nights I did not undress.

I was glad of it. He lay with the marble egg given to him by Miss Brawne in his hand. Women keep such an egg by them when they sew, to cool their fingers. He held that marble hour after hour, day after day. It soothed him as nothing else did. He wanted to know why he was still living, when everything was finished for him. This posthumous life, he called it.

He was sorry after he said it. 'My poor Severn, you have enough to do without listening to my misery.'

We had a piano carried upstairs so that I could play for him. He loved Haydn.

'Don't you hear that they are the same, Severn: the piano, and the fountain? Listen. But what am I thinking of? You cannot listen to yourself play, any more than a blackbird can hear itself sing.'

I was there as the days wore him down. His other friends, Dilke and Brown and Reynolds and the rest, they were far away in England. Now we fight over his memory like cats. But it was to me that he spoke. I wiped the sweat off his face and washed him and changed his linen. I told him about the sheep that roamed over the graves. He smiled. He never tired of the sheep, the goats, the shepherd boy and the violets. The next day he would ask again, as if he'd already forgotten. But I don't think he forgot. Words were like notes of music to him. He liked to hear how they fell.

'Sometimes I think I am already buried, with flowers growing over me,' he said as he stared up at the ceiling where the painted flowers swarmed.

Signora Angeletti became suspicious. She waylaid the doctor, asking what was wrong. Was it consumption? 'I am a charitable woman, but I must think of my other lodgers.'

I didn't know the laws of Rome then. She feared that they would strip her rooms and burn everything. I suppose she was right, but she was compensated. She lost nothing.

I heard the patter of Signora Angeletti's voice from the mezzanine. We were in her hands. No other boarding house would take us now: he was too obviously ill.

He understood Signora Angeletti very well. She gave us a bad dinner, not long after we came, and he threw it straight out of the window on to the steps. A crowd of urchins came from nowhere and scrabbled for it.

'She won't serve us such stuff again,' he said, and he was right. She had given us rubbish, to see if we were willing to swallow it. I wished I had his firmness. I was nervous with Signora Angeletti, and she knew it. In those ways he was more worldly than I was.

Yes, they made him a plaster saint of poetry, with his eyes turned up to heaven. They fight over his memory, shaping it this way and that. But I remember how he rocked with laughter when that dinner splattered on the marble steps!

'My best plate!' screamed Signora Angeletti.

But he said, 'If that plate is the best you have, signora, then I am very sorry for you.'

After that the dinners were always hot and good.

I've told the story of those months so many times that they hardly seem to belong to me. If I say that they were the high point of my life, you will misunderstand me. You may even accuse me of cruelty. A man lay dying, and I say it was the high point of my existence? How can I recall those months of agony and dwindling hope, except with a shudder?

I remember the nights chiefly. We set the candles so that as one died, the next one would light from its burning thread. Once he said that there was a fairy lamplighter in the room. The flame would burn down until it seemed about to collapse on itself. He watched intently all the while. When the next sprang up and began to bloom, he would allow himself to close his eyes.

When I was very tired the room seemed to sway and the noise of the fountain reminded me of our voyage from England. Sometimes I fell asleep for a few seconds and really believed that I felt the motion of the ship under me.

I remember one incident which I have never written down, or spoken of even. I was in the small room which was intended for my studio. I thought of his words: *You should be painting, Severn! Here you are in Rome and you do not paint at all.*

I was standing at the table, going through my sketch-book. It contained a few studies which I hoped might be worth further work. I had sketched the cemetery for him. The pyramid of Caius Cestius, with the young shepherd sitting on the grass. But I had never shown him the sketch. How can a man say to another: *Look, here is the place where you will be buried. Just there, where that shepherd sits and dreams.*

I decided to be buried there too, beside him. My heart grew easier then. I felt no more estrangement from him.

As I turned the pages of my sketchbook, a cruel truth hit me like a blow. The reason I could not paint was not so much my cares for the invalid as my fear that I would never paint well enough. Here I was in Rome, the heart of the painted world. Here were my masters all around me. Nothing I achieved could ever equal one of Bernini's marble coils.

The noise of the fountain grew louder. It was drowning me. It told me to give up, to stop pretending that there was merit in my pitiful daubs or in the travelling scholarship I'd been so proud to win. Rome would wash me away, as it had washed away a thousand others, leaving no trace. I seized hold of the leaves of my sketchbook, meaning to rip them out so that no one would ever guess the contemptible folly of my ambitions.

At that moment I felt a touch on my shoulder. A clasp, a warm, wordless, brotherly clasp. The fingers gripped my shoulder and then shook it a little, consolingly, encouragingly.

I knew straight away that it was him. God knows how he had dragged himself out of that bed and come to find me. I could not imagine how he'd guessed at my anguish. I said nothing. His clasp was enough. After a moment the grip of the hand tightened, and then left me.

He was going back to bed, I thought. But there were no retreating footsteps. I looked over my shoulder. No one was there. He could not possibly have moved so fast. I hurried to the bedroom and there he was, deeply asleep. I stared at his face and I knew that he was dying, not weeks or months in the future, but now. How had I not recognised it before?

I sat down by the bed. My sketchbook was still in my hand. I got up again, noiselessly, and fetched what I needed from the little room. I was ready to draw him now.

The noise of the fountain. The sound of a pencil moving. His breath. A long, dragging pause. Another breath. You can live an entire life between one breath and the next. That's where my life was spent, in one night, in one room. The rest is memory.

The following stories have been previously published:

'The Medina' appeared in *Good Housekeeping* (2001). 'Rose, 1944', 'Esther to Fanny' and 'Whales and Seals' were previously published in the collection *Rose, 1944* as part of the 'Pocket Penguin' series (Penguin, 2005). 'With Shackleton' was originally published in the Asham Awards Anthology (2006). 'At the Institute with KM' first appeared in the anthology, *New Writing 13* (Granta, 2007). 'Where I Keep My Faith' was published in the anthology, *Freedom* (Amnesty International, 2009). 'Girl, Balancing' appeared in the *Independent* (2009). 'The White Horse' appeared in the *Manchester Review* (2009). 'Wolves of Memory' appeared in the *Sunday Telegraph* magazine, *Seven* (2010). 'Protection' was originally published as part of the 'Penguin Specials' digital series (Penguin, 2011). 'A Night Out' appeared in *Woman & Home* (2011). 'All Those Personal Survival Medals' appeared in the *Daily Express* (2012). 'The Landlubbers Lying Down Below' was originally published as part of the 'Penguin Specials' digital series (Penguin, 2012) and also broadcast in the interval at the BBC Proms. 'Writ in Water' was originally published in *The Malarkey* (Bloodaxe Books, 2012) and first broadcast by BBC Radio 4. 'Taken in Shadows' was published in *The Malarkey* (Bloodaxe, 2012). 'Duty-Free' was published in the Asham Anthology, *Once Upon a Time There was a Traveller* (Virago, 2013). 'A Silver Cigar in the Sky' appeared on the Bristol website: www.bristol2014.com written for WWI ACE 2014 Bristol Arts Commission, the city's commemorative project to mark the outbreak of WWI (2014). 'Grace Poole Her Testimony' was published in the anthology, *Reader, I Married Him* (Borough Press, 2016). 'Cradling' appeared in *Good Housekeeping*. 'Portrait of Auntie Binbag, with Ribbons' originally appeared in *Woman & Home* and was then published in an anthology in association with a Breast Cancer charity (Transworld).

The following stories have been broadcast:

'Dancers' Feet' was originally broadcast on Radio 3 as 'Dropping the Pilot' (2008). 'Count from the Splash' was broadcast by Radio 4 (2010). 'Frost at Midnight' was originally broadcast by BBC Radio as part of the Earth Music Bristol Festival (2011) and also appeared in the *Radio Times*. 'Hamid in the Playhouse' was broadcast on Radio 4 (2013). 'Chocolate for Later' was broadcast as part of the Bristol Food Connections Radio 4 Festival (2014). 'The Musicians of Ingo' was broadcast by BBC Radio 3 during the Family Prom Interval.

Read on for an extract from
Helen Dunmore's final novel

Birdcage Walk

'The finest novel Dunmore has written.'
Observer

'A finely wrought psychological thriller.'
Daily Mail

'A blend of beauty and horror evoked with such
breathtaking poetry that it haunts me still.'
Guardian

'Compelling as ever.'
Daily Express

If my friends hadn't decided that I should have a dog I would never have opened the gate and gone into the graveyard. I always took the paved path between the railings: Birdcage Walk, it's called, because of the pleached lime trees arching overhead on their cast-iron frame.

In late summer the rosebay willowherb grew taller than the battered headstones and monuments. Every so often the graveyard would be strimmed and the stones would show naked. The tide of green would be stemmed for a few weeks, but it could never be held back. I once saw a man doing t'ai chi in a clearing, but usually only dog-walkers ventured among the graves. The church itself had been bombed to rubble during the war. In its place there was a lawn where children were not supposed to play ball games, and some rose trees planted in honour of a forgotten royal occasion.

I liked Birdcage Walk, especially late at night, when darkness and the rustle of nocturnal creatures gave an edge to the safety of the paved path.

I was still learning to be a dog-owner. I'd never considered becoming one, but when I was left alone I soon saw how uncomfortable my solitude was for everybody. Walking on my own was no great pleasure, and we had always walked. I thought of joining a ramblers' group, but I'd never liked being organised and so the idea melted away.

Jack had belonged to a girl I'd known from babyhood, the daughter of two dear friends. Nora was moving to Australia. I took Jack on a whim, perhaps because I couldn't think what else to do. And besides, everyone was so eager to match me with the dog, and they had been very kind since I was left alone. There was no question of taking on a puppy. Jack was five years old, perfectly trained.

It didn't seem like much more than an idea until the day Nora brought Jack round, with all the paraphernalia about which I knew less than nothing. We'd had a couple of introductory sessions, of course. I'd taken Jack for a walk, feeling an entire fraud. I knew what food he liked and that he must not have it more than once a day. But this time, when Nora left, she didn't take her dog with her.

So there we were, alone together. Jack was a mongrel, or mixed breed as they say now. He was rough-haired and had a strong little body and a pointed, foxy face which at the same time expressed a willingness towards the human which you would never find in a fox.

He took to me. I let him sniff my hand and I fed him and made him walk behind me through doorways –

Nora had told me this was important – and we began to go for long walks together. Everybody talked to me. It's a cliché, I know, but it's not until you've been left alone that you realise how very few people want to pass the time of day with a solitary and no doubt rather grim middle-aged man. I entered a little world which had obviously always been there, running parallel to the one in which I lived. I talked about Jack and enquired about Rosie, Dexter, Ebony, Skye. It was pleasant, but I still liked a solitary walk from time to time.

It was one of those long, slow summer dusks and Jack and I were the only creatures on Birdcage Walk. I heaved the gate open and Jack flashed away into the dense tangle of ivy, long grass, bramble, periwinkle and wild clematis. I could just see his hindquarters quivering in ecstasy as he explored a hole where a stone had keeled over. I whistled and he came to heel in a way which still astonished me – and, if I'm honest, delighted me.

We plunged on together through the graves. Some of the inscriptions were legible, some worn away. There was a particular type of stone which flaked off in layers, taking the inscriptions with it. Whatever care had gone into choosing the words, they did not matter now. It was hard to credit that real bones lay thick in the soil, but perhaps they too had dissolved. I wasn't sure how long it took. The graves were all more than a hundred years old.

Jack vanished beneath a wild rose bush, snuffling and then barking. I called him off and he came reluctantly. His look was so urgent, so abjectly enthusiastic that I didn't have the heart to keep him back. Let him dig if he wanted. It could do no harm, after all this time. I was careful. I was not one of those who festooned the iron railings with little plastic bags of dog crap. Jack barked again. He was looking back at me, as if he wanted me to come too.

I waded through the undergrowth, lifted a thorny branch and peered at the grave where Jack was digging. It sounds fanciful, but I half believed that Jack had brought me here for a purpose. The stone leaned only slightly backwards and the inscription was deep cut. I could not read it all but a name jumped out at me: Fawkes. For some reason I was curious. I suppose I thought of Guy Fawkes, and his awful fate, and the bonfires that still burned in his name. I bent down to look more closely. Jack was flurrying up earth with his paws but otherwise doing no harm as far as I could see. He had probably found a rabbit hole. I flattened the undergrowth with my boot and knelt down. Now I saw what I had not noticed at first: there was an object carved beneath the inscription. I puzzled over it, and then I saw what it was: a quill pen, beautifully drawn in stone. A craftsman must have done this. I ran my fingers over the inscription, for most of the words were hard to read. The script was flowing and copious.

To the Beloved Memory of Julia Elizabeth Fawkes,
Wife of Augustus Gleeson,
This Stone Was Raised on 14th July 1793
In the Presence of her Many Admirers.

And underneath, immediately above the quill, was written:

Her Words Remain Our Inheritance.

The inscription struck me as unusual. No dates of birth or death were given, and although Julia Elizabeth Fawkes was clearly married to Augustus Gleeson, she had not taken his name. Of course it was the many admirers who interested me most. She was a writer, clearly, but what had she written? I had never heard of her.

I called Jack to me. He came, whining and reluctant, but this time I was firm. We were going home.

I found nothing online about either Julia Fawkes or Julia Gleeson. They had quite vanished. I tried Augustus Gleeson too, but again I drew a blank. I decided to forget about them. Whatever Julia Elizabeth Fawkes's many admirers had cherished, it had disappeared as surely as the flesh from her bones.

There it would have ended, if there had not been an Open Doors day that September. One of the houses on the list was 18 Little George Street, which had never been open to the public before. The house dated from the mid-eighteenth century, and had later become a gathering place for poets and radicals. Coleridge had stayed there. Wordsworth had visited. Shelley had declaimed a poem on the top-floor landing and then attempted to slide down the banisters. Speeches had been made and it was believed there had been a printing press in the basement. The house still belonged to the same family, the Frobishers, but it had passed to a cousin who lived in Canada and wished to sell in due course. He had recently employed an archivist to go through the many papers which were lodged there. The archivist would be on hand on Open Doors day. There was some idea, according to the Open Doors leaflet, that the house might be bought by the City Council as a museum. I doubted that. This was probably my only chance to see it.

I planned my day carefully. I would go to Redcliffe Caves in the morning, have a bite of lunch down by the water and then go to 18 Little George Street as soon as it opened at one o'clock. Jack couldn't come. He would have loved the caves, but the multiplied sound of his barking might annoy other visitors, and I doubted that he'd be allowed into Little George Street. I noted with some amusement that I was already thinking like a dog-owner, with a faint resentment that anywhere should be off limits to Jack.

It was a mistake to come early. The house was busy and the archivist was engaged with a group of local historians. I looked around. The bones of the house hadn't changed much, as far as I could see. The Frobishers had clearly been happy enough with one magnificent, outdated bathroom and a separate lavatory with a cistern which must sound like Niagara Falls when the chain was pulled. The windows all had their original glass. I liked that: it pleased me to think that Coleridge had looked out of these windows. I lingered, but the historians were tireless, and I went away.

I was halfway home when I realised what a fool I'd been. The house might never be open again. It was entirely possible that Julia Elizabeth Fawkes had visited Little George Street. She was a writer. She was well enough known then to have had 'many admirers'. Was it possible that she had left some physical mark there? I felt that I owed it to Jack to search a little farther. After all, he had made me come to the grave.

It was almost three o'clock. The local historians had gone and the archivist was drinking a cup of tea, well away from the papers which he had spread out for display over a broad polished table. He looked up somewhat guardedly as I entered the room.

'I'm sorry,' I said, 'I don't want to interrupt your break.'

'Come in, come in,' he said with an alacrity which might have been a bit forced but which I pretended to take at face value. I turned over some of the papers. They meant nothing to me, but it would be polite to dwell on them for a few minutes.

'I'm interested in a writer who may have come to the house in the late eighteenth century,' I said at last, still looking at the papers.

'What was his name?'

'Julia Elizabeth Fawkes. She was a woman,' I added stupidly.

'Julia Elizabeth Fawkes,' he repeated. 'No. I don't believe I have seen any reference to her.'

'She had another name. A married name: Gleeson.'

'Gleeson ... Gleeson ...'

'She was married to a man called Augustus Gleeson.'

'Oh,' said the archivist, suddenly all keen attention. 'The pamphleteer, I assume?'

'I have no idea.'

'Let me just check ...' To my surprise, he ignored the laptop in front of him. 'I'll just have a look at the card index.' He got up, fetched a long dingy cardboard box and began to fossick about inside it. 'Gellborough ... Gifford ... Glanville ... Ah yes, I thought so. Gleeson.'

He pulled out a card and laid it in front of me. There was nothing but a name: Gleeson, Augustus Shovell, and a sequence of letters and numbers: 2nd F L/g R/H Bc Sh 2/R/14.

'I knew I'd seen something.'

'What does it mean?'

'Second floor landing, right-hand bookcase, second shelf from the bottom, 14 items in from the right,' responded the archivist. 'It isn't my system, of course. This card index must be forty years old at least. But so far, I've found it reliable. Any matter relating to your man will be there.'

'Could we look now?'

He glanced at the door. No one was coming. The interest of the day had peaked. I heard voices downstairs, then a door shut and they were cut off.

'Why not?'

He went ahead of me up the stairs.

The bookcases were glass-fronted, and locked. The archivist brought out his keys and selected one. It turned with difficulty and he had to prise the door open with a fingernail.

'It's all waiting to be properly catalogued,' he said apologetically. 'The card index is primitive. They want a digital archive, but of course people don't realise what an undertaking that is. And if the house is sold, then the collection must go to a museum.'

'You don't think the house will become one?'

He gave me a sharp look over his shoulder. 'It's not very likely, is it?'

He was kneeling now, searching along the rows and still talking. I looked over his shoulder and saw that while there were plenty of books there were also leather-bound boxes lined up on the shelves.

'I'm afraid this chap in Canada has absolutely no idea of what's involved. He thinks I can wave a wand and everything will be online – but the place is more or less untouched and that's what makes the job rewarding . . . Ah, here we are.' The box was unlabelled. He drew it out and undid the clasp. 'Here we are indeed.' A faint whiff of oldness reached me. 'I haven't got as far as this bookcase, you understand.' He held the box and peered into it. I could see nothing.

'May I look?' I asked, and at the same time I reached out smoothly. Without waiting for his permission, I took the box. In the bottom there lay a fragment of paper with writing criss-crossed over it. Most of the sheet had been torn away. The writing was smooth and flowing. It looked as if it ought to be easy to read, but I could not decipher it. I had the feeling, suddenly, that the archivist had not known the paper was there and did not want to share the discovery with me.

'I can't make head or tail of this,' I said and, as I had hoped, he responded.

'It's part of a letter. There, that's where the seal has broken. People often crossed their letters at the time. The post was very expensive and they wanted to fill the paper as much as possible. There's a trick to reading it, and of course you have to ignore the orthographic changes. Let me see. The light's not very good here, and the ink's faded. We might take it downstairs and have a look at it under the lamp, if you're interested?' His eyes peeped at me.

'I'd like that very much,' I said.

We settled at the broad table and he drew down the lamp so that it shone clear on the paper. Every so often he scribbled down a phrase; then he pored over the document again. He turned it, read again, jotted down his notes. I sat perfectly still, waiting.

At last he said, 'There's not much in it, I'm afraid. Rather frustrating. It breaks off and then the writing across – here – seems to refer to quite a different matter. It must be written by someone who knew Augustus Gleeson well, but unfortunately there is no clue to the writer's identity. Possibly my predecessor – the person who created the card index – knew more. He must have done, to give Gleeson's full name as a reference, since it isn't given in the document itself.'

'Would you read it to me?'

'For what it's worth – but it doesn't shed any light on the lady you mentioned. This is the first part:

' ... the Eagerness with which we read your
letter giving Assurance that you are safely come
to London. By Providence or the Act of Man
you have been preserved in health and safety.
Augustus, as you know, is staying with me at
Little George Street for the present, and the
Frobishers have been most Constant and Tender
in their Attentions to us Both. When Augustus
had read your letter he could not sit still but
must rise and walk about the room to express
his Emotion. How my Heart bounded, I
cannot ...'

The phrases galloped across my mind. All that long-dead emotion! Hearts bounding, eagerness, walking around the room – and it was all dead and gone, and no one left to know what any of it had meant. I would not have felt it so strongly, no doubt, if I had not been left myself, like the last speaker of a lost language that no one else understood.

The archivist was looking at me. I hoped that I had not spoken aloud.

'There is a little more,' he said.

'Preserve this Letter, my dear Susannah, as we
have done with every Word you wrote to us
from France. We lodge all Correspondence with

the Frobishers and I most Ardently Advise you to do the Same so that there will be a Memorial of these Perilous Times. For months Augustus has not picked up his pen. We can only console ourselves that our dear Julia did not live to see the Fate of her Unfortunate . . .

'The paper is torn just here.'

'Who was Susannah? Are her letters here too?'

'As far as I know there are none. Possibly the Frobishers destroyed them all. Unfortunately, without a surname—'

'Why were the times perilous?'

The archivist blinked, as if I had revealed an ignorance which forced him to reassess me. 'These were radicals, remember. It was the time of the French Revolution.'

I peered at the edge of the letter. 'Is that a "C"?'

'It may be. Or possibly a "D". The following letter may be an "H", but I'm guessing now.'

'Child, perhaps?' I said. There were many such deaths recorded in the graveyard: baby after baby, given the same name, born and dead within the year.

'It's unlikely. We know that Augustus Gleeson had a son, Thomas, and that he survived to adulthood. Gleeson alludes to him in a treatise on education, and calls him his only child. As far as we know, Gleeson never remarried.'

For months Augustus Gleeson had not picked up his pen. I wished that Jack were here. I would have reached

14

down and stroked his head, over and over, until my mind was quiet.

'There are several of his pamphlets in the City Library,' the archivist said.

'Are there?'

'He was quite well known in his day, I believe.'

'But there's none of her writing?'

'Not as far as I know.'

I touched the piece of paper. The words were faded yet they still tumbled across the paper, eager, impetuous, alive. But they weren't alive. The archivist and I were snuffling after something which no longer existed, like Jack in his hunt for imagined bones. Augustus had been left, as I had been left. But it was over for him: he was dead. They were all dead and they could no longer tell us what their words had been, before the paper had been torn across.

Even so, I touched the paper as if the heat of their lives might come off on my fingers.